# MURDER AT THE MYSTERY CONVENTION

The security guard knocked twice on the door to room 310 and then unlocked it with a key card. As soon as the door opened, the high-pitched whistle sounded even louder. He held the door open for Val.

She called out to Cynthia and got no response. The light in the entrance hall illuminated the doors to the closet and the bathroom on the left. The desk straight ahead was also visible. On it was an electric kettle with steam rising from its spout. Val darted toward it, Bethany trailing her. The instant Val unplugged the kettle, the whistling stopped.

She peered across the room at the bed. The duvet covering a mound on the window side of the bed told Val that someone was lying there, but the light wasn't bright enough for her to see more. "Cynthia?" she called. No answer.

"How could she have slept with that kettle shrieking? I hope she's okay." Bethany flipped a switch that turned on the nightstand lamps. She inched past Val and around the foot of the bed. As she approached the head of the bed, she yelped.

"Oh no! Val, I think she's dead!"

**Books by Maya Corrigan**

**Published by Kensington Publishing Corp.**

# Bake Offed

**A
Five-Ingredient
Mystery**

# Maya Corrigan

Kensington Publishing Corp.
www.kensingtonbooks.com

Dedicated to the hardworking organizers of mystery fan conventions, who make it possible for readers and writers to gather and share their love of crime fiction.

# CAST OF CHARACTERS

Paperback versions of books by Agatha Christie and mystery writers of her era often start with character lists. As an homage to classic mysteries, this book also has a cast list.

## Volunteers at the Maryland Mystery Fan Fest

Val Deniston—café manager who can't avoid dead bodies

Don Myer—Val's grandfather, recipe columnist, first-time bake-off competitor

Bethany O'Shay—mystery fest organizer, Val's best friend, first-grade teacher

Cynthia Sweet—recipe columnist, bake-off competitor, mystery book club member

Dave Proctor—bake-off competitor, a restaurateur without a restaurant

Trisha Turbek—tight-lipped volunteer with a face-hiding cap

Perry Macon—retired lawyer, mystery book club member

Birdie Natter—Cynthia's neighbor, snoop, mystery book club member

## Fest Attendees

Harrison Hawk—bookseller with a brain full of murder plots

Jordan Young—cozy mystery writer, Iraq and Afghanistan war veteran

Claire Rainey—consultant to historical novel writers, teacher

Greer Gordon—journalist and true-crime writer fixated on a year-old unsolved murder

**Others**

Bram Muir—Val's boyfriend, tech entrepreneur, Sherlock Holmes enthusiast

Meredith Waterbrook—Cynthia's stepdaughter, landscape designer

Nico Gonzalez—rookie hotel security guard

Eric Reddish—taciturn hotel bartender

Roy Chesterfeld—police detective, acquaintance of Val, Granddad, and Bethany

# Chapter 1

Val Deniston looked forward to a weekend of murder for pleasure. With discussions, contests, and games centered on crime and detection, the Maryland Mystery Fan Fest promised to be more fun than stumbling on real bodies. Val had done that all too often.

Her friend Bethany O'Shay, an avid mystery reader, had organized the weekend and coaxed Val and her grandfather into helping her. Val would monitor discussion panels and run the mystery trivia contest. Granddad would compete in the Deadly Desserts bake-off and serve as the charity auctioneer. Val printed a copy of the schedule from the fest's website and joined Granddad in the sitting room of the Victorian house they shared.

Lounging in his recliner near the sofa, Granddad was flipping through a thin paperback with yellowed pages to prepare for the bake-off. Each contestant had to assume the role of a famous detective's cook and make a dessert the sleuth might have eaten. He'd been assigned to play Fritz, chef to Rex Stout's food-obsessed detective Nero Wolfe. For the last week, Granddad had devoured Stout's mysteries from the 1930s and the following decades.

He slammed his book shut. "The bake-off organizer told Bethany I'd have no trouble finding a recipe, but the books only have fancy dishes with scads of ingredients. Nero Wolfe eats weird stuff like starlings, and it takes twenty of them to make a meal. I've gone through all his books I could scare up in Bayport. Not a single dessert in any of them."

Val perched on the sofa. "Dorothy could put in a rush order for more books." The new bookshop owner would go out of her way to help Granddad, her neighbor when she was growing up here. "How many Nero Wolfe books are there?"

"Almost fifty. Any dessert in them would probably have twenty ingredients, like the other stuff Wolfe eats." Granddad ripped off his bifocals, causing the tufts of white curls that fringed his balding head to stick out sideways. "How am I supposed to pretend to be a gourmet cook?"

Val didn't remind him he had extensive experience faking culinary expertise. Two years ago he could do little more than boil an egg when he wangled a job as a recipe columnist, calling himself the Codger Cook. "It's only for an evening. Wing it."

"You think I can get away with making one of my five-ingredient desserts?"

Bending the rules was nothing new for Granddad. "You can get away with it, but you won't win with it. The organizer who assigned you to play Nero Wolfe's chef might have a dessert in mind. I'll ask Bethany for the organizer's contact info while you look at the fest schedule."

She gave him the printout and called her friend, interrupting Bethany's tizzy over finding a weekend sitter for her spaniel, Muffin. If the fest hotel had allowed dogs, Muffin would have been among the attendees. After listening to Bethany's woes, Val asked her for the bake-off organizer's contact information. Bethany texted it to her.

"Here's the name, e-mail address, and phone number." Val showed Granddad her phone. "Do you want me to write this down or text it to you?"

He adjusted his bifocals. As he peered at her phone, his bushy white eyebrows rose halfway to what would have been his hairline if he hadn't lost most of his hair. "Cynthia Sweet organized this! I wouldn't ask *her* for advice. She ripped off my five-ingredient theme for her articles in the Baltimore newspaper. Her column, 'Granny Sweet's Pantry,' used to focus on cakes until she saw how popular my idea was and switched gears."

Val could have pointed out that several five-ingredient cookbooks had been published before he won the competition for the *Treadwell Times* recipe columnist. She could have also reminded him that he'd used her recipes, minus a few ingredients, to make his reputation as the local cooking guru. She opted instead to make sure he stood by his commitment. "I hope you won't pull out of the bake-off after all the times Bethany went along with your sleuthing schemes."

"Nah. Though Cynthia Sweet set me up for failure, I'm looking forward to a weekend away. Folks from Baltimore, DC, and Northern Virginia will go to the fest. I can give out my business cards and offer my services beyond Maryland's Eastern Shore."

When he'd handed out business cards around Halloween, he'd touted himself as a ghost buster. Val was almost afraid to ask. "What kind of services?"

"With my private investigator course and experience solving murders, I can be a consultant to mystery authors."

"First, you'll need to make a good impression. You only have a few days to decide on a dessert, find and test recipes, and practice your bake-off presentation."

He stared across the room at the bookshelves surrounding the fireplace. "I just remembered something. Your grandmother once made a cake from some Nero Wolfe thing she inherited from her favorite aunt. It's probably in the attic." He levered himself out of the chair and headed toward the stairs.

"Good luck on the hunt." The attic of the century-old house was crammed with junk and possibly a rare hidden treasure. When Val moved in two years ago, she'd envisioned sorting through all of it, but managing the athletic club café and moonlighting as a caterer had kept her too busy to tackle the daunting task.

She surveyed the books on the coffee table—crime novels her friend Bethany had given her, written by authors who'd be at the fest.

Val passed over the book with an exploding car

on the cover and one with a gun-toting woman sil-houetted in a dark alley. The third book, with a sepia-toned image of a woman in old-fashioned clothes on a bicycle, piqued her interest. The cover text described the main character as a woman who en-counters a murder while cycling across the coun-try in the 1890s. Val started reading and had got as far as the third chapter when the doorbell rang.

She went into the hall, peered through the side-light, and was surprised to see Bram Muir on the porch. He waved to her through the sidelight, a big smile on his face and a lock of brown hair falling over his forehead.

She flung the door open and gave him a long, welcoming kiss. "I didn't expect you, but I'm glad you're here. Did you eat yet? We did, but I could whip up some leftovers for you."

"I ate on the fly. I wish I could stay, but I have to get back to the bookshop."

"Your mom's doing okay, I hope." When Dor-othy broke her ankle on an icy sidewalk and couldn't work her usual long hours, mother and son had switched roles. Six weeks later, he still ran the shop with help from her, not vice versa. That meant Val didn't see quite as much of him as she had in his first three months in Bayport. And they'd had to postpone the Valentine's Day trip to Paris he'd planned for them.

"Mom's therapy is going well, but her ankle still aches, especially toward the end of the day." Bram took off his jacket and hung it over the newel post. "I'm here because your grandfather called and asked me to give him a hand moving something heavy. He didn't want you to hurt yourself trying."

Though she was on the small side at five foot three and slim, Val kept in good shape bicycling and playing tennis, but Bram's muscular build made him a far better mover. "You two will need a foreman—I mean, a forewoman—to oversee this operation."

"Lead the way. I've never been to the attic."

As they climbed to the second floor and up the narrow stairs to the dim and cobwebbed attic, she described Granddad's role in the fest bake-off.

The trunk he wanted to explore stood behind a stack of footlockers. Bram moved them to make a path. He had to use brute force to loosen the hasp and raise the lid of the old trunk.

Granddad rummaged in it for a minute and then shouted, "I've found it! I've found it!"

Bram's eyes widened. "Those were the first words Sherlock Holmes spoke. He was holding up a test tube when he said them."

Val smiled. A tech entrepreneur, Bram was also a Sherlock enthusiast and often brought his idol into the conversation. She couldn't see what Granddad had found because he was still bending over the trunk, but she was sure it wasn't a test tube. "Is it a Nero Wolfe book?"

Granddad straightened up and brandished his discovery. "That's what it looks like, but it's not."

Even in the dim light, Val could make out the image on the dust jacket and the words *Too Many Cooks* in big white letters and *By Rex Stout* in smaller black type. "So it's a Rex Stout book with a different detective than Nero Wolfe?"

"Nope." Granddad moved to stand under the single bulb that hung from the ceiling. He opened the cover of *Too Many Cooks* to reveal the title page, but there were no bound pages beyond it. Instead, it was a collection of loose cards. "It's a book-shaped box with recipe cards. I need better light to study the recipes."

"Let me see them." Val took the cards he held out and flipped through the first few. "Nero Wolfe's Baked Oysters in the Shell. Nero Wolfe's Terrapin Maryland. Nero Wolfe's Sponge Cake." She stared in amazement. "Eggs. Sugar. Lemon. Flour. Salt. Five ingredients, Granddad! You can bake it at the fest."

He grinned. "That'll show Cynthia Sweet she can't get the better of me!" He put the recipe cards back in the box. "There's gotta be a story behind this fake book. I'm gonna look it up online."

Back on the first floor, he thanked Bram for his help, went into the study, and sat down in front of the computer.

Bram took his jacket from the banister and put it on. "I may be able to squeeze out some free time on Sunday. The teenager who's working at the shop can put in more hours this weekend. Do you want to get together on Sunday, or will you be busy the whole weekend?"

"I promised Bethany I'd stay until after the gala luncheon on Sunday. Unless there's a massive traffic jam, I should be back no later than five."

He looked disappointed that she couldn't spare more time. "Let's plan on having dinner together. You're a good friend to give up your days off to help her."

"I'm happy to go for other reasons. I've never been to a gathering of writers and readers before, and I'll get out of Bayport for the first time since moving in with Granddad." Though Val loved the town where she'd settled after leaving her job in Manhattan, she'd welcome a change of scenery, the foothills of the Appalachians instead of the coastal plain.

Bram put his arms around her and held her close. "I'm sorry we couldn't make that trip to Paris on your Valentine's Day birthday."

"I'm sorry too, but taking care of your mother was what you had to do."

"We'll reschedule the trip as soon as she's got her stamina back."

"And Paris will be warmer than it would have been in February." Val kissed him goodbye, closed the door after him, and went back to the book she'd started.

Twenty minutes later, Granddad interrupted her. "There's good news and bad news."

"Let's get the bad over with."

"I got an e-mail from the publisher about my cookbook proposal. The editor liked it, but they'd just made an offer to another writer with a similar concept." His brows knit together and his eyes narrowed. "I'll bet Cynthia Sweet is that other person and she submitted an idea for a five-ingredient cookbook too."

Val tried to put a positive spin on his bad news. "Saying that a book competes with another one already in the works is a gentle way for a publisher to reject a proposal."

"You mean my book's no good, and they're lying so they don't hurt my feelings?"

"They're not lying. You're interpreting a *similar*

*concept* to mean five-ingredient recipes. The publisher requested proposals for cookbooks focused on the food of the Chesapeake Bay area. That's probably what they mean by a similar concept."

"Maybe you're right. You used to work for a cookbook publisher, so you know how they operate."

"I do. Unless you're a famous chef, it's hard to get a cookbook published because of the competition and even harder to make any money on it." This wasn't the first time she'd made that point. No harm in repeating it. "So much for your bad news. What's the good news?"

He held up his attic treasure. "This recipe box is worth a pretty penny. It comes from a publicity tour Rex Stout did when *Too Many Cooks* was serialized in a magazine in 1938. The publisher put on a lunch in a dozen cities. Each guest got one of these boxes as a souvenir. Inside is a menu card, a printed note from Rex Stout, and thirty-four cards with recipes for dishes mentioned in the book."

In her former life as a cookbook publicist, Val had heard of lavish publicity tours for celebrity chefs' cookbooks, but none could top that. "Did Grandma's aunt go to that lunch?"

"Nah. It was for folks in the business of promoting books. Philadelphia was one of the stops on the book tour, and that's where she lived. She mighta got the box at an estate sale or an antique shop or even from a neighbor. It's a collector's item now."

Worth a pretty penny, whatever that meant to Granddad. "How much would someone pay for that recipe box?"

"There's one on eBay with a dust jacket more beat up than this one. It's listed for two thousand dollars. A rare book dealer is selling one in better condition for almost twice as much."

"Wow." Val made up her mind to check the attic soon for other treasures amid the junk.

He held up the box. "This will make a good story to tell at the bake-off when I'm acting as Nero Wolfe's chef."

She was tempted to suggest he thank Cynthia Sweet for assigning him that role, but bringing up his nemesis might dampen his good spirits.

The fest hotel in Frederick County, Maryland, was an L-shaped building with an older red brick side dwarfed by a modern addition. Val and Granddad rolled their suitcases into the lobby that connected the two wings at four on Friday afternoon. They'd left the ingredients and pans for Granddad's dessert in the car because the bake-off would be held in a different location.

Granddad looked longingly at the small bar in the far corner of the lobby. "I could use a beer after two hours in the car."

"Let's get our room keys first. The check-in line is short now, but it may get longer." Val started toward the reception desk.

A sixty-something woman with a narrow face and long chin intercepted them. Her bottle-blond hair was tied with a pink velvet bow at the nape of her neck. "You must be Don Myer, the Codger Cook, and his granddaughter, Val. Bethany told me to be on the lookout for you two. I'm thrilled to meet you. I'm Cynthia Sweet."

From what Granddad had said, Val had expected the woman to resemble the evil Cruella de Vil. But no, Cynthia spoke with a honeyed voice and gave off a floral scent. Her flared dress featured huge red roses on a baby-blue background. "Nice to meet you, Cynthia."

"Hello." Granddad's voice was barely audible.

Cynthia reached into her rose-patterned quilted tote bag, pulled out a key card, and extended it to Val. "Bethany asked me to give you the key card for the room you're sharing with her. She went to the community center to make sure everything's ready for the bake-off."

"Thank you." Val put the card in her jacket pocket. "What's the room number?"

"I'm in 310, and it's the door after mine. The community center's kitchen will be available from five o'clock on for us to prepare our desserts."

Granddad peered with narrowed eyes at Cynthia. "For *us* to prepare our desserts? You're the organizer *and* a contestant?"

"That's right. I'm going to bake as Mrs. Hudson—Sherlock Holmes's landlady. The third contestant is Dave Proctor. He'll be playing Bunter, Lord Peter Wimsey's valet and cook. Dave went to the Culinary Institute, but he's never cooked professionally."

"What's he do for a living?" Granddad said.

"Restaurant management." Cynthia turned to Val. "You're not allowed in the kitchen. Only contestants."

Val guessed that Bethany had mentioned Val

was a caterer and Cynthia didn't want a pro help-ing Granddad with his dessert. "I appreciate your holding on to the key card for me."

"I'm glad you came early enough so I can make a cup of tea before the bake-off. Don't forget to stop for your fest badges in the foyer of the Poe wing." Cynthia pointed to the corridor to the left of the reception desk. "I'm going to freshen up. Bye now." She crossed the lobby to the elevators.

Val said, "Cynthia Sweet doesn't seem as bad as you made her out to be."

Granddad got in line for room registration. "Synthetic Sweet should be her name. She's like a sugar substitute that leaves a bad aftertaste. It's un-fair to organize the bake-off and then compete in it. She probably asked her best pal to judge the contest."

"No. Bethany picked the judges from the fest volunteers, and the audience will also get to vote. I think you're prejudiced against Cynthia."

Before he could reply, the desk clerk beckoned him. Granddad requested and received a room on the third floor, where Val and Bethany's room was. Once he had his key card, he and Val went into the Poe wing. A gray-haired man at the fest table di-rected them to check in with the younger woman next to him for their badges.

They got in line behind a slim, sandy-haired man. When he advanced to the table, he gave his name as Dave Proctor.

Val tugged Granddad's sleeve and whispered, "The man in front of us is the third contestant in the bake-off."

"I'll introduce myself to him if I get the chance."

The woman at the fest table handed Dave an envelope and muttered something to him with her head down.

When he stepped to the side, Val gave her name to the woman, expecting a friendly welcome to the festival. Instead, all she saw was the brim and the crown of a purple hat with *Trisha* embroidered on it. Granddad moved over to talk to Dave while the woman thumbed through a long box of envelopes.

Without looking up, she thrust an envelope toward Val. "Here's your packet. In it you'll find your name tag and tickets for the Deadly Desserts bake-off tonight, tomorrow's box lunch and evening reception, and Sunday's gala luncheon. You don't need tickets for the movies at nine each night—*Murder on the Orient Express* tonight and *Clue* tomorrow night."

"Thank you. Could I pick up my grandfather's packet too?" Val pointed to him. "He's over there. His name is Don Myer."

Trisha raised her head and turned to look at Granddad through glasses that dwarfed her face. The name tag pinned to her gray sweatshirt identified her as Trisha Turbek. She wore her long brown hair pulled through the ponytail hole of her baseball cap, like Val's high school friends used to do, but Trisha had to be twice the age of a high schooler.

She hunched over the box again and drew out a second envelope. "You'll get a detailed schedule with the room locations and a fest tote from Perry Mason." She pointed to the man with thick gray hair at the table with her.

"Not Mason, *Macon*." He held up his name tag. "Perry Macon."

Trisha didn't bother looking at it. "Sorry. My grandmother watches *Perry Mason* reruns, so that's what's in my brain."

Standing nearby with Dave, Granddad glanced at the man at the fest table. "You mean you're not the famous defense lawyer?"

"I'm a not-famous retired lawyer," Perry responded solemnly.

"Come over and meet Dave, Val." Granddad introduced his bake-off competitor to her. The round-faced man with light, tousled hair gave her a winning smile, a nice change from the fest's aloof greeters.

She smiled back. "Glad to meet you. I'm looking forward to tonight's bake-off." Dave was about half Granddad's age and, with a Culinary Institute background, would probably make stiffer competition than Cynthia.

"Such a fun idea. Chefs to famous sleuths." Dave turned to Granddad. "Do you compete in cooking contests often?"

"Nope. I'm in this one 'cause Val's best friend is running the show and recruited me."

Val was about to turn Dave's question back on him when his phone played a tune. He excused himself, said he'd see them at the bake-off, and walked toward the lobby with the phone against his ear.

Val gave Granddad his envelope. "Your tickets and name tag are inside. We need to pick up the rest of our fest kit from Perry."

Perry raised his head from doing a crossword puzzle. "Check the spelling on your name tags. We found some with typos and had to go to the hotel's business center to print new ones." He handed each of them a red tote bag with *Maryland Mystery Fan Fest* written in black on it. "The program booklet is inside. All the events will be in this wing except for tonight's bake-off in the community center."

"What's the best way to get there?" Val said.

"It's a fifteen-minute walk or a five-minute drive. Are you driving?" When she nodded, he recited the directions.

They were simple enough that she didn't need to jot them down. As she listened, two older women gave Trisha their names. The volunteer made eye contact and conversed with them. Trisha's changed demeanor mystified Val.

She thanked Perry for the directions and looked for Granddad. He'd stepped away from the table and opened his fest envelope.

As she approached him, he was staring at his name tag and a slip of paper. "Did they misspell your name, Granddad?"

He shook his head. "Follow me."

Once they were back in the lobby, he handed her the paper. The words on it were printed in an italicized font.

As she glanced at it, the spelling error in the first word popped out: *Sabatage is Sweet's signature dish. Guard your ingredients and your batter.*

"Still think I'm being unfair to Cynthia Sweet?" Granddad whispered. "That woman is trouble, and I'm not the only person who knows it."

# Chapter 2

Val handed the anonymous note back to Grand-dad and glanced around the busy lobby. The line in front of the reception desk had grown, and people milled around, dressed to the hilt. From the conversation snippets Val heard, they were at the hotel for a wedding reception. "Let's talk upstairs." She and Granddad threaded their way around chair groupings and massive potted plants toward the elevators.

After getting off the elevator on the third floor, Val walked past Cynthia's room, stopped at the next door, and took out the key card Cynthia had given her. It didn't unlock the door.

"Let me try," Granddad said. He had no better luck. "Your key mighta been demagnetized. You can always leave your stuff in my room and get yourself a new key after the bake-off. The line at the front desk won't be as long then. We gotta leave for the community center soon."

"Cynthia said she was in 310. Maybe I misunderstood her and my room is on the other side of hers." Val knocked on the door of 310.

By the time Cynthia answered the knock, Granddad had rolled his suitcase to his room at the end of the hall.

Cynthia confirmed that Val had tried the right door. "The card must have been keyed wrong. One of mine didn't work either and—" She broke off, her eyes widening. "The front desk gave me two keys to my room. I might have given you one of them by mistake. When I came up here after talking to you, the card I tried didn't open my door. But the other card that I had in my bag worked. Let's exchange keys and try them again."

Both doors opened. Val saluted Cynthia. "I'm glad you solved that mystery."

A piercing whistle came from the open door to Cynthia's room. "Sorry. That's my kettle. I always take it when I travel. Teatime!" She disappeared into her room.

Val left her suitcase on the bed, joined Granddad in his room, and explained the key mix-up.

He sat down at the desk and held up the slip of paper that warned him against his bake-off rival. "I've been trying to figure out what to do about this. I'll stay as far away as I can from Cynthia in the kitchen so she can't sabotage my dessert. And I'll watch her like a hawk in case she sabotages Dave's dessert. I wonder if he got the same warning I did or if he already knows about her. She might be notorious in bake-off circles."

"It can't be easy to tamper with someone else's dessert without the other contestants noticing." Val sat down in the armchair by the window. "The whole thing could be a hoax, some joker stirring up trouble. Maybe Dave got a note saying you would sabotage his baking and Cynthia got one saying he would sabotage hers. You'll all be guarding against one another in the kitchen."

Granddad looked lost in thought. "I'd planned to get a quick bite after putting my cake in the oven. But now I gotta stay there to protect it from her."

"I'll drop you off at the community center, pick up a pizza, and bring it back there for you and your competitors to share."

"Okay. Do I have time for a beer before we leave?"

Val checked her watch. "A quick one, but if you really want to show up Cynthia, you'll spend the time reviewing your presentation. The official judges choose the best-tasting dessert, but the audience votes too. They'll be influenced by the presentations. It's worth putting on a good show."

"You're right. I'll go over my notes now."

Passing up a cold beer to prep for the bake-off meant he was determined to defeat Cynthia.


After dropping off a pizza for the bake-off contestants, Val grabbed a quick dinner of veggie lasagna and a salad at the hotel's restaurant. She went up to her room, unpacked, and changed clothes. A black pencil skirt, an electric blue sweater, and low heels replaced the black slacks, white top, and athletic shoes she'd worn to work this morning.

She arrived at the community center thirty minutes early. A woman at the door to the meeting room checked her name badge against a list of attendees and took her ticket. Val surveyed the room already half filled with fest goers. At the front was a dais with a long table where the contestants would sit and the lectern from which they'd speak.

At the back of the room, people lined up near urns to fill paper cups with coffee or tea. Some attendees stood talking amid the circular tables for six in the room, and others had already chosen seats. Two tables were occupied by women wearing hats—straw boaters with wide ribbons, cloches, and fascinators made of feathers and flowers. Val scanned the crowd and noticed a woman in a purple cap—Trisha, the volunteer from the fest table. She might know who else had access to the envelope she'd given Granddad with the anonymous note in it. Val watched where she sat down and hurried to the table.

"Okay if I join you?" Val put her hands on the back of the chair to the left of Trisha's.

The volunteer gave a brief smile. "Sure."

"By all means. Do sit down." The stout middle-aged man sitting to Trisha's right nodded. He wore a gray three-piece suit with a red bow tie. The hair fringing his mostly bald head was jet-black, like his thick eyebrows. With the right mustache, he could have passed for Hercule Poirot. "I'm Harrison Hawk, the fest's book vendor. My establishment is in Alexandria, Virginia. I offer a curated collection of new and antiquarian popular fiction with emphasis on the mystery genre."

Harrison struck Val as a man who'd never use one syllable when five would do as well. She assumed that *antiquarian* meant *used.* "I'm Val Deniston, one of the volunteers. I live in Bayport, Maryland, on the Eastern Shore near the Chesapeake Bay."

"Trisha is also a volunteer. Sadly, we'll only have five at our table. One of the Marples commandeered a chair so she could squeeze in at another table."

Val wasn't sure what he meant. "The Marples?"

He flicked his wrist toward the women in hats. "My name for them. They come to mystery gatherings dressed to kill at a country-house party. Mind you, I have nothing against Agatha Christie on the page. But a mass of Miss Marples attired for tea at the manor house is rather daunting."

Val smiled. "No one will get away with any crimes this weekend with that many Miss Marples among us."

Harrison turned his attention to an African American man passing by the table. "Looking for a place to sit? Come join us." He pointed to the chair next to his.

"Thank you. I will." The tall man in a navy blazer and chinos folded himself into the chair. Though his dark skin was unlined, his goatee with a touch of gray suggested he was on the far side of forty. "I'm Jordan Young."

Harrison gave him Val's and Trisha's names and introduced himself and his business. "Are you a mystery author or a fan, sir?"

"Both. The third book in my crime series just came out."

"If I may hazard a guess as a mystery aficionado, you write about a private investigator or perhaps a policeman who resembles you physically—tall, broad-shouldered, handsome. Your detective metes out rough justice on mean streets."

Jordan chuckled. "Sorry to disappoint you. My series features an amateur sleuth, a woman who's a hairdresser, modeled after my mother. The books are set in my hometown in Southern Maryland. My mother says a salon is the place to learn everyone's secrets. She prodded me to write mysteries set in one and even gave me a few plots."

"Men who write cozies are a rare breed. Delighted to have you among us." He pointed to the only all-male table in the room, where one man wore a Stetson and another an Indiana Jones hat. "The anti-Christies at that table would not be as welcoming to a cozy writer."

Val laughed. "They call themselves that? Because they hate Agatha Christie's books?"

"That's what *I* call them. They'd never commit the heresy of hating the Queen of Crime at a mystery fest, but they do scorn books that aren't the shoot-'em-up, blow-'em-up type."

Jordan said, "I had all I wanted of shooting and blowing up in a previous life. I served in Iraq and Afghanistan before I retired from the military."

A woman about Val's age came to the table, asked if the remaining seat was available and then sat down. Like Val, she had curly hair, but hers was a lighter color, caramel to Val's cinnamon. It was also longer, falling in spirals rather than springing out like Val's corkscrews.

Harrison introduced everyone to her and passed out his business cards.

The newcomer said, "I'll have to check out your bookshop in Alexandria. We're almost neighbors. I'm Claire Rainey from Arlington."

"Are you a mystery writer?" Harrison said.

She shook her head, making her curls bounce for a moment before they fell back in place. "I teach history. I'm here to talk about doing research for fiction set in earlier eras. I worked with a writer of a private-eye series on her first historical book set in the Renaissance. The book's coming out soon. I also edited a first-time author's mystery set in the 1890s. It was just published."

Val thought about the historical mystery she'd just started. "Was it the book about the bicyclist in bloomers?"

Claire's face lit up. "Yes! The author will be on the historical mystery panel with me tomorrow afternoon." She looked around the table. "Who else is on a panel?"

Jordan raised his hand. "I'll be talking about my hairdresser series on a cozy mystery panel Sunday morning."

Harrison pointed to himself. "Tomorrow afternoon I'll be on a panel, educating the audience about collecting rare books, particularly classic mysteries."

Val silently apologized to him. *Antiquarian* was apparently the right word after all, meaning not just old, but rare enough to be valuable. "I'm going to conduct the mystery trivia contest on Sunday morning with a nice prize for the winner, in case you need an incentive to come."

"I need no incentive," Harrison said, "but alas, I cannot compete in the trivia game. I'll be handling the bookshop alone on Sunday morning. My assistant can't get here until mid-morning. I could, however, supply you with some questions if you'd like, nothing terribly abstruse."

"Thank you. I'd appreciate that." Whether Val would use any of his trivia was another matter.

Claire turned to her. "You must spend a lot of time reading mysteries if you can make up questions about them."

Looking at her full face, Val had a feeling that she'd met Claire before, or someone who resembled her. "To come up with a trivia question, it's enough to know an odd fact. You don't need to be an expert. I used to run pub trivia when I lived in New York City."

Jordan looked across the table at her. "What else did you do in the city, Val?"

"I was a cookbook publicist."

Trisha perked up, showing her first reaction to anything said at the table. "That must have been interesting. What do you do now?"

"I manage a café, cater on the side, and work on my cookbook." Although lately she'd spent more time helping Granddad with his. She'd decided against telling her tablemates she was related to a bake-off contestant, hoping to hear honest opinions on the desserts. Trisha might remember seeing her and Granddad together at the fest table this afternoon, but she hadn't mentioned it yet.

Val turned to the volunteer. "Where do you live, Trisha?"

"Not far from here. I'll be going home each night, not staying at the hotel."

It would take more than a single question to get Trisha talking. Val persisted. "Then you're familiar with the area. Tell us something that most visitors don't know." She expected to hear about a good local restaurant or a trail with a beautiful vista.

Trisha hesitated. "The Poe wing, where the fest is being held and all the attendees are staying, was built a hundred years ago. Supposedly, the ghost of a woman who was murdered here haunts it."

"Was the woman murdered when the hotel was first built or later?" Claire the historian said.

"Who saw the ghost, and what did it look like?" Jordan the mystery writer said.

Trisha held up her hands, palms out, as if to stop an onslaught. "Don't ask me. I don't believe in ghosts. Anything about them goes in one ear and out the other."

Val didn't believe in ghosts either, but she'd read her share of ghost tales. "I take it her killer was never caught. That's the usual story. The murder victim returns to earth to find justice and haunts the scene of the crime."

"If that's so," Harrison said, "a more recent victim might be haunting the hotel—a man, not a woman. A year ago, the hotel hosted an interactive murder mystery dinner. The guests had to solve the murder of the groom at a wedding. His bride was the chief suspect. That same night, a man who'd attended the dinner was found dead in his room. His wife, who'd argued with him after the show, was a suspect."

Val hadn't heard about this murder, but news from a different part of the state didn't necessarily travel across the Chesapeake Bay.

Jordan stroked his goatee. "A fake murder followed by an actual murder. Sounds like the plot of a book."

"It really happened," Trisha said. "It was in the newspaper. Everyone thought the wife did it, but no one was arrest—" She broke off as someone tapped the microphone to test it.

Val saw her friend Bethany at the lectern, dressed in the neon colors she favored for her first-grade classes. She wore a shift with op-art images like Andy Warhol's Marilyn Monroe panels, except Bethany's dress featured Edgar Allan Poe's haunting face. Perfect for a mystery fest.

She spoke into the microphone. "We'll be starting in fifteen minutes. You may want to get yourself coffee or tea from the back of the room before the contestants come out. After the presentations, you'll get to sample the desserts."

Harrison and Trisha already had drinks and remained at the table. Val was in the decaf coffee line when her phone dinged. She read a text from Granddad—*Meet me in the hall near the restrooms. Now. Important.*

What had happened? Val hurried out and followed the sign for the restrooms. Granddad was pacing outside the restroom doors. "What's wrong?"

"Cynthia went to the restroom ten minutes ago. A little later, I did too. We had to walk through the meeting room to get there. I was right behind her going back. A volunteer stopped her at the door because Cynthia didn't have her name tag on, but she had her fest envelope. She took it out of her purse and ripped it open." He held up a slip of paper about the same size as the one he'd found in his envelope. "This fell out of her envelope onto the floor. She didn't notice, just flashed her name tag and went into the room. I don't know if I should show this to her."

Val took the piece of paper and read the note. *A Sweet way to go—bake offed at the bake-off.*

# Chapter 3

Val stared at the note. Could *bake offed* mean *killed?* The capital *S* on *Sweet* made it clear that Cynthia Sweet was the target.

"You have to show this to her, Granddad." Val handed the paper back to him. "It's definitely a threat."

He cringed. "If I do that, she might accuse me of writing it. No one else saw the paper fall out of her envelope. My fingerprints are on the note."

She couldn't argue with his reasoning. "We should tell Bethany. She can show Cynthia the note without saying who found it." Val texted her friend.

Within a minute, Bethany met them in the corridor and read the note. "No one would try to attack Cynthia in a room packed with witnesses. This is a sick joke or an attempt to intimidate her. Dealing with adults is so much harder than handling kids." Looking frazzled, Bethany ran her fingers through her ginger-colored hair. "But I can't ignore it. I have to give her this note and let her decide what to do. If she wants to back out, we'll go ahead with two bake-off contestants, but I'm not calling the whole thing off."

Val doubted Cynthia would pull out without making a fuss. "What if she decides the show must go on, with her in it?"

"The community center can station a security guard in the room. I'll call the volunteers together and tell them a contestant received a vague threat. They can watch the people around them and yell for the guard if anyone behaves strangely or acts menacing."

"Your watchers might include your culprit," Val said. "Who else but a volunteer could have slipped that note into Cynthia's envelope?"

"If that's the case, I'm giving the culprit notice that a lot of eyes will be on him or her. I'll be scanning the room from the dais." Bethany turned to Granddad. "Would you also keep your eyes on the room from there?"

"Yup."

Val went back to the table, wondering what Cynthia would decide. Two minutes later, Bethany stepped up to the microphone, said there would be a short delay, and called the volunteers and committee members to the building's entrance hall. Val and Trisha joined the others for the see-something-say-something message. Bethany made sure that each table had at least one volunteer. Even with sixteen volunteers on alert and the security guard at the back at the room, Val was uneasy, her heart beating faster than usual, and her jaw clenched as she and Trisha returned to their seats.

At the microphone again, Bethany welcomed everyone to the Deadly Desserts bake-off. "The contestants will take on the roles of cooks who prepared food for three famous detectives, Sherlock Holmes, Lord Peter Wimsey, and Nero Wolfe. You'll all get to sample the treats the contestants baked and vote for your favorite. Winners will be announced at Sunday's gala luncheon. Without further ado, let me introduce Cynthia Sweet, a recipe columnist in Baltimore. She has created a sweet that Mrs. Hudson would have baked at Baker Street."

Bethany yielded the lectern to Cynthia, who wore a white pinafore apron over her flowered dress and a small, ruffled cap on her head. As she began her presentation, Val watched the people at the tables around hers for sudden moves.

Cynthia's syrupy voice reverberated through the room. "Mr. Holmes and Dr. Watson always enjoyed my hearty English breakfasts of eggs, toast, and rashers, what Americans call bacon. There were days, though, when Mr. Holmes ate little. Once he even fasted for three days. He broke his fast with my biscuits. And my biscuits gave another man the strength to go on after he collapsed of hunger at Baker Street. Biscuits in England are what Americans call cookies. That is the dessert I've made for you this evening— sweet lemon-glazed biscuits. And, of course, I would serve a proper cuppa with it."

Cynthia described the process of making perfect tea in painstaking detail—using water just off the boil, prewarming the pot and the cup, steep-

ing for the proper length of time. Val saw signs of
boredom in the audience but no signs of trouble.

Harrison fidgeted and muttered, "Why is she
going on and on about tea?"

When Cynthia asked if anyone had questions
about biscuits or tea, he rapped on the table and
stood up. "I don't like to quibble but . . . in sixty
stories Holmes rarely drinks *tea*. Mrs. Hudson serves
him coffee in the morning, though he does take
tea in railroad stations." Harrison sat down.

Cynthia squared her shoulders and thrust out
her chin. "Well, Mrs. Hudson drinks tea." She
matched Harrison's tone of outrage and then
switched into her usual dulcet voice. "I hope
you've all enjoyed my presentation. Now I'd like to
say something on a personal note. I'm thrilled to
be among so many successful writers, and I want to
announce that I will soon join your ranks. I just
learned that a publishing contract is in the works
for my cookbook, *Granny Sweet's Five-Ingredient Recipes*."

Val saw Granddad turn rigid, his lips set in a
grim line. He managed to clap politely as Cynthia
ended her presentation. Fortunately, he wasn't the
next contestant at the microphone, and he had
time to regain his composure before speaking.

Harrison didn't join in the applause for Cynthia. "I hope her dessert is better than her presentation."

Claire looked across the table at him. "I think
we should judge the desserts on their own merits."

Val gave her high marks for fairness and for taking on Harrison. If Val hadn't read the note about
sabotage at the bake-off and Granddad hadn't poi-

soned the well, she, too, would have defended
Cynthia against the pompous Harrison.

Cynthia returned to her seat on the dais when
the next contestant, Dave Proctor, stepped up to
the lectern.

He looked and sounded like an escapee from
*Downton Abbey.* As Bunter, Lord Peter Wimsey's
valet-cook, he wore a white shirt with a wing collar,
a black tie and vest, and a white apron tied at the
waist, similar to the bistro apron Val wore when
working at the café. His sandy hair was parted on
the side and slicked down.

He spoke with a stiff upper lip. "Lord Peter
drinks tea in the afternoon and evening, though
he always starts his day with my incomparable coffee. His words, not mine. As for sweets, His Lord-
ship enjoyed the petit fours at a soiree supper.
This evening I've made petit fours decorated for
this occasion."

Val listened intently as he described the process
of making petit fours, something she'd never
done, but he didn't explain what made them special for the occasion.

As Dave wrapped up his presentation, Jordan
said, "With that accent, he must hail from England."

Claire smiled. "By way of Chicago. He does a
good imitation of BBC English."

Trisha said, "You know him?"

Claire shook her head. "Besides history, I studied linguistics, especially regional speech. He grew
up in the Midwest. Figuring out where people come
from is my superpower. What's yours, Trisha?"

The volunteer tapped her pointed nose, her

most visible feature under her hat's long bill. "My sense of smell." She lowered her voice. "My nose tells me that Harrison smokes a pipe. His tobacco has hints of vanilla extract in it."

Val didn't pick up even a whiff, but Trisha, sitting next to Harrison, was closer to his tobacco aura.

Dave returned to his seat on the dais, and Granddad, wearing a chef's toque, walked to the lectern, carrying his book-shaped box of Nero Wolfe recipes. Val noticed the turned-up hem of his bib apron. Yikes! He was wearing it inside out. The prep room must not have had a mirror. Too bad Cynthia or Dave didn't tell him he needed a wardrobe fix.

Granddad stepped up to the microphone. "You've heard from a landlady who cooks and a manservant who cooks. I am someone whose only job is to cook. Fritz Brenner, personal chef to Nero Wolfe." Granddad touched his toque. "Mr. Wolfe is a gourmet and a detective. We both feel strongly about food. We often wrangle about the many ingredients that go into his typical meal. Because he wolfs down generous helpings at three meals a day, he has little room for desserts and nothing to say about them. I had to consult someone else before deciding on this evening's dessert."

Granddad whipped off his toque, took off his apron, and turned it to the opposite side. Val grinned when she read the words emblazoned on it—*Codger Cook.*

He returned to the microphone. "Now I'm speaking for myself, a recipe columnist in search of a dessert Nero would agree to eat. I found what

I needed in the fifth Nero Wolfe book, *Too Many Cooks*, the first mystery ever to include recipes. Rex Stout's promotional tour for the book included fancy lunches in a dozen cities. Each lunch guest got a recipe box that looked like a book." He held up the recipe box. "Inside are thirty-four recipe cards for the dishes mentioned in the book. The box is even rarer than a first edition of the book."

Harrison half-stood and craned his neck for a better look at it. The dealer's eyes smoldered with lust.

Granddad put the box on a shelf under the lectern's slanted top. "The recipes in the box include one for a sponge cake that I believe would be too bland for Nero's palate. I got an idea for serving that cake when I remembered the first words Rex Stout put in Nero's mouth—*Where's the beer?* There's a man after my own heart."

"My heart too," one of the anti-Christies shouted.

Granddad beamed. "My dessert is tiramisu with a twist. I whipped together mascarpone, cream, and coffee liqueur, and then soaked the sponge cake in the secret ingredient for Nero and Rex—stout." He showed the audience an amber bottle he'd pulled from under the lectern. Then he held up a parfait glass with layers of cake and mascarpone cream in it. "It's beeramisu!"

The audience applauded, led by the anti-Christies' standing ovation. Val was proud of Granddad's inventiveness. He'd come up with a unique dessert combining two five-ingredient recipes, one for the cake and the other for his tiramisu with a twist. The stout came as a surprise to her. She hadn't detected it when she'd sampled his dessert at home,

though she'd noticed the coffee flavor was less obvious than usual in a tiramisu. The anti-Christies
might like a dessert that tasted more strongly of
beer, but the rest of the audience would probably
prefer the subtle flavor of Granddad's concoction.

Bethany announced that volunteers would bring
the desserts to the tables. She thanked the bake-off
contestants and said they'd stay for a while in case
anyone in the audience wanted to talk to them.
She remained on the dais, scanning the crowd.

Fest volunteers brought the dessert samples to
the tables—a lemon-glazed "biscuit," a petit four,
and a plastic cup of beeramisu with a tiny taster
spoon for each attendee. They also received a ballot for voting on their favorite dessert. Val started
by eating the one she found least appealing in
looks. The lemon cookie was sweet on the outside
and rock-hard on the inside, like the woman who
made it, at least in Granddad's estimate. Cynthia
must have overworked the dough.

The petit four looked pretty, a cake cube with
strawberry jam and cream filling, covered all over
with pink icing, and a swirl of red icing on top.

Harrison peered at the others' dessert plates.
"Aha! Notice that the red icing on each little cake
is in the shape of a Clue board game weapon.
Mine is a gun."

Val examined the icing on her petit four. It looked
like a tiny noose. The others had a knife, a lead pipe,
and something that was either a candlestick or a
wrench. Petit fours suitable for the occasion, they ri-
valed Granddad's dessert for inventiveness. Granddad's dessert tasted better in Val's biased opinion.

She noticed her tablemates scraped every last bit of it from their small plastic cups.

As soon as Harrison finished his desserts, he rushed to the front of the room, where people clustered around the contestants. While the others conversed after filling out their ballots, Trisha took a while to fill out hers, not just checking off a favorite, but writing notes on it. Val waited, hoping for a chance to ask the volunteer if she knew who'd stuffed the fest envelopes and therefore could have slipped in anonymous notes. That chance never came. Trisha folded her ballot, said good night, and left the table with a tote the size of a diaper bag over her shoulder. Val figured the volunteer was anxious to get home. But no, she headed toward the dais.

Val joined Bethany at the back of the room near the exit door. "You managed the program well."

"Thank you. I hope Cynthia leaves soon. I won't relax completely until she goes back to the hotel. I'm not responsible for what happens there."

"You're not responsible no matter where she is. It was her choice to stay. Did she take the note as a hoax?"

Bethany rolled her eyes. "She took it as a challenge. I guess cooks who enter contests hunger for fame. She said people go to great lengths to win a bake-off."

"That sounds like a dig at Granddad and Dave. She'd better not go around implying that Granddad had anything to do with the threatening note. He received one that accused her of cheating." Val told Bethany what the note to Granddad said.

Bethany frowned. "I don't believe Cynthia would risk her reputation to tamper with a rival's dish. Someone at this fest has it in for her."

Val glanced at the dais. The crowd there had thinned. "When you get back to the hotel, meet me at the bar and I'll buy you a drink. You look like you could use one."

"Yes, but I might fall asleep before I finish it. See you later."

At nine thirty, when Val and Granddad went into the hotel lobby from the parking lot, they couldn't find three seats together at the bar. The six bistro tables near it were also taken, but a three-some looked ready to vacate theirs.

Val snagged it after a brief wait. She pointed to the canvas bag Granddad was carrying. "You want me to take that upstairs while you hold the table?"

"Nope. I'll keep it with me." Though he'd stowed a box with his mixing bowls, cake pans, and leftover ingredients in the car, he'd insisted on bringing the bag inside with him. It contained the props he'd used for his presentation—the apron, the toque, and the recipe box.

Val went to the bar to get his beer and glasses of wine for herself and Bethany. Cynthia was on a bar stool at the base of the U-shaped bar. She'd changed out of her Mrs. Hudson dress and into magenta lounging pants and a matching loose top. Dave Proctor sat next to her in his formal clothes, minus the apron he'd worn as Bunter and minus his British accent. Val didn't recognize the

man who sat on Cynthia's other side, but just beyond him was a woman who couldn't have been at
the bake-off without Val noticing her. The long
black hair, lipstick the color of dried blood, and
nose rings would have made her memorable. Val
had seen people in their teens and twenties who
favored that style, but this woman was well into
middle age. Beyond her, two of Val's bake-off tablemates, Claire and Harrison, sat along the right
side of the U.

While Val waited for the drinks, two women
praised Dave on the cleverness of his weapon-
decorated petit fours. Cynthia swiveled her bar
stool away from him, her lips pursed.

By the time Val brought the drinks to the table,
Bethany had arrived.

She proposed a toast. "Here's to you, Mr. Myer.
You were the hit of the bake-off. So many people
wanted to talk to you afterward."

"Thank you." He took a long swallow from his
frosted mug. "One of the folks who came up to me
afterward was the guy in the fancy suit, the one sitting at the bar now. He wanted to buy my Nero
Wolfe recipe box on the spot. He offered me three
hundred dollars."

Val wasn't surprised at the lowball offer. "Harrison Hawk, antiquarian mystery book dealer. I was
at his table for the bake-off. I assume you turned
him down."

"Yup. I told him the box wasn't for sale, but he
could buy one online for ten times what he offered me. Guess he thought I didn't know the
value of what I had." He peered under the table.

"Just checking that my bag is still there. If he comes near our table, I'm gonna grab that bag and hold it with both hands."

Bethany laughed. "He's not going to steal it."

"No?" Granddad took a swig of beer. "Even after I told him the box wasn't for sale, he kept eying it. I stuck it under the table to put temptation out of his way."

A middle-aged woman with thick gray hair approached him. "Aren't you the man who was involved in capturing the killer at Poe's grave? And in getting to the bottom of those murders right before Christmas?" Her robust voice must have carried to the people at the bar and nearby tables. They quieted, apparently waiting for Granddad's answer.

He grinned. "That's me. And those weren't the only crimes I've solved."

"Let's hope you don't have another one to solve this weekend. Last time this hotel hosted a bunch of mystery fans, there was a murder here, and the killer is still at large."

Bar stools and heads swiveled toward her.

Cynthia broke the silence. "I was here when that murder happened. I knew from the start that the police suspected the wrong person."

The gray-haired woman took out a business card and handed it to Granddad. "I'm a journalist, Greer Gordon. I write true-crime books in addition to a newspaper column focused on crime. We should talk sometime."

She went over to the bar, abandoning him for Cynthia. Dave gave up his seat next to Cynthia and Greer took it.

Granddad folded his arms. "I'll bet Cynthia doesn't know anything about that old murder. She was just jealous of the attention I got."

With his Bunter tie askew, Dave walked past their table, carrying a half-full highball glass. He stopped to greet them.

Val said, "Good job at the bake-off."

Bethany nodded. "I loved your British accent."

"Thank you." He ran a finger under the neck of his dress shirt. "I'm looking forward to getting out of the butler monkey suit."

Granddad said, "I didn't get around to asking you this when we were making our desserts. The envelope with my name tag also had a note in it. Did yours?"

Dave shook his head. "I just grabbed the tag and tickets out of the envelope and tossed it. What did the note say?"

Bethany answered before Granddad could. "It was advice about the bake-off. It's over now, so *it doesn't matter.*"

Granddad took the hint and said no more about the anonymous note.

Dave held up his glass. "I'll come back for another of these when it's less crowded. Maybe I'll see you all then."

As he left, Bethany said, "The bar will be even more crowded later, after the movie ends." She leaned toward Granddad. "The less said about the anonymous notes you and Cynthia received, the better. Now that we came through the bake-off okay, the rest of the weekend should be a breeze."

With Cynthia and her harasser still around, Val felt an ill wind blowing, not a gentle breeze.

When they finished their drinks, they took the elevator up to the third floor. A minute after Val and Bethany went into their room, they heard a knock on the door. Val opened it.

Granddad stood there wide-eyed with his mouth downturned, like the icon of a frowning face. "Come in. What's wrong?" Val closed the door behind him.

"My Nero Wolfe recipe box is gone. It isn't in my canvas bag."

Bethany frowned. "When did you last see the box?"

"After the bake-off, when folks in the audience came up, I stuck the box in my bag under the table." He folded his arms. "Three steps down from the dais, where the crowd was, someone must have reached under the table and pulled it out when everyone crowded around."

Val conjured an image of his canvas bag under the table and his chef's hat sticking out of it. "The bag was on its side. Maybe the box fell out, and I didn't notice it on the floor when I picked up the bag. Is the community center still open, Bethany?"

"No, but I'll call over there first thing in the morning and ask them to look for the box. It'll probably turn up tomorrow, Mr. Myer."

Val could tell he was frustrated at having to wait until the next day. "The box could have slipped out of the bag on our way here. Why don't you look in the car, Granddad? I'll go back to the table where we had drinks and check if the box is under it."

They took the elevator down together and then went separate ways.

Approaching the bar, Val distinguished Cynthia's voice amid the hum of conversation. Her speech was slurred, and Val picked up only a word here and there—*heirloom, poisoning, turtle*. What could Cynthia be talking about? She had her back to the bar and one hand extended, as if showing a ring. The people around her blocked Val's view of it.

Val approached the table where she'd sat earlier and asked the couple there to check if there was anything under it. They found nothing on the floor. But someone might have noticed the recipe box and taken it before they sat down. Harrison had coveted it earlier. He was still at the bar next to Claire. Val was surprised to see Trisha in her monogrammed baseball cap at the far end of the U-shaped bar and almost hidden by a large espresso machine. The volunteer lived nearby but apparently wasn't anxious to go home.

Granddad returned from the parking lot with empty hands.

"The recipe box is probably at the community center," Val said to him on the elevator. "Forget about it until tomorrow and get a good night's sleep. I'll meet you in the hotel restaurant at seven thirty for breakfast."

"Okay, but I don't expect to sleep much," he grumbled. "My room's right across from the vending alcove with an ice machine. Whenever anyone gets ice, it makes a racket."

Val shrugged. "Most people don't need ice in the middle of the night." And not much woke Granddad once he fell asleep.


Val woke up to a high-pitched noise. It wasn't piercing like a smoke alarm, but still the whining whistle was annoying. The clock on the nightstand between her bed and Bethany's read 12:05. Her friend was stirring but still asleep. Val got up to check the source of the noise.

It was loudest near the wall between her room and Cynthia's. Val recognized the sound—the kettle that had whistled in the afternoon. Cynthia must have put on water for tea, forgotten about it, and gone down to the lobby. Or maybe her bar drinks had put her into a deep sleep.

Rather than risk waking Bethany by calling the front desk from the room, Val decided to deal with the problem herself. Fortunately, her PJ bottoms looked more like joggers than jammies. She zipped herself into a warm-up jacket and put on her black flats.

Stuffing her key card in her jacket pocket, she crept out of the room and knocked on Cynthia's door. After half a minute, Val knocked again. Still no answer. She took the elevator down two floors and looked around the lobby.

No sign of Cynthia, but two men sat at the bar—Jordan Young, the dark-skinned war veteran turned cozy-mystery writer, and the pale, light-haired Dave Proctor. He'd exchanged his Bunter vest, tie, and dress shirt for black joggers and a gray T-shirt. The small duffel bag on the floor next to him suggested he'd changed clothes to visit the hotel's fitness room before his nightcap.

Val went over to them. "Hi. I'm looking for Cynthia Sweet. Have you seen her?"

Jordan swiveled toward Val, a beer bottle in his hand. "Remind me who she is."

Dave said, "Mrs. Hudson at the bake-off. She was here earlier. By the time she left the bar, she'd had a few." He mimed drinking. "She's probably sleeping it off."

Jordan pulled out the stool next to his. "You want to join us, Val?"

Before she could answer, the beefy bartender spoke up. "I'm sorry. We closed at midnight. You're welcome to sit here, but I'm not pouring anything else tonight."

"No problem. You guys have a good evening."

Val crossed the lobby to the front desk and reported the persistent noise from the room next to hers. The clerk called the room. When he got no answer, he summoned a security guard and asked him to accompany Val to the third floor and check on the problem.

The man in a gray uniform shirt and pants looked more like a college student than a security professional. As he waited with Val for the elevator, he introduced himself as Nico Garcia and asked her to describe the noise.

"It sounds like a whistling kettle. I heard it this afternoon when the woman in the room was making tea."

They got into the elevator, and he pressed the button for the third floor. "I wouldn't want the lady to wake up and see a strange man in her room. If she doesn't answer the door, would you mind going in and unplugging the kettle?"

"I don't mind."

As they got out of the elevator on the third floor, Bethany was standing there, wearing sweatpants and a bulky sweater. "I was just going to look for you, Val. A weird noise from Cynthia's room woke me up." She eyed the guard. "What's going on?"

"We're checking on the noise you heard," Val said.

The security guard knocked twice on the door to room 310 and then unlocked it with a key card. As soon as the door opened, the high-pitched whistle sounded even louder. He held the door open for Val.

She called out to Cynthia and got no response. The light in the entrance hall illuminated the doors to the closet and the bathroom on the left. The desk straight ahead was also visible. On it was an electric kettle with steam rising from its spout. Val darted toward it, Bethany trailing her. The instant Val unplugged the kettle, the whistling stopped.

She peered across the room at the bed. The duvet covering a mound on the window side of the bed told Val that someone was lying there, but the light wasn't bright enough for her to see more. "Cynthia?" she called. No answer.

"How could she have slept with that kettle shrieking? I hope she's okay." Bethany flipped a switch that turned on the nightstand lamps. She inched past Val and around the foot of the bed. As she approached the head of the bed, she yelped. "Oh no! Val, I think she's dead!"

# Chapter 4

Bethany skittered away from the bed, brushed past Val, and then stumbled as she went around the desk. She steadied herself with one hand on it and the other on the wall behind it.

The security guard came toward them. "You say she's dead?"

Bethany nodded. "Her eyes are open. She's staring at the ceiling."

He walked purposefully around the bed to the side where Cynthia was lying. Val stayed rooted while Nico leaned over the bed for a closer look at Cynthia. His broad shoulders kept Val from seeing what he was doing. Just as well. As long as she didn't look, she could hope that Bethany had been wrong. Though Val had come across dead bodies previously, it wasn't an experience she wanted to repeat. They had been murder victims. That didn't mean Cynthia had been murdered, but Val felt queasy, remembering the *bake offed* note.

It seemed an eternity before Nico stood up straight. "She's dead alright." He pulled out his cell phone. "I gotta call 911. They'll dispatch the EMTs and the police."

"The police?" Val's stomach lurched. "Was she attacked? Do you see any blood or bruises?"

"No, but when someone dies with no one else around, the police always come. I know that 'cause I majored in criminal justice, and I'm studying to be a policeman." He frowned in concentration as if trying to remember his coursework. "You ladies can leave. What's your room number in case the police want to talk to you?"

Relieved, Val said, "We're both in 312." Probably the police would have no reason to talk to her if Cynthia had died of natural causes. But if she hadn't, Val would tell them about the note. She turned to leave and was surprised to see Bethany bending over, clutching her middle. "Are you okay? If you're going to be sick—"

"Let's get out of here." Bethany straightened, her arms still wrapped around her stomach, and rushed out to the corridor.

Val had her key card ready. She opened the door to their room and stepped aside to let her friend go in. "Can I get you anything?"

Bethany shook her head. "Shouldn't you go tell your grandfather about Cynthia?"

Val hesitated. He'd be upset if she didn't at least try to give him the news. "I don't want to wake him up, so I won't call him. I'll tap on his door. If he's awake, I'll tell him about Cynthia. Otherwise the news can wait until morning."

Bethany hurried into the bathroom. Val went out the door and down the corridor to Grand-dad's room. She knocked on his door, waited half a minute, tried again, and still got no response. He must be sleeping better than he'd expected. She retraced her steps.

Bethany was in bed with her eyes closed. Had she fallen asleep in exhaustion? Or was she faking sleep because she didn't want to talk about finding Cynthia dead? Val shed her jacket and slipped off her shoes. She'd showered before going to bed earlier, but now she wanted to do it again to scrub off the last half hour. That wouldn't work. She settled for splashing water on her face. As she came out of the bathroom, she heard noises in the corridor. She cracked the door open and saw emergency responders rushing from the elevators toward Cynthia's room. Nico let them in.

Across from Cynthia's room, a small woman with wispy white curls peered out her door. "I wonder what's happening in there." She pointed to Cynthia's room.

"So do I." Val closed her door.

She collapsed on the bed, but had trouble falling asleep. She pushed aside the duvet and switched pillows. The linen on the other bed rustled as Bethany turned and tossed. A murmur of deep voices came through the wall between Cynthia's room and theirs. Val was tempted to put her ear to that wall, but she was too tired to get out of bed. She couldn't unplug her brain as easily as she had the kettle. How could Cynthia be lying dead with her kettle whistling? Maybe she'd put on water for tea, lain down because she felt ill, and died of a heart attack or a stroke. But the anonymous note made it hard for Val to accept that explanation.

Val woke up at seven when the alarm on her phone went off, feeling as if she hadn't slept most of the night. She rolled over and saw Bethany sitting on the other bed. "Ready for the busy day ahead?"

"I'm trying to decide how to handle Cynthia's death. I hate to put a damper on the fest by talking about it at the opening session."

The fest goers relished death on the page, but they hadn't anticipated the real thing. Val wondered how they would react. She swung her legs over the side of her bed. "You can't pretend it didn't happen. Anyone in the lobby when the EMTs and police arrived or left would know something was going on. And an older woman across the hall saw where the responders went."

"Birdie Natter. She's a volunteer, nosy and gossipy. She poked her head out of her door when I came up to drop off my suitcase yesterday." Bethany massaged her temples as if she had a headache. "Can I get by with a brief announcement? *I'm sorry to tell you that Cynthia Sweet passed away last night in her room.* How does that sound?"

"Okay, but can someone else say it? If you make the announcement, people will hound you for details, especially if it gets out that you have the room next to Cynthia's."

"I don't want to spend today reliving what hap-

pened last night." Bethany sprang off the bed and
paced the room. "The fest chairwoman should
make the announcement after she gives the welcome. I'll write it down for her so she doesn't turn
the job over to me."

"Good plan. I'd like to grab a table in the restaurant before it gets too crowded. You want to have
breakfast with Granddad and me? He's meeting
me at seven thirty."

"I'll join you there after I shower and get dressed."

Val put on jeans and a pullover. Hoping to fit in
a morning walk before the fest's opening session,
she took her sweat jacket with her.

A crowd in the hallway leading to the restaurant
made her glad she'd come early for a table. This
was Val's first time in the hotel's new wing. With a
lower ceiling than in the Poe wing, the narrow corridor crammed with people awakened her claustrophobia.

She lined up behind the Stetson-wearing anti-
Christie she'd noticed at the bake-off. He was with
a man whose clothes came from the big-and-tall
department. From somewhere ahead of them, the
voice of a woman carried toward Val.

"Have you heard what happened to Cynthia
Sweet, Mrs. Hudson from the bake-off?" The
woman paused for a response Val couldn't hear
and then continued. "I don't know much about it
myself, but I saw an emergency team go into her
room last night, and the police too. I knocked on
her door this morning, and there was no answer."

Val concluded the woman had to be the gossip
Bethany had mentioned, Birdie Natter. Val couldn't
see the woman's face but glimpsed wisps of white

hair peeking out from under a large hat. With its crown decorated with leaves and feathers, it looked like a nest. Maybe Birdie always wore a nest on her head.

She continued to talk. "I'm afraid something bad has happened to her. The hotel won't tell me anything. I'll just keep asking folks until I find someone who knows."

The Stetson man ahead of Val elbowed his companion. "Mrs. Peacock in the hotel room with a candlestick?"

"No. With a teapot." Both men guffawed.

While Birdie talked to a man leaving the restaurant, Val hunched down, put up the hood of her sweat jacket, and edged into the restaurant. She snagged a secluded table in the restaurant's far corner. Granddad arrived five minutes later, with Bethany right behind him.

Once the three of them were seated, a perky teenage server came over to pour coffee and take their breakfast orders. Bethany asked for a cinnamon-raisin bagel with cream cheese to go, Val ordered French toast with fresh berries, and Granddad requested a skinny omelet, turkey sausage, toast, and fruit. Before Val moved in with him and weaned him off his unhealthy diet, he'd have ordered a cheese omelet, bacon, and a muffin. She was sure he still indulged in red meat and sweets when she wasn't around, but not often.

As soon as the teenager left, Granddad said, "A woman outside the restaurant says the police went into Cynthia's room last night. Do you know what that's about?"

"Yes, I tried to tell you last night, but you didn't

answer when I knocked on your door." Val gave him the details.

The news shocked him into silence, but he recovered after a few sips of coffee. "Mighty strange, her dying a few hours after getting that nasty note."

Bethany jerked back in her seat. "Why? Cynthia was lying there like she died in her sleep. The security guard said he didn't see any blood or injuries."

Granddad shrugged. "That doesn't eliminate poison. Did you notice a glass or any medicine on the night table?"

"Her face is all I remember, and I wish I didn't." Bethany guzzled water as if to wash away the memory.

Val said, "I didn't get close enough to see Cynthia or the night table."

"What was on the desk?" Granddad persisted. "Anything to eat or drink?"

Val closed her eyes, trying to picture the desk surface. "Near the kettle was the usual hotel coffeemaker with the paraphernalia that goes with it and a small teapot that must have been Cynthia's. Two key cards were there, and a cell phone was plugged into a charger."

He stroked his chin. "Was anything strewn around the floor?"

Like a murder weapon? "Nothing I saw, Granddad. There were no signs of a struggle in the room. The only thing I noticed on the floor was Cynthia's big, quilted tote bag."

Bethany bit her lip. "Her shoes were near the bed. I stepped on one and almost tripped." Her eyes glistened with tears. "It's bad enough she died during the fest. Murder would be worse. It wouldn't be fun to talk about murders in books if a real one happened."

Granddad sipped his coffee. "You can't predict what mystery fans will do when they find out someone died unexpectedly. Some of them will just assume it was murder and start snooping."

Val leaned toward him. "That's exactly what *you're* doing."

He glanced at her teary-eyed friend. "I'm sorry for dwelling on it, Bethany. Breakfast is on me."

"Thank you. And I'm okay. Really." Bethany looked at her watch. "I hope they hurry up with my bagel. Fest registration starts at eight. I have to make sure that we have enough volunteers at the table and that the AV is set up for our opening session."

"Text me if you need help with anything." Val pointed to the server coming toward them with a tray. "Our breakfasts are here."

Bethany picked up the bagel the server delivered to her. "Off to work." She left the restaurant.

A minute later Val caught sight of the journalist who'd stopped at their bar table last night. What was her name? Greta? No, Greer. Tucking into his breakfast, Granddad didn't notice her. "Keep your head down, Granddad." Val took a bite of her French toast and focused on her plate.

Her attempt at invisibility didn't work.

Greer approached their table. "Good morning! Have you seen Cynthia Sweet anywhere? She was supposed to meet me for breakfast."

Val said quickly, "No, we haven't seen her." Ironically, the journalist had posed an easy question to answer truthfully, while Birdie's question—*what happened to Cynthia?*—would have put Val on the spot. The score stood at one for the nosy amateur and zero for the professional interviewer.

Greer said, "I'll look around the lobby. Maybe she's waiting there for me. Have a good one, you two."

Granddad watched her leave the restaurant. "She said she wrote about true crime. She's after information about the murder here a year ago. Cynthia no sooner claimed to know something about it than Greer was all over her. Other people heard Cynthia say that too."

Val could tell the wheels were turning in his head, grinding out a motive for someone to kill Cynthia. "The people at my bake-off table said the crime occurred after a murder mystery dinner. Cynthia might not be the only one here who attended that dinner."

"One murder makes the hotel an attraction. Two makes it a place to avoid." Granddad went back to eating breakfast, and so did Val.

The next time she looked up from her plate, Trisha was approaching their table. She again wore the baseball cap with her name on it. "It's the beeramisu chef! I didn't get a chance to talk to you after the bake-off. I loved your routine and your dessert."

Val stared at the previously bashful volunteer now bubbling over with friendliness. Yesterday her well of words had been nearly dry. What had primed the pump?

Granddad grinned. "Thank you very much. I enjoyed it myself."

"Did you get your recipe box back?"

Granddad squinted at the volunteer. "No. I've been looking for it. Do you know where it is?"

Trisha pushed up her oversized glasses. "Cynthia had it last night. I guess she didn't have a chance to return it to you. It was in the big flowered tote bag she carries."

Granddad frowned. "I don't understand how the box could have gotten there."

Trisha hesitated and then said, "When everyone was crowding around you after the bake-off, she reached down under the table. She knocked over her bag and yours. A couple of her things spilled out on the floor near your recipe box."

Val didn't see that as evidence Cynthia had taken it. Why would she? "Did you see her put the recipe box in her bag?"

"I didn't stick around to watch her pick up the stuff, but I saw it, or a book with a similar cover, in her bag later."

Val rated the possibility of a similar cover as close to zero.

Granddad glanced at the volunteer's hat. "Thank you, Trisha. It was nice of you to tell me about the box."

"No problem. See you later. I gotta get to work at the fest table."

"Just a second," Val said. "Do you know who filled the envelopes containing our name tags and tickets?"

"I'm not sure. When I got to the fest table, an older woman was giving out the envelopes. She was peeved at me for being a little late. She told me she'd spent all morning getting everything ready and wanted to rest before the bake-off. She might have filled the envelopes."

"Do you remember her name?"

"Something weird. Oh yeah, Birdie." Trisha took two steps away from the table and then turned back. "Why were you asking? Was something missing from your packet?"

"Nothing was missing." Val certainly wasn't going to explain why she'd asked. "Thanks, Trisha. See you later."

Granddad folded his arms as the volunteer left. "So it was Cynthia, not the book dealer, who stole my box."

"Don't accuse her of stealing. She might have picked it up by mistake and not even realized it." She ignored his skeptical look and continued. "It's still worth asking if the box is at the community center. Trisha could have been wrong about what was in Cynthia's bag."

"Okay, but I'm not holding out hope. If the police have Cynthia's bag and my box is in it, I can claim it. The whole audience last night saw me with that box."

"The police might not give it to you anyway. They're probably required to turn everything over to Cynthia's family. You'll have to convince her heirs to give it back."

He speared a piece of sausage. "Sounds like I won't get it back anytime soon."

If ever. As Val tackled her French toast again, she looked around the restaurant. She recognized a few people from the bake-off. Harrison Hawk, the book dealer Granddad had been ready to accuse of theft, was gesturing broadly at a table with an older couple and a young woman. Jordan Young, the war veteran, was sitting with the women Harrison had dubbed the Miss Marples.

Val pointed out Claire Rainey standing near the restaurant entrance. "At the bake-off, I sat next to that woman with the curly hair. She helps authors of historical mysteries get the details right. Okay if I ask her to sit with us?"

"Fine with me."

Val stood up, went over to Claire, and greeted her. "Would you like to join my grandfather and me for breakfast?"

"I'll join you, but I've already eaten breakfast. I came down for a cup of coffee with real milk. I hate the creamer stuff they put in hotel rooms."

Val brought her to the table. "This is my grandfather, Don Myer." She noticed no flicker of recognition as Claire looked at him. "He played Fritz, Nero Wolfe's chef."

"I'm Claire Rainey." She extended her hand to Granddad. "I enjoyed your presentation last night and the dessert you made. Are you really a gourmet cook?"

"Nope. I stick with five-ingredient recipes, like the ones I put in my newspaper column." He held up his cup, signaling the server to bring coffee to the table, and turned back to Claire. "Val says you help writers get their history right. What's your process?"

"I review manuscripts to make sure that the language is appropriate for the time. I also check that the food, drinks, clothing, and jewelry are accurate for the historical period." Claire stopped abruptly. "Speaking of jewelry, I want to ask Cynthia Sweet about the ring she was showing off at the bar last night. She said it was from the Renaissance. Have you seen her?"

As the server arrived to fill their cups, Val exchanged a look with Granddad. They hadn't told Greer the journalist or Trisha the volunteer about Cynthia. No reason to switch gears. "We haven't seen her this morning. A ring that old must be worth a lot."

"Absolutely, but her ring isn't as old as she thinks." Claire added milk to her coffee. "From what I could see, it's Renaissance revival jewelry from the late nineteenth century. Though it's not a museum piece, it's a lovely antique ring with an intricate design."

Val wished she'd had a chance to see it. "What does it look like?"

"The band is gold. It has a gold turtle on top with diamonds of different shapes on its shell."

Granddad sipped his coffee. "A diamondback terrapin, the official Maryland state reptile. I noticed she was wearing a big ring when we were making our desserts last night. I figured it was gaudy costume jewelry."

Val couldn't imagine baking with a big ring on. "Diamonds and dough get in the way of each other."

Granddad frowned. "Are you sure they were real diamonds, Claire?"

She shrugged. "I'm not a gem expert, but I saw a similar ring on *Antiques Roadshow*. It was in the shape of a salamander and encrusted with diamonds, big ones on the top and smaller ones around the bezel and down the sides. Both that one and Cynthia's are poison rings."

Granddad's fork full of omelet stopped halfway to his mouth.

The seemingly unrelated words Val had overheard Cynthia say in the bar now made sense. She was describing her jewelry—*heirloom, turtle,* and *poison ring,* not poisoning. Had poison caused her death?

# Chapter 5

Granddad put down his fork. "What exactly is a poison ring, Claire?"

"A poison ring has a hinge like a locket. You flick it open and there's a compartment, a little deeper than the one in a locket." Claire mimicked opening a hinge on a phantom ring.

Granddad's eyes lit up. "Like the ring in the movie *Casablanca*. A man flips it up to reveal a symbol of the French resistance."

Claire nodded. "Rings with hidden chambers have been popular since ancient times and have many uses. Poison is just the most dramatic one. Hannibal supposedly avoided capture by the Romans by swallowing poison he'd kept inside his ring. During the Renaissance in Italy, the infamous Borgia family used such rings to slip poison into their enemy's wine."

"So the ring wearer is the poisoner, not the one

poisoned." Granddad looked disappointed. "What else would someone put in the compartment?"

"People carried scented pomade to block noxious smells." Claire raised her hand to her nose. "It might hold pills or strands of a loved one's hair. Cynthia said it was a family heirloom. I'd love to hear the story behind it." Claire finished her coffee. "I have a pile of papers to grade before the sessions start."

Granddad said, "Then you'd better get to work. The coffee's on me."

She stood up. "Thank you for that and for sharing your table." She left.

"I hope to get to her panel this afternoon." Val put down her cup. "I'm going to the Poe wing to sign up for the panels I want to monitor and to see if Bethany could use an extra pair of hands."

"Tell her I'm available if she needs help." Granddad signaled the server for the check. "Just in case Trisha was wrong, I'll call the community center when it opens to see if anyone turned in the recipe box. I'll catch up with you later."

Val was already assigned to monitor the last panel of the morning. She put her name on the schedule for Claire's panel in the afternoon. The fest table was well staffed, and Bethany needed no help with room setup. Val had free time for a stroll outside. Walking through the lobby toward the hotel exit, she noticed Birdie perched on the edge of a chair, looking ready to pounce. Val hunched down and quickened her step toward the exit.

A man stepped into her path. "Val! Great to see you again."

She stared up at Roy Chesterfeld, a sheriff's

deputy she'd met in Southern Maryland. In his early thirties, Roy had thick blond hair and a face made for Hollywood. She was used to seeing him in uniform, but today he wore casual clothes. "What brings you here, Roy?"

"My family's from this area. I moved back last year to join the police department as a detective."

"Congratulations on your promotion." Detectives wore plainclothes, so he might be on duty. "Are you looking into last night's death here?"

"Uh-huh. It appears to be from natural causes, but when I read you were the first person on the scene, I decided the case might need a second look. You have a history of finding murder victims." He gave her a wry smile. "Just teasing, but I need you to give me the details."

Val scanned the lobby filled with people wearing fest badges. Birdie Natter's beady eyes were trained on her and Roy. "How about we talk outside? We'll have more privacy than in here."

"Sounds good. Beyond the patio at the back of the hotel, there's a pond with a path around it." They walked through the lobby and past the bar. He opened the door to the patio. "I saw the poster in the lobby about the mystery fest. I'd rather not have amateur sleuths eavesdropping on us. Are you here for the fest?"

"I'm a volunteer, not the kind of fan a lot of people here are." They walked quickly by two smokers standing just outside the door. "The woman who died, Cynthia Sweet, was also here for the fest."

"I didn't know that." He matched her pace as they headed toward the pond. "According to the report I read, you heard a whistling noise coming from her room around midnight. What happened after that?"

Val described going to the lobby and returning to the third floor with the security guard. "Bethany met us in the hall. I'm rooming with her, and by then the noise had woken her up too."

"The report mentioned a roommate but not by name." His smile revealed even white teeth. "I'll make time to catch up with Bethany this weekend."

And possibly renew their relationship after he'd broken it off? Bethany had fallen hard for him a year and a half ago and didn't need him complicating her life now. Should Val stick her nose into this? Maybe just the tip of it. "Bethany won't have much free time because she's running the fest, but I can update you about her. She's doing really well. The PTA at her school has nominated her for a teaching award." Val looked up and caught his eye. "And she's seeing a guy who's perfect for her."

Regret flitted across his face and disappeared. "I'm glad for her. Now, back to what occurred last night."

"There's not much more to tell." The path around the pond was lined with yellow daffodils. She'd always thought of them as happy flowers, a sign that spring had come, but they didn't lift her spirits this morning as she detailed what led the guard to call 911.

"What happened after he made that call?"

"Bethany felt sick, so she went back to our room. I knocked on the door to my grandfather's room to tell him about Cynthia, but he slept through my knocking."

Roy grinned. "Your grandfather's here too. How's he doing?"

"Great. He competed in the fest bake-off last night. So did Cynthia. I want to report that they both received anonymous notes. His was a warning and hers a threat." Val quoted the notes.

"Her note sounds like trash talk, not a threat. *Bake offed at the bake-off* is a way of calling her a loser."

The detective's interpretation surprised Val. Had she, Granddad, and Bethany overreacted? Being at a fest devoted to murder mysteries might have influenced them. Val was too embarrassed to tell Roy they'd marshaled an army of volunteers to foil a possible attack. And yet, the woman was dead. "I'd be more inclined to take the wording as an insult if Cynthia was still alive this morning. Unless you have proof that she died of natural causes, you might want to examine the note. It's probably in her hotel room."

"The officers who responded last night bagged everything in that room. If she had the note, it's in our possession."

Did the police suspect foul play? "Is it standard procedure to remove everything from a room after someone dies of natural causes?"

"We didn't have a doctor to sign a death certificate attesting to the cause." Roy remained silent for a moment, as if deciding whether to say more. "And there was another reason to scoop everything up. She died alone in a hotel room. A year ago in the same hotel, a man also died alone in his room. He was murdered. There are similarities and differences between the two deaths. That was my first case here, and it's still open. I know who did it, but we don't have a witness or any forensic evidence to prove it."

His rigid jaw told Val that the open case bothered him. "Last night at the bar, Cynthia mentioned that murder. She announced that she was here when it happened. In her opinion, the police investigation focused on the wrong person."

"What?" Roy steered Val to a bench along the path. "What else did she say?"

"That's all I heard."

"Who else might have heard Cynthia say that?"

Val shrugged. "Lots of people were in the bar. She was speaking loudly, like she wanted attention. I don't know how many people heard her because the bar was crowded and noisy."

He pulled out his phone. "Can you give me the names of anyone who was near her?"

She visualized the people at the bar. "Dave Proctor, Harrison Hawk, Claire Rainey, Trisha Turbek—no, wait, Trisha wasn't there until later. Greer Gordon, a journalist who'd been talking to Granddad, rushed over to talk to Cynthia. Greer told us this morning that she and Cynthia were supposed to meet for breakfast."

Roy looked up from thumbing a text message. "Was anyone else sitting close to Cynthia when she brought up that murder?"

"No one whose name I know. A woman with goth makeup and long black hair sat nearby. I didn't see her at the bake-off last night or in the restaurant this morning. I doubt she has anything to do with the fest."

"The bartender might have heard what Cynthia said too. About what time was that?"

"Best estimate, nine forty-five."

Roy's phone buzzed, and he stepped away from the bench to take the call.

Seconds later Val received a text from Granddad: *Recipe box not at community center. Saw YouTube of the poison ring on the antique show. Worth 7-8 thou a few years back.*

And it might be worth more now. When Roy returned to the bench, Val told him about Cynthia's ring and the appraisal Granddad had found of a similar one. "Cynthia showed it around the bar last night. I didn't see it, but someone described it to me. Did the police find it in her room?"

"It wasn't on her finger. I'll get someone to sift through the stuff we bagged."

"Could you ask them to look for something else too?" She described the Nero Wolfe recipe box and told Roy what Trisha had said about Cynthia having it. "Granddad would like to get it back. He has a sentimental attachment to it, but it's also prized as a rarity, worth a few thousand dollars."

Roy whistled and thumbed a message into his phone. "Hard to believe a box of recipes would sell for that much. You'd better hope Cynthia's heirs don't know the value of the box or your grandfather might have trouble getting it back."

Taking the heirs to court to get it back might cost more than the box was worth. "Do you know who Cynthia's heirs are?"

He shook his head. "We're trying to track down her next of kin. The only person she had listed as an emergency contact is her husband. He's been dead almost a month."

"I'll try to find out if anyone at the fest knows about her family." Val glanced at her watch and stood up. "I should go. I'm supposed to help Bethany with the festival kickoff."

As they retraced their steps back to the hotel, Roy said, "What's new with you? Still managing the café at the athletic club?"

She nodded. "I've added a sideline, catering small parties or dinners, usually in people's homes."

"Still going out with the same guy?" His tone was nonchalant.

She glanced at him and saw only his profile. His straight-ahead look suggested he had no stake in her answer. Fine with her. "No, but I'm seeing someone else."

"Darn. I didn't manage to catch you in between them."

Flirting was a reflex for him, but not for Val. She was glad his phone rang, cutting off the banter.

He walked next to her with the phone up to his ear and grunted a few times. "Thanks. I'll call you later with instructions." He put the phone back in his pocket. "I have bad news. No ring and no recipe box among Cynthia Sweet's belongings. And no video cameras in that old wing of the hotel. Any theories on who could have stolen those items and when?"

"*When* is easier than *who*. The whistling kettle narrows down the time. I'm guessing she invited someone for tea last night. She let the person into the room, started the tea, and then didn't feel well. She went to lie down, or maybe her guest helped her into bed. Then she died. Her guest didn't want to report her death and rushed out after grabbing a couple of souvenirs."

"Why leave the kettle on?"

Val shrugged. "Maybe the water hadn't boiled yet. Unplugging the kettle's not foremost in the thief's mind. Getting away is."

"Who drinks tea at that hour?"

"Cynthia. At the bake-off, she gave a talk about making tea properly. She said she traveled with her own kettle, pot, cup, and teas."

"So a friend who came for tea stole the ring?" He shook his head. "The security guard let you into her room. Other hotel staffers could have gained access, but let's focus on him because we know he was there. Were you in a position to see him the whole time?"

Val balked at the idea that Nico would have stolen anything from Cynthia. "The guard studied criminal justice. He must know he'd be the first suspect if anything went missing."

"You didn't answer my question. Was he in your sight the entire time?"

"I looked away when he checked to see if Cynthia was dead, but he couldn't count on my doing that. Bethany and I were standing there, and the room lights were on."

"Could you see the night table from where you were?"

"No." Roy's question suggested he thought the ring might have been on the night table within easy reach of Nico, but that wasn't the only stolen object. "The guard couldn't have taken the recipe box. It's the size of a hardback book, too big to fit in his pockets, too bulky to shove under his shirt. He had no reason to think it had any value, unlike the people who went to the bake-off." Especially Harrison Hawk, the book dealer.

"Any burglar would take a valuable ring. It's easy to conceal and to fence diamonds and gold." Roy thought a moment. "That's not true of the box. It's a rare thief who'd snatch two such different things. I'll need to talk to the woman who told you about the ring to get a description of it. What's her name?"

"Claire Rainey. Are you thinking there might be two thieves rather than only one with a taste for rings and recipes?"

"I'm not sure," he said as they approached the hotel's patio.

Val wondered if the missing recipe box interested him at all. She owed it to Granddad to prod Roy a bit. "Trisha Turbek is the woman who saw the recipe box in Cynthia's bag, in case you want to follow up with her. She's easy to spot in her purple baseball cap with her name on it."

Back in the lobby, he shook Val's hand. "Thank you for your help. Without you I'd still be inquiring into an unattended death. Now it's looking like a criminal investigation of at least grand theft, if not something even more serious."

"Val!" Bethany bustled across the lobby. "I wondered where you were. We need to—" She broke off and eyed the man next to Val. "Hello, Roy."

"Bethany!" He approached with his arms extended as if ready to embrace her.

She stepped back, her expression stony. "What

are you doing at the mystery fest? Promoting a
book about your exploits?"

He looked taken aback. "I'm not promoting a
book. I'll let Val fill you in." He gave them a curt
nod and headed to the reception desk.

Bethany looked wary. "What's going on, Val?"

They were standing in the busiest part of the
lobby, in the path from the elevators to the Poe
wing. Val whispered, "I'll tell you, but not here.
Come with me."

"This fest has too many mysteries," Bethany muttered.

# *Chapter 6*

As Val and Bethany crossed the lobby, Grand-dad emerged from an elevator. Val motioned for him to come along with them. They huddled near the bar, which wasn't yet open.

Val explained Roy's new job and his interest in Cynthia's death. "He said that the circumstances of her death resembled last year's murder at this hotel, but he stopped short of saying the police suspected murder this time. I brought up the note Cynthia received before the bake-off, but he didn't see it as a threat. Even if Cynthia died of natural causes, he has a related crime to investigate. A thief might have been in her room last night."

Bethany turned pale and gaped at her. "A thief?"

"A valuable ring she was wearing last night has disappeared." Val described the ring. "Roy's theory is the security guard took it when he went to check if she was dead."

Bethany shook her head. "No way. The guard was pretty shaken up. Roy's just reaching for an easy solution."

Val agreed that the detective had hit on the simplest explanation. Any other one required answering a number of questions. How and when did the thief enter Cynthia's room? Why did Cynthia put on water for tea and then climb into bed? "I know you don't want to think about this, Bethany, but when you saw Cynthia lying there, did you notice what she was wearing?"

"The duvet covered her except around the shoulders. She still had on the reddish-purple top she wore in the bar." Bethany glanced at her watch. "The opening session's starting soon. Unless you really want to go to it, Val, I need someone at the fest table to check in latecomers. The volunteers who've been there for the last ninety minutes will explain what you need to do. Another volunteer will take over after the opening session."

Granddad spoke up. "I'll help if you're short of volunteers."

"Thank you, Mr. Myer."

Val remembered what she'd intended to ask Bethany. "One more question before you take off. Roy said the police were having trouble getting in touch with Cynthia's relatives. Is there anyone at the fest friendly enough with her to know about her family?"

"Talk to Birdie Natter." Bethany started to walk away, stopped, and whirled around. "Cynthia was going to help Birdie put out snacks in the hospitality room after the opening session. Why don't you take Cynthia's place? You'll have Birdie all to yourself." She hurried toward the Poe wing.

Val groaned. "I've avoided Birdie all morning. Now I have to figure out how to wring information from her without giving her any. I hope she likes to talk more than she likes to pry."

Granddad looked distracted. "Did you tell Roy about my recipe box?"

She nodded. "The police didn't find it in the room."

"Whoever stole the ring took the box too. Your average burglar goes for small, valuable things— cash, drugs, jewelry. An old recipe box wouldn't appeal to that sort of thief." Granddad stroked his chin. "But a thief who really wants the box might also steal a ring. He'd expect the police to treat the incident like a typical burglary and not focus on him."

"When you say *him*, you mean the book dealer. But maybe someone else coveted that box too. Harrison can't be the only collector here." Val remembered her new duties. "You want to keep me company at the fest table?"

He nodded. When they went into the Poe wing, they saw Harrison putting up a sign outside a small room that identified it as the bookshop and listed the hours it would be open. This morning he wore a vest and bow tie, but no jacket. They greeted him.

"I keep seeing you two together." he said. "Do I detect a family resemblance around the eyes?"

"He's my grandfather."

"You were incognito at our table last night, Val. You didn't tell us you were related to Nero Wolfe's gourmet chef. While we're on that subject"—Harrison gave Granddad a toothy smile—"I'm still interested in that recipe box. I'll be in the bookshop most of the day should you want to resume negotiating."

"I can't resume what I haven't started," Granddad muttered after Harrison disappeared into his room full of books. "He has that box. That was a ploy to convince me he doesn't."

Val didn't bother to respond. Regardless of anything she might say, Granddad would hold on to his fixed opinion until another one took its place.

Beyond the bookshop was the ballroom where the opening session would be held. Val peeked into it and estimated a hundred and fifty people were already seated. Bethany stood on the raised platform at the front of the room, talking to a woman who was probably the fest chair.

Trisha was the only volunteer still at the fest table. She gave Val instructions for checking in latecomers and left. Val was surprised to see her go toward the lobby rather than the ballroom. She probably needed caffeine after ninety minutes of saying the same thing over and over.

Granddad sat down on the metal folding chair next to Val's and grunted. "The volunteers would stick around longer if the seats weren't so hard."

With the ballroom doors still open, Val heard a woman test the microphone and then call for attention. As the audience quieted, someone closed the doors to the room.

A couple ambled toward the table. Val gave them

the envelopes with their badges and a fest tote. "The opening session has just started." She pointed to the ballroom.

As they went into the ballroom, Greer nearly mowed them down on her way out.

The journalist clutched her phone, tapped furiously on it, and then barreled toward Granddad. "Do you know anything about the announcement they just made in there?"

Granddad faked wide-eyed innocence. "I didn't hear it. What did they say?"

"Cynthia Sweet died last night. Now I know why she didn't meet me for breakfast."

With her voice echoing through the empty corridor, it was no surprise that Harrison joined them. "Cynthia Sweet is dead? What happened?"

Greer said, "She was found in her hotel room, but they didn't say what caused her death."

"Have you ever attended a gathering of mystery lovers before?" When the journalist shook her head, he continued. "At these events, the report of a death might be part of a mystery game, a mock murder. The person who submits the best solution to the mystery wins a prize. You might find clues left in the hospitality room or on the message board." He pointed to the board on an easel.

Greer rolled her eyes. "This is no game. I was standing near the hotel front desk when a man flashed his ID and asked for the manager. I recognize a cop when I see one. Cops don't show up for murder games."

"On the contrary, madam. I was at a mystery conference where the police re-created a murder scene in the hotel garage with a dummy victim. They evaluated everyone's analysis of the clues. Let me give you a hint about this case. Doubtless it's a classic locked-room mystery. There are seven explanations for a death in a room locked from the inside."

Granddad took the bait. "What are they?"

"Poe invented the most bizarre one—death by a wild animal coming down the chimney." Harrison held up his hand to tick off the others. "Accident. Suicide rigged to look like murder. Poison gas. A mechanical trap that springs when the culprit is elsewhere. A culprit outside the room, shooting bullets of ice or frozen blood through the window. And finally—"

"Real deaths interest me, not fictional ones." Greer hurried toward the lobby.

Harrison shrugged. "She doesn't realize how often life imitates art. People have actually attempted murders that imitate the ones in Agatha Christie's books."

Val decided against going down that rabbit hole with him. "What's the seventh locked-room solution?"

"The victim is drunk or drugged and appears to be dead. The first person to get near the victim commits the murder, which is assumed to have occurred earlier. I can point you toward some excellent locked-room mysteries when you come to the fest bookshop." He glanced at his watch. "It will be open in precisely sixteen minutes. Hope to see you later."

When he disappeared into the bookshop, Granddad said, "He sure likes to show off how much he knows, but none of that applies to this case. Hotel door locks engage when someone closes the door from the inside or outside. Unless you had to break a chain or bolt to get into Cynthia's room, it's not really a locked room. Was Cynthia's door bolted?"

"No, and most women alone in a hotel room *would* bolt the door before going to bed. Putting the water on for tea suggests she wasn't ready to go to bed yet. Or maybe she just wasn't thinking clearly. She sounded tipsy when I went back to the bar last night."

"Someone coulda been in the room with her when she died, maybe Harrison. He follows her to her room, waits a moment, and then knocks on her door. When she opens it, he apologizes for his remarks at the bake-off about Sherlock Holmes not drinking tea."

"Then what? She forgives Harrison and asks *him* in for tea?"

Granddad shrugged. "Or she closes the door on him. Either way, he slaps tape on the latch, like the Watergate burglars did, and the door lock doesn't engage. He waits until she's likely to be asleep, sneaks in, and helps himself to the box and the ring. End of story if it's just a theft, but what if she's not asleep or she wakes up and catches him in the act?"

"Your scenario is as plausible as Harrison's locked-room plots."

"He went through all those plots to put us off the scent."

A string of latecomers deprived Val and Granddad of the privacy they needed to talk more about Cynthia's death.

The ballroom doors soon opened. As the mystery fans poured out, Val left Granddad at the fest table and hurried to the hospitality room, anxious to find out what Birdie knew about Cynthia. The older woman in the elaborate hat was already in the room.

Val went in. "You must be Birdie. Hi, I'm Val Deniston. Bethany sent me to—"

"To take poor Cynthia's place." Birdie squinted through her granny glasses. "You pop up everywhere."

Val could have said the same to her. "Bethany told me you knew Cynthia pretty well. I'm sorry you lost a friend."

"Thank you. She lived next door to me in our condo building. We were also in the same book club. I founded that book club ten years ago. She was our newest member."

The older woman's emotionless words convinced Val that Birdie hadn't lost a friend, only a neighbor. Val pointed to the bags of prepackaged snacks on the table. "Shall we start putting out the nibbles? Why don't you put out the sweet ones at one end of the table, and I'll set out the salty ones at the other end."

Birdie broke into a large box of cookie packets. "Cynthia baked the most delicious cookies and dainty cakes. She invited select neighbors to her place for tea and sweets a couple of times a week. I only got to enjoy her treats at our book club meetings. I'll miss those."

But she wouldn't miss the woman who made the

treats? Val piled up snack packs of pretzels and cheese crackers. "What kind of books does your club read?"

"We like crime." Birdie made an overlapping cascade of shortbread packets from back to front on the table. "Mysteries, thrillers, romantic suspense, whatever the person choosing the book that month likes."

Hmm. Birdie might not be the only one at the fest who knew Cynthia. "Is anyone else from your book club here this weekend?"

"Perry Macon. He always picks a legal thriller." She groaned. "Not my favorite. He's a retired lawyer."

"I met him yesterday when we checked in for the fest. Was he the one who filled the envelopes with the badges and tickets for each person?"

"We did it together, and it took a long time. We had to check the registration forms to find out which tickets to put in each envelope. They charged extra for anything involving food—the bake-off, tonight's wine-and-cheese reception, and tomorrow's gala luncheon. They should have raised the price for the fest and included all that."

So either Birdie or Perry could have slipped the anonymous notes into the envelopes. "Sounds like a big job for just the two of you. No one else helped?"

"Cynthia gave us a hand with the last bunch when she arrived."

Val couldn't think of any reason Cynthia would write a note that accused herself of sabotage. "How long were you and Cynthia neighbors?"

"Not quite a year and a half. Her husband, such a nice man, died last month. Now she's dead too."

Finished with the cookie cascade along the table's edge, Birdie was lining up milk chocolate miniatures end to end, like cars on a freight train. "Sometimes one spouse goes, and the other soon follows, but usually with couples who've been together for a long time. Cynthia and *this* husband were newlyweds when they moved into my building. Before that she lived in a rowhouse with her second husband."

"What happened to him?"

"Died. I'm not sure how long *they* were married, but she didn't waste much time finding another man. She buried two husbands within two years."

Birdie made it sound as if Cynthia had wielded the shovel to dig their graves. "That must have been hard on her," Val said. "How did her husbands die?"

"The last one of a heart attack, the one before that fell down the stairs. She said he'd gotten quite frail." Birdie sorted the candy miniatures by type, separating milk chocolate from dark. "Her last husband, Austin, was a perfect gentleman."

Val was surprised at the depth of Birdie's knowledge about Cynthia. "Was his surname Sweet?"

"No, that was her birth name. Good thing she kept it instead of changing her name each time she got a new husband. She married and divorced young. She didn't find the second husband for years, until she went for older men. With the third one barely in the ground, she was already trying to find his replacement." Birdie leaned toward Val and said softly, "She brought a man back to her condo the week before last. And yesterday afternoon, a man visited her hotel room."

"Did you recognize him?"

"How could I? All I saw was his leg a second before the door closed. I'd gone to my room to nap and thought I heard someone knocking on my door. I opened it just in time to see the man disappear into Cynthia's room."

Val pictured Birdie running to her door, ready to peer out at the slightest sound in the corridor. Scatterbrained though she seemed, she was a mine of information and must know something about her neighbor's family. "Did Cynthia have any children?"

"Not of her own, only adult stepchildren from her marriage with Austin." Birdie lined up the dark chocolates on a parallel track with the milk chocolate train she'd made. "He was in our book club too. Most of us liked him better than her. We all went to his funeral. His son and daughter wouldn't have anything to do with Cynthia."

Val struggled to sound casually curious. "Why were they so against her?"

"Their mother was barely cold in the ground before he married Cynthia. Austin's daughter, Willow, lit into Cynthia at the funeral." Birdie closed the space between her and Val. "The ladies' lavatory at the funeral home had a small anteroom for primping. I'd just gone in when I saw Cynthia and Willow arguing in the room with the stalls and sinks. I didn't want to interrupt a private conversation."

So she stayed out of view and eavesdropped, and now she wanted to share. More than willing to listen, Val prompted her, "Could you hear what they said?"

"I wasn't trying to, but I couldn't help it. Willow said, *It doesn't belong to you. It was my mother's, and she meant me to have it.* And Cynthia said, *Your father inherited it from her, and he gave it to me. That makes it mine now.*" Birdie hissed the words she claimed the irate women spoke.

"Any idea what they were arguing over?" A ring, perhaps?

Birdie shook her head. "It got worse from there. Willow screamed at Cynthia, *You took my father off his diet. You killed him with carbs and sweets!* Cynthia yelled back, *That's slander. Say that again, and I'll sue you, you witch.* Only instead of *witch*, she said something that rhymes with it. I left the restroom, and Willow stormed out a few seconds later."

Val was impressed with Birdie's memory . . . or maybe her imagination. "Where does Willow live?"

"A Baltimore suburb, I think."

Birdie returned to lining up candy miniatures. If only her trains of thought were as precise and connected as her chocolate trains.

Val set out packets of trail mix, wondering how often Birdie had peeked out of her door last night. "We both heard the emergency personnel come down the corridor last night. Did you hear anything going on before that?"

Birdie looked up. "Like what?"

"I heard a high-pitched sound like a whistle around midnight."

"So did I. It was in my dream. I was on a train that was whistling. When I woke up, I heard the whistle, but then it stopped. I had trouble falling asleep again and was still awake when the emergency squad came through."

Her story made sense to Val. The whistling hadn't been loud enough to bother Birdie across the hall until Nico opened the door to Cynthia's room. Val had then pulled the plug on the kettle, silencing the whistle. "Did you look out into the corridor any other time last night?"

"Before I go to bed, I always check the hall in my apartment building to make sure no one is lurking around. I did the same thing last night here in the hotel."

"What time?"

Birdie frowned in concentration. "It was after 11:45, but before midnight. Yes, that's when I saw her."

That was fifteen minutes or so before Val heard the kettle whistling. "You saw Cynthia?"

"Definitely not. The woman I saw was walking toward the ice machine at the end of the corridor. Cynthia didn't use ice. Her teeth were sensitive to the cold."

But she could have gotten ice for someone she expected to visit her. Did Birdie have any other reason to rule out Cynthia? "Any clue who the woman in the hall was?"

Birdie bit her lower lip. "I'd rather not say. Nobody would believe me anyway." Birdie glanced at her watch and reached under the table for a carpet-bag Mary Poppins would have been proud to own. "The first panels are about to start. I hope you don't mind finishing up here."

Val didn't mind that, but Birdie's dodging bothered her. Before Val could ask another question, Cynthia's neighbor hurried out of the room.

Val was going to follow her, but a hotel server blocked the doorway with a beverage cart. By the time he maneuvered the cart into the room, Val had no hope of catching the chatty woman who'd suddenly zipped her lips.

# Chapter 7

Val puzzled over Birdie's refusal to identify the woman she'd seen last night. Why did she expect skepticism if she named the woman? Maybe she saw someone who resembled a movie star or another famous person. Or she might have dreamed that the hotel ghost was haunting the third floor. Saying she'd seen a ghost would make most people question her sanity. Or could she have withheld information so she'd have a dramatic exit line? After a brief acquaintance, Val couldn't guess what motivated Birdie's sudden silence.

With the hospitality room set up, Val ambled toward the fest table, anxious to tell Granddad what she'd learned about Cynthia from Birdie. Retired lawyer Perry Macon, not to be confused with Perry Mason, sat there filling in a newspaper crossword puzzle. Next to the newspaper was a business card for Don Myer, Problem Solver and Senior Sleuth.

Granddad must have been touting his skills to his replacement at the fest table.

Val couldn't pass up the chance to talk to a member of Cynthia and Birdie's book club and one of the fest's envelope-stuffers.

She approached the table. "Hi. I'm Val Deniston. You were here yesterday afternoon when I checked in."

He lowered his reading glasses and peered at her over the top of them. "Ah, yes. Your grandfather said you might stop by looking for him. He's waiting for you in the lobby."

"Thanks. Birdie told me that you and she were in the same book club with Cynthia. My sympathy on losing one of your members."

"We've lost two members recently. It was a real shock when Cynthia's husband died, and now this. She was . . . quite a presence at our club." The lawyer's pause suggested he chose his words carefully. He added, "Our meetings won't be the same without her."

Val noticed his eyes straying back to his crossword. She declined to take the hint. "If you have a moment, Perry, I think you might be able to help with something. A police detective told me they haven't yet located Cynthia's next of kin. Birdie said Cynthia had no children of her own, but she had a stepdaughter, Willow. I didn't catch her last name. If you know it, I'll pass it on to the police."

"Same last name as her father—Waterbrook." Perry sipped coffee and studied Val over the rim of his insulated paper cup. "Funny you should ask about Willow. I saw a woman at the hotel reception desk this morning who reminded me of her."

Val tried to hide her surprise. Could the hostile stepdaughter have been in the vicinity when Cynthia died? "What does Willow look like?"

"More like an oak than a willow. Tall and strong, in her forties, reddish-brown hair. However, she may not be the person the police need to contact. A blood relative, no matter how far removed, would have precedence over a stepchild for the final arrangements."

What had prompted Perry's comment? "Do you know of any blood relatives?"

He put down his pen and removed his glasses, apparently giving up on returning quickly to his crossword. "I know what she told our book club. After Austin died, she received a letter from an unknown cousin, asking that they arrange to meet. The family had split apart because of a feud that went back generations. Cynthia asked our opinions on how to respond to the letter, though I think she'd already decided to ignore it."

"Because of the feud?"

Perry tilted his head to one side and then to the other, as if weighing his response. "Partly. From what she'd previously said about her family, *forgive and forget* wasn't in her DNA. This person hadn't contacted her until Cynthia was about to come into some money. Understandably, she assumed she had a sponger for a cousin."

Now that Cynthia was dead, that sponger might inherit her money. "I hope Cynthia didn't shred the letter with the cousin's contact information. Do you happen to remember his name?"

"*Her* name is Loren Davis. That was Cynthia's

great-aunt's name after her marriage. The rift between the two branches of the family began with
that marriage. Cynthia described her whole family
tree, but I tuned her out. My wife might remember."

If she did, she'd be another source of information about Cynthia that Roy could tap. "Is your
wife at the fest?"

"No. She's a piano teacher and gives lessons on
Saturdays. She almost quit the book club because
of Cynthia's grandstanding. Whatever news anyone else shared, Cynthia had a story to top it. She
was rather inventive. At a recent meeting, Birdie
announced that she'd traced a family member
back to the American Revolution. Cynthia immediately boasted of having an ancestor on the
*Mayflower*." He rolled his eyes.

Cynthia had behaved the same way in the bar
last night. When Granddad's role in solving a murder attracted attention, she one-upped him by
claiming she knew more than the police about the
murder at the hotel a year ago. And Granddad
had seen through her.

"You think Cynthia invented a *Mayflower* ancestor?" When Perry nodded, Val said, "Did Birdie
also invent *her* ancestor?"

Perry responded with no hesitation. "Birdie ex-
aggerates, but I doubt she'd make up a story from
scratch."

A pair of fest latecomers hurried to the table. As
Perry checked them off his list and gave them the
envelopes with their badges, Val thought about another of Cynthia's attempts to wow the crowd at

the bar—flashing her unusual ring and claiming it was centuries older than it was. A mistake or a tall tale? Not that it mattered. Except that someone hearing her might have assumed the ring was even more valuable than it was. And now that ring had disappeared.

Perry invited the latecomers to attend any of the panels in session farther down the corridor. They thanked him and hurried off.

Val asked Perry if he and Birdie had been the only ones stuffing the fest envelopes. "Cynthia helped us out as we were finishing up. Why do you ask?"

Val decided to trust him with the truth, though not the whole truth. "My grandfather's envelope contained a slip of paper with an unsigned personal note. We're wondering who put it there. Did anyone else have access to those envelopes once you filled them?"

"Not while I was around, though possibly when I took a break. Trisha was here while I was gone." He tapped on Granddad's business card. "Your grandfather hyped his detection skills. Sounds like you're an amateur sleuth too. Is the policeman friend you mentioned real or was that just an excuse to snoop?"

His tone made his disdain for amateur sleuthing clear. "My police friend is real." Val showed him Roy's card.

Perry adjusted his glasses. "Detective Roy Chesterfeld."

"I'm going to pass on what you said about Cynthia's cousin to him. He may want to contact you. Do you have a card?"

Perry took one out of his wallet and gave it to her. "I've closed down most of my law practice, but I've kept the phone numbers."

She glanced at his card, which identified him as practicing Trust and Estate Law. "Thank you for your help, Perry."

"No problem." He went back to filling in crossword squares.

Val stepped away from the table and texted Roy that she had information about Cynthia. He responded that he'd meet her in the lobby in a few minutes.

She found Granddad in the lobby, sitting on a sofa.

He looked up from poking at his phone. "That took a while."

"It was worth it." She sat down next to him. "Roy's meeting me here. You can listen when I tell him what I found out. How did your stint at the fest table go?"

"Only one latecomer. A few folks came by the table to check if any clues in the murder game were at the table."

"Harrison was right about how mystery fans would interpret Cynthia's death."

"Dave Proctor stopped by the table too. He's over there now." Granddad pointed to the man who'd played Bunter. He was sitting at the far end of the lobby, barely visible behind a tall potted plant. "He wasn't at the opening session and didn't know Cynthia was dead until he heard talk about it in the corridor. He asked me if it was true. He's been in that armchair for a while, reading his phone or staring into space. He's a young fella, probably hasn't dealt with sudden death before."

"He's not real young. He could be ten years older than I am."

"That's young to me. And here comes the even younger detective."

Roy strode across the lobby and shook hands with Granddad. "The last time I saw you, sir, you were trying to prove you could slip poison into my soup bowl with no one noticing."

"What do you mean trying? I succeeded." Granddad's eyes twinkled. "Val tells me you've come up in the world of policing. Congratulations!"

"Thank you. The hotel has turned over the event planner's office to me. Let's talk there."

They followed him to a small room with two straight chairs facing the desk Roy had claimed. She summarized her conversation with Cynthia's neighbor, glossing over Birdie's comments about Cynthia's marriages. Roy listened intently as Val told him about the argument Birdie had overheard between Cynthia and her stepdaughter. "Her name is Willow Waterbrook. I also talked to Perry Macon, another member of the same book club as Cynthia. He'd seen a woman in the lobby this morning who resembled Willow."

Roy thumbed notes into his phone. "Very helpful."

"I have only begun to be helpful," Val said. "Birdie has the room across from Cynthia's. She glimpsed a man going into Cynthia's room yesterday afternoon, but she couldn't describe him because his back was to her. She also saw a woman in the hall toward midnight but refused to tell me who. Birdie said no one would believe her if she identified the woman."

"You gotta put the screws on Birdie, Roy." Granddad smiled.

"I'm sure Roy will use charm rather than coercion." As long as his patience with the talkative Birdie held out.

"Not everyone falls for my charms." Roy gave Val a pointed look. "I won't put the screws on an elderly woman. I have to interview her anyway as Cynthia's neighbor. I'll get her to talk about what happened last night without mentioning you as my source. Anything else?"

Val nodded. "Cynthia recently received a letter from a distant relative named Loren Davis." Val relayed what Perry had told her and passed his business card to Roy.

Roy glanced at it. "I'll ask the officers who are searching Cynthia's home to look for the letter. Without that, though, I don't have enough information to locate this relative."

Granddad had said little, but he'd fidgeted since they sat down. "You make any progress tracing the stolen ring or my recipe box?"

"I talked to Claire Rainey and got a detailed description of the ring. We can circulate the description to jewelers and hock shops. We'll also monitor online sales. I haven't talked to the woman who saw your recipe box yet." He swiped at his phone. "What's her name again?"

"Trisha Turbek." Val doubted he'd made a note of it earlier. The vintage ring was worth the detective's time, but not the recipe box.

Apparently reaching the same conclusion, Granddad slumped in his chair. "Any word on what killed Cynthia?"

"Nothing definitive." Roy leaned back in the desk chair. "The initial examination revealed petechiae, tiny red spots on her body caused by broken capillaries. They show up on the face of someone who's been strangled, but they weren't on her face. They can also occur as a side effect of some medications or as a result of suffocation."

Granddad sat up straighter. "From being smothered by a pillow?"

"Pillow, hands, plastic bag over the head. It takes about five minutes to kill someone that way. People being smothered usually struggle for a few minutes, and the struggle leaves marks. She had none. Of course, a victim who's drugged or intoxicated will fight less, if at all, and show no marks."

"Won't the autopsy tell you if she was smothered?" Val said.

"Not necessarily. The tox screen will tell us what meds or drugs were in her system, but a case for suffocation is usually made by other evidence, like a pillowcase with the victim's saliva on it and evidence that the culprit was at the scene."

Granddad said, "I'll go to the bar later and schmooze with folks. Find out who was there last night with Cynthia, when she left, and whether anyone was with her."

Roy gave him the okay sign, a circle with his thumb and index finger. "That's fine, as long as you tell me what you find out. People don't find you threatening. They'll say things to you they might not say to me." He turned to Val. "What are your plans?"

"This morning I'm monitoring a panel about the legacy of Edgar Allan Poe, Arthur Conan Doyle, and Agatha Christie."

"I devoured Sherlock Holmes stories when I was a teen." Roy reached into his pocket and pulled out a protein bar. "If Sherlock were on this case, I can guess what he'd say. He'd bring up the curious incident of the key cards on the desk."

Val had often heard Bram recite the phrase Roy had adapted: *the curious incident of the dog in the nighttime.* The curious incident was what the dog didn't do—bark, the animal's normal reaction to an intruder. The lack of a bark, a negative clue, led to the culprit's identity.

Val had seen nothing odd about the key cards in Cynthia's room, but she hadn't picked them up or tried to use them.

Granddad broke the silence. "I'll bite. What's curious about the key cards?"

Roy unwrapped his snack. "They have no fingerprints on them."

# Chapter 8

Val tried to make sense of the detective's disclosure. How could Cynthia's key cards have no fingerprints? "Cynthia must have used a card to get into her room. Why would she wipe off her own fingerprints?" When neither Granddad nor Roy responded, Val continued. "She might have washed off something sticky, like lotion or toothpaste, but unless she held the card by the edge, she'd still leave a print on it."

Granddad said, "Someone else mighta used a key to get into her room to steal stuff, and then wiped the prints off. But how did that person get hold of her card?"

Val shrugged. "She could have dropped it or left it at the bar. She was loosey-goosey with her belongings. In the afternoon she accidentally gave me a key to her room. It's hard to believe she wiped off one card and someone else wiped off the other."

Roy laced his hands behind his head. "What's the alternative? One person wiping off both cards. Why? Any theories, Val?"

She kept her first thought to herself: *Isn't it your job to come up with theories, Detective Roy?* "I'll take a stab at it. The person with Cynthia's key card assumes she's asleep, uses it to gain entry, and drops it on the desk. The intruder finds the diamond ring on the night table, pockets it, and then when Cynthia wakes up, silences her. Or else she's already dead. Worried the police might fingerprint everything, the culprit wants to wipe off the card with his prints on it, but there are two identical cards on the desk. So he wipes off both and—" Val broke off. Her scenario had a fatal flaw. "I still can't explain the teakettle."

Roy grinned. "'Ay, there's the rub.'"

Val groaned at his pun, hiding her surprise that he'd quoted from Shakespeare.

Granddad stroked his chin. "I got it! I can explain the whole shebang. The key cards, the recipe box, the teakettle, how Cynthia died. It all fits together." He folded his arms and basked in his cat-who-got-the-cream moment.

Val was used to his routine of following up a dramatic statement with a lengthy silence, leaving his listeners in suspense.

Roy was not used to it. He drummed his fingers on the desk. "Lay it out for us, please."

"The murder came first. The theft was a distraction. This hotel is full of folks who devour mysteries like an addictive drug. They know all about clues and red herrings. I think one of them came up with a plot to commit the perfect murder. First, kill a woman in a way that leaves hardly any trace and could be a natural death. Then, in case there's a suspicion of foul play, make it look like a burglary gone bad by stealing the ring, the recipe box, and maybe a few other things you don't even know about."

Val waited for Roy's reaction to this scenario, but his mouth was occupied with munching a protein bar. He was leaving it up to her to point out Granddad's plot holes. Where to start? "In the spur-of-the-moment scenario I described, the flustered killer lost track of which key he used and wiped off both. Wouldn't your killer, executing a plan for the perfect murder, know which key card needed to be wiped off?"

"Wiping off both keys was a fancy touch to tease the police," Granddad said. "I think Cynthia opened her door to the murderer and put on the water for tea. Then the killer pushed her onto the bed, smothered her, and arranged her body to look like she died in her sleep."

"Why didn't the killer turn off the kettle?" Val said.

Granddad shrugged. "These days most kettles shut off when the water boils. The murderer probably didn't realize it would whistle. Not turning it off was a mistake because it pinned down the time of her death. To figure out whodunit, you just gotta track Cynthia's movements and her contacts from the time she left the bake-off to when her body was found." Granddad rested his case with a smile.

Roy crumpled the protein bar wrapper. "Interesting theory, but I'd look for a motive beyond mocking the police by committing the perfect murder. Greed is the number one reason people kill. The murderer wants what the victim has—money, spouse, job. Grudge is a close second as a motive, whether it's cold revenge or hot road rage. Then there's passion, crimes committed for love, lust, or obsession." Roy threw his snack wrapper into the trash. "Protection is also a reason to murder. The killer gets rid of someone who poses a threat."

Granddad folded his arms, his smile gone. "Trying to commit the perfect murder doesn't rule out another motive. The anonymous notes before the bake-off came from a person with a grudge against Cynthia. At the bar she claimed to know more than the police about the murder here last year. That would make her a threat to the person who got away with it."

Roy nodded. "You're on the right path with that. But you both made the assumption that the thief and the killer are the same person. I'm not convinced of that."

Val knew why—he had another candidate for the theft, the easiest person to blame. "The security guard might have had an opportunity to steal the ring, but he had no chance to wipe the key cards and, as I said earlier, nowhere to hide the recipe box."

Roy shrugged. "I assume the murderer wiped

the key cards. I also assume Cynthia's ring was stolen. She wore it earlier in the evening and now it's gone. The recipe box is in a different category. One person claimed to see something similar to it in Cynthia's bag. That's not proof she ever had it."

Roy's phone, sitting on the desk, played a tune. He glanced at it. "I have to take this. Thank you for your help. I'm sure you already know not to repeat anything we said in this room."

"Hmph," Granddad muttered as he led the way out of the room. "Roy's not even trying to find my recipe box."

"A week ago you didn't know the recipe box existed, and now you're hung up on it." Val thought of a way to soften the blow of losing his newly found treasure. "Your homeowners' insurance might cover some of the loss since the box came from the attic." Of course, he'd have to jump through hoops to establish its value and condition, but if he persisted, he'd probably get some money.

"Your grandmother would want it to stay in the family. She was fond of her aunt, and so was I. Finding that box brought back a lot of memories. Money can't do that."

"I understand." Val wouldn't part with Grandma's china for the same reason. She thought about Willow, Cynthia's stepdaughter, and the argument Birdie had overheard. Willow probably had a sentimental attachment to the keepsake that her mother had intended for her and that Cynthia wouldn't give up.

Val checked her watch. "It's time for me to set up the speakers' table for the Edgar-Arthur-Agatha panel Bethany assigned me to monitor. Are you coming with me?"

"Nah. I'm going to track down folks who saw Cynthia last night to find out what time she left the bar. Besides Dave and Greer, do you remember who was at the bar when Cynthia was there?"

"Harrison, Claire, and later on Trisha sat on the side of the bar, not close to Cynthia. There was also a woman with a mass of dark hair, heavy eye makeup, and nose piercings. I haven't seen her this morning. Maybe she had nothing to do with the fest and checked out of the hotel already."

"I'll keep an eye out for her. She should be easy to spot. I gotta talk to the bartender too, but he's on the late shift and doesn't come in until four." Granddad pulled a folded sheet of paper from his shirt pocket and adjusted his bifocals. "The schedule says box lunches will be available in the ballroom at twelve thirty. I'll meet you there after the panel you're monitoring."

Val hurried to the room where the panel would be held, set out water for each panelist, and checked that everyone who came in had fest ID badges. Then she sat in the back of the room.

The panel began with a discussion of the three mystery writers and their famous sleuths—Poe's Dupin, Conan Doyle's Holmes, Christie's Poirot and Miss Marple. Then the moderator described a crime scenario and asked the panelists to outline the methods each would have used to figure out whodunit. As they talked, Val's mind wandered to questions that hadn't even come up in their talk with Roy. Who had written the anonymous notes?

Did the woman Birdie saw in the hall have anything to do with Cynthia's death and the theft of the ring?

Val brought her thoughts back to the present just in time to hold up one hand with her fingers splayed, signaling the panelists that they had five minutes to wrap up the session.

When the panel ended, she cleared the table at the front of the room so it would be ready for the first afternoon panel. Then she hurried to grab a box lunch and join Granddad in the back of the ballroom, where tables and chairs were set up. He was at a small table with his bake-off rival Dave Proctor.

When she sat down, they were already half-finished with their lunches. Yesterday she'd seen Dave in passing at the fest table and in the bar, and at a distance when he was on the dais. Now she had a chance to study him. He had a baby face, round and slightly plump, with faint crow's feet at the corner of his eyes and some graying at the temples. Last night, playing the English manservant Bunter, he'd plastered his hair down. Today his hair was spiky on top. He looked forty pretending to be thirty.

"Your grandfather's been telling me about your café and catering," he said. "How long have you been doing that?"

"Only since I moved to the Eastern Shore two years ago." Val unwrapped her sandwich. "What about you? Have you been in this area a long time?"

"No. I came here last year from Napa Valley."

"Val's boyfriend just moved to Maryland from

Silicon Valley," Granddad said. "Is that far from Napa?"

Dave shook his head. "About a two-hour drive."

Val remembered Claire's comment that his British pronunciation came by way of the Midwest. Was she right about that? "Are you originally from California?"

"No, I grew up in Chicago, but I left there as soon as I was on my own. Spent a few years in New York and then Los Angeles."

So Claire had been spot-on about his origins. As Val opened her water bottle, she noticed two women at the next table peering at him. "How did you get into the restaurant business, Dave?"

"I went to the Culinary Institute in Napa and interned in a restaurant at a winery. I worked my way up to food and beverage manager. My girlfriend was the pastry chef. Everything was going great." Dave's eyes glazed over as he stared beyond Val, as if willing himself into the past. "Then a forest fire burned down the winery."

She'd seen photos online of a California winery with its crop incinerated. "That's terrible. I'm sorry."

"It was a real kick in the teeth. After that my girlfriend wanted to move back to the East Coast. Shereen was fed up with earthquakes, droughts, and fires. We live between Baltimore and Wilmington, Delaware, where she works as a pastry chef. I'm the weekday manager at a restaurant in Baltimore."

A step down from food and beverage manager at a winery restaurant. Val drank water, washing down a bite of her turkey and avocado sandwich.

"How did you get involved in making a Deadly Dessert here?"

"I'm planning to open my own restaurant, so I spend my weekends getting to know the culinary culture here at food fests and cook-offs. I met Cynthia at one of them. We got to talking, and she asked me to be part of this." Dave shifted his chair closer to the table and leaned toward Granddad. "I liked her, but not everyone did. She and I were both semifinalists at a bake-off six weeks ago. Another contestant whose cake turned out bad accused Cynthia of sabotaging it."

The same accusation the writer of Granddad's anonymous note had made. Val almost choked on her sandwich.

Granddad's eyes grew round. "*Sabotage* is a strong word. Who was the contestant?"

"Patty Cook, a food blogger. I should say *vlogger*. She has a popular video channel. She made a Mexican hot chocolate cake, hot as in spicy, with chipotle powder, ancho powder, and cayenne. Her cake was so peppery that a judge spit it into his napkin."

"Why didn't she taste it as she was going along?" Granddad said.

Dave shrugged. "Most people avoid tasting dough because of the raw eggs. Besides, she'd made the cake previously and won other bake-offs with the same recipe. She claimed that she turned her back to take a call and Cynthia dumped hot pepper into the batter."

Val's tongue tingled at the thought. "How did Cynthia respond?"

"Calmly. She said, 'You must have measured wrong.' I don't see how Cynthia could have gone near the other woman's batter or icing without anyone seeing her." Dave bit into what was left of his sandwich.

Granddad stroked his chin, a sign that an idea was brewing. "You remember the big, gaudy ring Cynthia wore last night when we were making desserts? Did she wear it at that other bake-off?"

Val knew what he was thinking. Cynthia might have filled the ring's compartment with something like ghost pepper, two hundred times hotter than a jalapeño. She didn't need to go near the batter or icing. She could just add the powerful pepper to the spices her competitor had already measured out and arrayed on the counter. Val imagined Cynthia surveying the ingredients for the hot chocolate cake. Like a Renaissance noble surreptitiously adding poison to wine or food at the table, she could have flipped open the catch on her ring and released her secret ingredient.

Dave finished chewing before answering Granddad's question. "Yes, Cynthia wore the same ring, kind of fancy for baking. I thought it must be her lucky charm. Why do you ask?"

"Because it's missing, and so is my Nero Wolfe recipe box."

Dave raised an eyebrow. "Weird things to steal."

"Cynthia talked about the ring at the bar last night and suggested it was quite valuable." Val wasn't sure how long Cynthia had talked about the ring. "Did she mention it when you were with her?"

Dave shook his head. "I wasn't exactly *with* her at the bar. We got to the hotel after the bake-off at the same time. She asked me to save her a seat at the bar while she went to her room to change clothes.

Then we had a drink together. A gray-haired woman came up and wanted to interview her about a murder that happened here a year ago. I gave her my seat, and that's when I saw you guys."

He'd told them he planned to return for another drink, but how soon had he done that? Val had seen him at the bar when she went down to notify the front desk of the whistling coming from Cynthia's room. "Were you there when Cynthia left?"

"I went back to the bar right before that. She was soused. She almost fell when she got off the bar stool. A woman with black hair and clothes kept her upright on the way to the elevator. I was going to give her a hand, but another woman offered. It was better if two women went with her in case she needed help getting to bed."

Val nodded. "I saw the raven-haired woman sitting next to Cynthia at the bar when I was there. What did the other woman look like?"

"I didn't get a look at her face then or earlier, when she was checking people in for the fest. Glasses, ponytail, purple baseball cap."

With *Trisha* written on it.

One of the women who'd been eying Dave from the neighboring table approached him. Her shoulder-length white hair framed a face that was smooth except for smile crinkles around her eyes and mouth. "Excuse me. My friend and I thought you looked familiar. Were you in the soap opera *The Young and the Reckless*, if you don't mind my asking?"

"I don't mind at all. I'm just surprised you recognized me. I was on the show for barely a year."

"You were one of my favorites. I was so sorry when they killed you off."

"I was even sorrier than you." He gave her a wry smile. "Thank you for your kind words. I appreciate them."

"You're very welcome. I hope to see you on TV again soon." She returned to her table.

"Not much chance of that," Dave mumbled.

"You were an actor," Val said. "Is that what you were doing in New York?"

He nodded and stuffed the final piece of his sandwich into his month. Apparently, he'd rather not talk about his acting experience.

Harrison Hawk came over to the table and handed Val a folded piece of paper. "Here are a few questions you might use to challenge the trivia players tomorrow."

"Thank you." Val tucked the paper in her shoulder bag.

"I'm still looking for clues to solve the weekend's mystery. I have a new theory after seeing the two of you together." Harrison pointed at Dave and Granddad. "Do you remember the movie *Who Is Killing the Great Chefs of Europe?* This could be a variation—*Who Is Killing the Chefs to the Sleuths?* Cynthia was the first to go, but you two might be next."

Dave's jaw dropped, and Harrison whirled and walked away.

Granddad said, "Don't mind that guy. He thinks the fest is staging a murder game. Like at those murder mystery dinners where the audience is supposed to figure out whodunit."

"A game? You mean Cynthia's not really dead?"

Dave's features relaxed, his jaw less tense, his eyes less prominent.

Was he relieved because he'd believed for a moment that he might be the next victim, based on Harrison's scenario, or because he now thought Cynthia was alive? Val hated to give him the bad news. "It's not a game. Cynthia is definitely dead."

Dave's body sagged. "I'm cursed."

# Chapter 9

Val and Granddad exchanged surprised looks across the small table. If, as Dave had said, he'd only recently met Cynthia, why would he view her death as a curse?

Granddad tapped his ear. "I'm not sure my hearing aid's working right. Did you just say you were *cursed*, Dave?"

The younger man looked up from cradling his head. "Yes. Whenever I get close to success, the rug is pulled out from under me. Story of my life. In New York I had a lot of auditions that came to nothing. My juiciest role was as the dead body in *Law & Order*." He smiled ruefully.

Val remembered her neighbor in New York saying she would die for that role. "Isn't that a sought-after part?"

"As a stepping-stone, not a last hurrah. When I moved to LA and got a job in a soap, I expected it would keep me busy for years and lead to better roles. Didn't happen. Then my future at a restaurant went up in smoke." Dave munched on the chocolate chip cookie from his box lunch.

Val noted that even Culinary Institute graduates would resort to packaged cookies as comfort food.

Granddad leaned toward Dave. "Everyone has setbacks, son. I lost my fish store when a supermarket opened and undercut my prices. Lost my video store when folks switched to getting movies in their mailboxes. But I had what really mattered— someone to love and share my ups and downs. Sounds like you've got that too."

Dave smiled. "Yes, and that's what keeps me going."

"How does Cynthia come into your hard-luck story?" Granddad's question echoed what Val was wondering.

"Ever since moving East, I've been looking for a backer so I could open my own restaurant. Cynthia told me she had some money coming to her and she'd invest in my place."

"That's why you were moping in the lobby this morning," Granddad said.

"It wasn't just because I lost a backer. Cynthia resembled my mother." Dave bit his lower lip. "Mom died of cancer when I was in college."

So the curse of Cynthia's death was its reminder of his earlier terrible loss. "That must have been awfully tough," Val said.

Dave nodded. "I don't understand how people can think of death, especially murder, as entertainment."

"You're not a mystery fan?" Granddad said.

"No, but my mother was. She spent her time reading mysteries and ghostwriting girl detective books." Dave brushed cookie crumbs from his lap. "Whatever problem I had, her cure was to hand me a mystery. She fed me the classics—Poirot, Nero Wolfe, Lord Peter and Bunter. I was more interested in what they ate than their detecting."

Val said, "You played Bunter to the hilt, and your dessert was a great hit."

"I have to give Shereen credit for the recipe and the idea of creating Clue weapons with icing. She's a terrific pastry chef. With her in the kitchen, our restaurant can't fail." Dave reached into his shirt pocket. "Here's my card, in case you or someone you know might want to invest in a surefire business."

He thanked them for sharing their table with him and left.

Granddad scratched his head. "Worst pitch I ever heard. *My life is cursed and everything I touch turns to dust, so how about financing my next venture?*"

Val laughed. "His pitch flopped, but you hit the jackpot. You found out when Cynthia left the bar last night and who was with her. The woman in black might be gone, but the one with the purple hat and ponytail is still here."

"Talking to Trisha is high on my afternoon list. And calling Dorothy to see how she's handling her first Saturday back in the bookshop. It'll be a lot busier today than on the weekdays." He stood up. "What are you going to do?"

"I'll research Patty Cook. A food vlogger should

be easy to find online. But first I have to monitor the panel on historical mysteries. It's starting in ten minutes."

As she was leaving the room with Granddad, the war veteran who wrote cozy mysteries about a hairdresser was coming in. She introduced the two men. "Jordan writes a mystery series set in Southern Maryland."

Jordan extended his hand to Granddad. "Glad to meet the bake-off star in person. Your beeramisu was my favorite dessert."

"Thank you. You enjoying the fest?"

"Not the way I'd like. I've been in my hotel room all morning working on the next book. I have a full-time job, so I write at night and on the weekends. Aside from the panel I'm on tomorrow, I'm only leaving my room to eat."

"And drink," Val said. "You were at the bar last night."

"That was my reward for reaching my daily word count before midnight. On the elevator down just now, I heard a couple of people talking about a woman who died in her hotel room. Was she the one you were looking for last night?" When Val nodded, he said, "Sorry. Was she a close friend?"

"No, just an acquaintance." Val didn't want to explain why she was looking for someone she barely knew. "Are you going to the wine-and-cheese reception this evening?"

"You bet. I'm looking forward to that. Now I'd better grab one of those box lunches before they all disappear."

"Nice meeting you, Jordan. See you this evening." Granddad glanced down the corridor at the fest table. "Darn. Trisha's not the volunteer on duty now. I'm going to stake out the lobby. Maybe she'll pass through it."

Val wished him luck and headed toward the room where the historical mystery panel would be. Just before the panel began, she spotted Birdie slipping in. Maybe Val could catch her after the panel and coax her to describe the woman she'd seen in the hall last night.

The first panelist, author of the bicyclist mystery Val was reading, talked about the inspiration for her historical mystery and the research she'd done. She gave a shout-out to Claire, sitting next to her, for pointing out words and objects in the story that weren't used before the twentieth century.

The second panelist described her series in which a minor noble's widow and her maid solved murders in 1920s England. Val's mind wandered to what Dave had said about Cynthia's rival accusing her of food tampering. Could Patty Cook have come to the fest and somehow managed to slip anonymous notes into Granddad's and Cynthia's envelopes? Wouldn't Cynthia have recognized Patty at the fest? Not if she were in disguise. Val thought about the woman at the bar who'd looked ready for Halloween, with her mass of witch hair and vampire-like makeup. She and Trisha had given Cynthia a hand. Had one of them stayed longer and been alone with Cynthia?

Val tuned back into the panel when her table-mate at the bake-off, the historian Claire Rainey, began speaking. Claire talked about the research that authors of historic mysteries needed to con-

duct. Most writers of historical fiction took the
time to study the clothing that their characters
would wear but neglected domestic details—what
food they ate, how it was prepared, what utensils
were used, what time they had meals, where they
ate them, and how they were served. Claire said
she became aware of how complex this subject was
by taking a college course on the history of food in
which the students had to prepare meals that
would have been served during Medieval, Renaissance, and Victorian times.

Val had taken a course like that too. An image
flashed into her mind of Claire organizing a Renaissance dinner. That's why she looked familiar.
They'd taken the same course, Val as one of the
few non-history majors in it. She'd spent most of
her time in the kitchen preparing the food for the
feast.

When the session ended, Val postponed talking
to Birdie and rushed instead to the speakers' table
to confirm her recollection. Yes, she and Claire
had graduated from the same Virginia college and
taken the same history of food course. With a line
of people waiting to speak to her after the panel,
Claire suggested she and Val meet in the hospitality room in twenty minutes to talk about their
shared college experience and what they'd done
since then.

Val used the time to fetch her laptop from her
room, grab a table near the back of the hospitality
room, and search online for the bake-off contestant who'd accused Cynthia of cheating. It took no
time to find a video of Patty Cook demonstrating a
recipe. She was a perky woman with long, bouncy

hair that cascaded around her face in waves, a winning smile, and a friendly manner. She appeared to be in her early thirties. And her cooking tips were sound. Val was so engrossed in the video that she was startled when Claire leaned over her shoulder.

"Hey, Val. You're watching Trisha doing a cooking video?"

Val paused the video. "Trisha?"

"The woman who was at our table at the bake-off."

Val pointed at the screen. "She isn't Trisha. She's a video blogger named Patty Cook."

"Would you play a little more of the video please?" When Val restarted the video, Claire closed her eyes for twenty seconds, opened them, and said, "She has the same voice as Trisha. Patty and Trisha are both nicknames for Patricia."

Val paused the video again, freezing Patty Cook's face. "She doesn't look like Trisha."

"People can change their looks more easily than their voices. I didn't recognize your voice after a dozen or so years of not hearing it. But after hearing Trisha talk yesterday, I can identify her voice today."

Val studied the woman on the screen and visualized how she'd look with big glasses on her nose, her hair pulled back into a ponytail, and a baseball cap pulled down. Yes, the woman in the video could be Trisha. And her access to the fest envelopes while Perry Macon took a break had given her the chance to slip anonymous notes into them. The disgruntled Patty Cook hadn't donned a long black wig and thick makeup to disguise her identity in the bar last night. She'd come to the fest with a different hairdo, huge glasses, and an alternate name spelled out on her cap.

"I'd have never guessed that Trisha was the woman on the screen, but I see the similarity now." Val closed her laptop.

Claire sat down across from her. "It's odd she never mentioned she makes cooking videos."

Not so odd if she wanted to avoid being identified as the bake-off contestant who'd clashed with Cynthia. Enough about Trisha. "What have you been up to since we graduated, Claire?"

"I spent a couple of years studying at the Sorbonne in Paris. A magical time. When I came back to real life, I went into a Ph.D. program in history. The academic life wasn't a perfect fit for me, and I became a freelance historian."

"What does a historian for hire do?"

"Research whatever part of the past anyone wants dug up. Write histories of organizations and families. Dig into archives for homeowners who want to register their properties as historical buildings to get tax breaks. And I recently translated a French historical novel into English. That's in addition to substitute teaching and helping historical fiction writers." Claire looked fixedly across the table at Val. "Your turn. How did you end up running a café on the Eastern Shore?"

"I ran in the New York City rat race for ten years. I worked in a coffeehouse, edited cookbooks, and became a publicist for celebrity chefs before I moved to Maryland two years ago. I expected to help Granddad sell his house for a smaller place. He wouldn't sell, and I realized I didn't want to leave, though I envy the time you got to spend abroad." A wistful thought about her cancelled trip to Paris with Bram crossed Val's mind. "Hard to believe we were in the same graduating class and didn't get to know each other."

"I was off campus for a year in France. My major was Medieval and Renaissance Studies. I studied whatever interested me from different departments."

"I majored in American Studies for the same reason." Val noticed Bethany across the room.

Claire smiled. "You and I have a lot in common. I'm glad you figured out where we'd met before, and we've had the chance to reconnect."

Bethany had come up behind Claire in time to hear what she said. "I hate to interrupt you, Val, but your grandfather might need help at the fest table. Trisha took a break and didn't come back."

"I'll give him a hand." Val introduced the women to each other. After they shook hands, she said, "Sorry for running off, Claire."

"Not a problem. I need to grade papers anyway." Claire stood up. "Hope to see you both for wine and cheese."

"You look frazzled, Bethany," Val said as they left the hospitality room. "Can you rest before the reception? Go to our room and put your feet up?"

Bethany's phone chimed. "There's your answer. People have been texting me all day." She read a message and frowned. "I have a problem to fix. But then I'm going up to the room. I want to make a video call to Muffin."

She was going to chat with her spaniel? "How does that work?"

"The dog sitter's expecting my call. Muffin recognizes my voice and, if I say 'Look,' she'll gaze into my eyes even when I'm on a screen, and she'll know I haven't abandoned her. See you later." Bethany hurried down the corridor in the opposite direction from the fest table.

Val joined Granddad at the table and sat down in the chair next to his. "Did Trisha tell you anything before she ran off?"

"Yup. I got her talking about what happened last night when Cynthia left the bar. She was unsteady on her feet, but at least she remembered her room number. After Trisha and the other woman got her to the door, Cynthia couldn't find her key card in her bag. The other woman took the bag, got the key, and opened the door. The two of them helped Cynthia to her bed. She just wanted to lie down. She slipped off her shoes, climbed in, and refused any more help. Trisha and the other woman left the room at the same time."

"Did she tell you anything about the other woman?"

"Trisha noticed the woman's face studs were pasted on. The rings hanging from her nose and lips were clipped on."

Made sense to Val, who was too squeamish to have anything pierced except her earlobes. "She wanted the look without the pain. Or else she faked the piercings to draw attention away from how she usually looked. Did they both go back to the bar after leaving Cynthia?"

"They went separate ways. Trisha took the elevator to the lobby and drove home. The other woman waited for the elevator going up."

"So she was staying at the hotel. Roy could probably get a list of people who had rooms on the fourth floor. That's as far as the elevator goes."

Granddad looked skeptical. "*If* she had a room there. She mighta taken the up elevator just to ditch Trisha."

"Did you ask Trisha where the woman put the key card after using it to open the door?"

"Uh-huh. She said she paid no attention to that. I asked her if she noticed my recipe box while she was in Cynthia's room. That set her off. She said she'd told me what she knew about the recipe box and she wouldn't stand for me cross-examining her any more. She flounced away, leaving me here to do her job."

"You hit a nerve," Val muttered as some fest goers came to the table with questions they could have answered if they'd looked at their schedules.

The volunteer who was supposed to take over for Trisha arrived early, so Val and Granddad left for the lobby. As they went by the hotel reception desk, Roy was escorting a middle-aged woman into the makeshift office he was using. She matched Perry Macon's description of Willow Waterbrook. Tall and sturdy, she had chin-length auburn hair that hung straight down.

Val nudged Granddad. "The woman with Roy might be Cynthia's stepdaughter."

"I hope she keeps him busy. That'll give me a chance to talk to the bartender before Roy scares him into him watching his words." He glanced at his watch. "The bartender's shift will be starting soon."

Val pointed to a love seat and chair in the lobby. "Let's sit over there. I want to tell you who Trisha really is and why you shouldn't believe anything she says." Once they were seated, Val explained how Claire had recognized Trisha's voice as Patty Cook's. "Trisha's the contestant Dave talked about who accused Cynthia of sabotaging her cake."

Granddad wanted to see Patty Cook on video before accepting Claire's opinion.

After looking at the video, he still wasn't convinced. "Hard to believe that Cynthia didn't recognize her and neither did Dave. They both saw her at that previous bake-off. And she was checking in people for the fest yesterday."

"Yes, and the whole time Dave was there, she kept her head down. I'll bet she did the same when Cynthia checked in. Trisha stayed away from her last night at the bar until Cynthia could barely see straight and needed help. Trisha's glasses, ponytail, and hat with her name on it fooled both Cynthia and Dave."

But Granddad wasn't listening. He whispered to Val. "The woman who was with Roy is staring at us."

The redhead in black cargo pants and a quilted flannel shirt jacket took tentative steps toward him. "Excuse me. You're Don Myer, aren't you?"

"That's right. This is my granddaughter, Val Deniston. And your name is—?"

"Willow Waterbrook. I believe you knew my stepmother, Cynthia Sweet."

Val remembered Birdie's description of the scene between Cynthia and her stepdaughter. Hard to imagine this soft-spoken woman in a screaming match at her father's funeral.

Granddad said, "I met your stepmother yesterday for the first time before the bake-off we were in. I'm sorry for your loss."

Willow pressed her lips together as if holding back her words. After a moment, she said, "Nothing compares to the loss I felt four weeks ago when my father died. I hope you can help me with a problem." She glanced at the people crisscrossing the lobby. "Can we talk somewhere more private?"

Granddad turned to Val. "Your room?"

Val shook her head. They might interrupt Bethany's video call with her dog. "Let's go to yours instead."

As they waited for the elevator, Val cast sideways glances at Willow. Her crow's feet and forehead lines weren't deep, but two red spots on her otherwise clear face stood out. The tiny bruise near her nostril and a sore beneath her lower lip could be where she'd clipped on rings that mimicked body-piercing jewelry. If Cynthia's stepdaughter had donned a black wig and put on a goth face last night, she couldn't have come up with a better way to transform her appearance.

# Chapter 10

Granddad offered Willow the armchair in his room and eased himself into the desk chair. Val sat down on the bed, wondering what problem had prompted Cynthia's stepdaughter to ask an amateur sleuth for help. Probably it had come out of her meeting with the professional detective investigating Cynthia's death.

Willow sat ramrod-straight in a chair meant for lounging. "I'm asking for your help because I know you by reputation. A friend told me you solved a murder the police assumed was an accident. And I've heard about another case you worked on."

Maybe the one Greer had mentioned last night in the bar? Before Val could ask which case Willow meant, Granddad spoke up. "Is this about a murder?"

"Cynthia's death is apparently under investigation. The police called me because I was the only near kin they could locate. I assumed they needed me to sign some papers." Willow gripped the arms of the upholstered chair tightly. "The detective in charge of the case spent most of the time grilling me. He told me he'd reviewed the hotel's registration records and asked why I'd reserved a room here for the weekend and then checked out this morning."

Granddad tugged on his earlobe. "It's standard practice for the police to look at hotel records if there's an incident. That doesn't necessarily mean murder. Coulda been a theft or another crime."

Val was surprised he hadn't asked why Willow was at the hotel, as Roy had. Instead of cross-examining her, Granddad was trying to relax her. He must have noticed how wound up she was.

Willow drummed her fingers on the arm of the chair. "The detective went beyond the hotel records. He was digging up dirt. Someone gave him the idea that there was bad blood between Cynthia and me."

Oops. That someone was Val. She kept her eyes trained on the room's gray carpet, hoping her blush would go unnoticed. In telling Roy what Birdie had overheard, she'd given him hearsay on top of hearsay. But suppose Birdie had embellished what she'd overheard or even made it up? In the future Val wouldn't rush to the police with information until she'd confirmed it with another source.

"So you got along fine with your stepmother?" Granddad said.

"Far from it. When my mother died eighteen

months ago, my husband and I offered to remodel our house so my father could have his own space. He was on a strict diet and had to eat at set times. He was fine with our plan. Then he met Cynthia." Willow winced as if the thought of her stepmother pained her. "He brought her to dinner to meet the family. She went on about her blog, food columns, cookbook, and the cake she'd brought for dessert, which she insisted my father eat or she'd be insulted. My father was diabetic. The next day my brother had a heated talk with my father and called Cynthia a gold digger. When Cynthia found out, she refused to see my brother or me ever again."

Granddad murmured sympathetically.

Willow continued. "Dad couldn't bring himself to get rid of my mother's things. He asked me to do it and take what I wanted while he spent a few days with an old friend. An antique ring my mother had inherited and promised to me wasn't with her things. My father came back from that weekend married to Cynthia. She had a wedding band on one hand and my mother's ring on the other."

Val glanced at Willow's hands, surprised at her long, thin fingers, perfect for showing off a ring, but she wasn't wearing one. "Didn't your father know the ring was meant for you?"

"He'd forgotten. When I reminded him, he said he'd tell Cynthia the ring was on loan to her and she should give it to me. I had no hope she'd ever turn it over, but I couldn't hold that against him. Unlike my brother, I stayed in touch with my father. We'd meet in the public library while Cynthia was busy perfecting recipes for her cookbook."

"Getting together with you must have meant a lot to him." Val noticed tears welling in Willow's eyes. "Can I get you some water?"

"Yes, please. Tap water's fine."

Val grabbed the two large glasses near the ice bucket. As she filled them with water for Willow and Granddad, she remembered Birdie's account of Cynthia and Willow arguing at her father's funeral. They must have been talking about the ring, possibly the poison ring. Val delivered the water and sat down again on the bed.

Willow crumpled a tissue in her hand and sipped her water. "A few months ago, Dad was upset because Cynthia left the ring in a theater restroom. Fortunately, an honest person turned it in. Then she left it in the bathroom at a friend's house. She treated the ring that meant so much to me like it was hers to lose. The next time she forgot it, she might not get it back."

"She wore a ring last night with a turtle and gems on it." Granddad said, "Is that the one?"

Willow nodded.

When would she start leveling with Granddad? Val decided to force the issue. "You saw Cynthia showing off that ring at the bar last night. She didn't know who you were because of your wig, heavy makeup, and fake piercings. You helped her to her room when she drank too much." And maybe Willow had helped herself to the ring.

If Granddad was surprised, he hid it well, his eyes fixed on Willow.

She cleared her throat. "I knew Cynthia would be at the fest. She and Dad had registered for it months ago. She'd left my ring in a bathroom at least twice before. I hoped she'd do the same this weekend. I got a hotel room, didn't register for the fest, and just hung around in my disguise. Anytime she came out of a restroom, I'd go in and look for the ring. And I kept an eye on her in case she left it somewhere else."

Granddad looked at her over the top of his glasses. "That's why you were at the bar?"

She nodded. "I sat two seats away from her and didn't talk to anyone because I was afraid she'd recognize my voice. By eleven she was smashed, and I wasn't worried she'd recognize me. She couldn't walk straight. She leaned on me and a young woman named Trisha. We took her to her room."

Granddad prompted, "What happened when you got there?"

Willow's account of finding the key card and opening the door matched Trisha's. "Cynthia took off her shoes and fell back onto the bed with her legs dangling over the side. Trisha was driving home and anxious to leave. I asked her to help me get Cynthia all the way in bed. Between us, we got her settled and pulled the cover over her. Cynthia mumbled something and closed her eyes."

"Was the ring still on Cynthia's finger at that point?" Val asked.

Willow said nothing for a moment, biting her upper lip. "It must have been. She had it on in the bar."

So after stalking her stepmother to get that ring,

Willow couldn't say for sure where it was when she was that close to it? Unlikely. Val didn't press her as the police would, but switched to a question Willow might answer truthfully. "Where did you put Cynthia's bag after you found her key in it and opened the door?"

"On the floor at the side of the desk."

Exactly where it had been when Val saw it an hour later. "What did you do with the key card?"

"The detective asked the same question, and my answer is why I'm in trouble." Willow took a long gulp of water. "I'd put the key card in my pants pocket, but I didn't realize I had it until I was getting ready for bed. I went back to Cynthia's room to return the key—in disguise, of course."

It occurred to Val that Willow, made up like Dracula's bride, could have been the woman Birdie had seen in the hall last night.

Granddad looked up from the pad where he was jotting notes. "What time did you go back to Cynthia's room?"

"I looked at the clock on my nightstand before I left. It was 11:43. My room's on the fourth floor, and the elevator came fast. I got to Cynthia's room in less than a minute. She didn't respond when I knocked, so I let myself in. I called her name. When she didn't answer, I crept over to the desk and left the key card there. Then I glanced at her in bed. Her eyes were open, but not looking at me. I went closer and saw she was dead."

Val was too stunned to say anything.

Granddad broke the silence. "Some folks sleep with their eyes open. Back when I was in the army, one guy in basic training did that. The first time

we saw him in the bunk, we thought he was dead
and tried to revive him." Granddad tapped his pen
on the notepad. "Did you turn up the lights to
make sure she was dead or try to revive her?"

"No. The light in the hall was good enough. I
saw death up close when my mother passed. I didn't
need a spotlight on it. I assumed a heart attack or
a stroke had killed Cynthia." Willow gulped more
water. "I should have called 911, but I panicked.
I'd illegally entered the room of a woman who'd
died suddenly. No one would call us friends, and a
case could be made that I'd stalked her. I'm not
proud of this, but I bolted. I wasn't in the room
more than a minute before I ran out."

With or without the ring? Val saw no point in
asking. If Willow had taken the ring, she wouldn't
admit it. "Did you notice anything on the night
table?" When Willow shook her head, Val continued. "When you left the key card on the desk, did
you see another one there?"

"I have no memory of that. The shock of finding Cynthia dead blotted out most of what happened before and after. I remember turning away
from her and getting into the elevator. Everything
in between is a blank."

Unless she was lying, Val would have to give up
on the idea that Birdie had seen Willow in the hall.
The woman Birdie had spotted was walking toward
the ice machine and stairwell at the end of the
hall, the opposite direction from the elevator. "Are
you sure you took the elevator?"

"Yes. I saw a tall African American man with a
goatee waiting for a down elevator."

Had to be Jordan Young heading to the bar,

where Val had seen him half an hour later. He couldn't have missed Willow in her goth outfit if they were both waiting for an elevator on the third floor.

A raucous clatter from the ice machine dispensing cubes across the hall startled all of them.

Granddad made eye contact with Val. "You didn't believe me when I told you that machine would wake me up at night, and it did." He swiveled the desk chair so he faced Willow again. "When you were trying to find the key card in Cynthia's bag, did you see something in it that looked like a book or a box about the size of the book?"

"No." Willow was drumming her fingers on the chair arm again. "The detective said he had reason to believe Cynthia died later than when I left her room. He didn't explain his reason, but I know he's wrong."

Val knew the reason. The whistling kettle hadn't woken her until five after midnight, suggesting Cynthia must been awake close to midnight to plug it in. What Val didn't know was why Willow put so much emphasis on the time. "What will you do if the police charge someone with killing Cynthia after you left the room?"

Willow looked pensive for a moment and then met Val's steady gaze. "I would sign an affidavit and testify in court that she wasn't alive then. I wouldn't let an innocent person be punished. But if the police can't find anyone to blame for Cynthia's death at the later time, they might come back to me as the only suspect." She turned to Granddad. "That's why I want to hire you."

He frowned. "To do what?"

Willow shifted to the edge of the chair. "Find another suspect. Someone who could have gone to her room after 11:15, when Trisha and I left her in bed, and before I went back."

Granddad stroked his chin. "I'll try to find out if anyone was seen near her room in that time frame, but I'm going to do it with an open mind about when she died."

Really? Val couldn't see the point of it. Finding someone near her room didn't turn that person into a suspect in the absence of a motive. "Do you know of anyone with a grudge against Cynthia besides—" Val broke off before saying *besides you.* "Anyone she harmed?"

Willow shrugged. "There must be slews of people she treated badly. She was totally self-centered."

Granddad reached down for his briefcase on the floor. "I have my standard contract here. I'll fill in the blank areas to say what I'm going to do for you. You can take it with you, look it over, and if you agree, let me know."

Willow said, "I'm impressed by how prepared you are. I don't do any work without a contract either."

Val couldn't understand why Granddad was jumping on this "opportunity." She'd want to know more about Cynthia's stepdaughter with her sketchy story before taking her on as a client. As Granddad filled in the specifics on the contract, Val said, "What kind of work do you do, Willow?"

"Landscape design."

Val glanced at Willow's sturdy walking shoes. "You like the outdoors then."

"Yes, and the creativity of the job. Except for

when I scope out projects, I work mostly on a computer, drawing up plans." Willow took the contract Granddad held out to her. "Thank you. I'll look at it over a cup of cappuccino downstairs. Here's my contact information." She pulled a business card from a wristlet that had just enough room for a phone, driver's license, and assorted cards.

Val envied the woman's ability to make do with a small purse, but she had overflow space in the capacious pockets of her cargo pants. She must also have deep pockets of another sort, given that she hadn't asked Granddad what he'd charge her.

He gave Willow his business card. As he walked her to the door, Val moved from the bed into the armchair.

Granddad returned and leaned against the desk. "After listening to her, we've got a lot to chew on."

"And some of it's hard to swallow. Two women disguised themselves to keep Cynthia from recognizing them. Willow and Trisha both had something against her, and they took her to her room together. Then they left the room at the same time." Val imagined what the book dealer with a database of mystery plots in his brain would make of that. "Harrison would say Willow and Trisha were in cahoots to kill Cynthia and alibi each other."

"But Willow admits to pocketing the key and going back."

"Then she insists Cynthia was dead half an hour before anyone else saw her dead and hires you to back her up. Why does she care when her stepmother died?"

Granddad looked up at the ceiling as if the answer hung there. "Maybe Willow has an alibi for the earlier time, but not for the later time. Or she really believed Cynthia was dead. Most people haven't encountered an open-eyed sleeper like my army buddy. "

"Willow didn't even bother to check if Cynthia was breathing. Despite what she said, I think she gave in to temptation and took the ring."

"Off Cynthia's finger?" Granddad looked askance. "If she wasn't dead, that would wake her up."

"Not if she'd drunk a lot. And maybe the ring wasn't on her finger. Cynthia was probably in the habit of removing the ring before getting into bed. Or she might have gotten up after she was put to bed, slipped off the ring, and left it on the night table or in the bathroom."

Granddad sat down in the desk chair. "Willow also had the chance to grab my recipe box. She said it wasn't in Cynthia's bag, but that could be a lie."

Val couldn't imagine why Cynthia's stepdaughter would want it. "You told everyone at the bake-off how valuable the recipe box was, but Willow wasn't there to hear it. She's not registered for the fest and couldn't have gotten in."

He took off his glasses and pinched the bridge of his nose. "But Trisha was there and knew the value of the box. Suppose she was lying when she said it was in Cynthia's bag? Trisha had the chance to snatch the box herself and make Cynthia look bad."

"Both Trisha and Willow resented Cynthia. One or both of them might be thieves, but is either of them a murderer?" Val stood up and paced the room. "We know someone was in Cynthia's room after they were, based on the kettle whistling and the keys. Willow left one key. Two keys were there when Bethany, the guard, and I went in, and both were wiped clean of fingerprints. The kettle was whistling. And Cynthia was definitely dead."

Granddad put his glasses back on. "Someone might have a stronger motive to want her dead than those two women did. Roy put greed ahead of grudge as a motive. If he's following the money, he's looking for Cynthia's heirs."

"He'd need to see Cynthia's will to find out who the heirs are. If she didn't make a will, Roy would have to locate her cousin who came out of nowhere. The next time I see Roy, I'll ask if he's made any progress on that. I'd also like to track down Birdie and coax her to tell me more about the woman she saw in the hall last night."

"I want to talk to the bartender, but I need to do something else first."

Val suspected Granddad needed a nap. He usually took one in the afternoon at home. "See you later."

When she got off the elevator, she noticed Willow in a wingback chair near the bar. A cup and saucer were on the small side table next to her. Val passed the reception desk and had just gone into the Poe wing when someone came up behind her.

"Miss! Miss!"

It took her a moment to recognize the security guard who'd let her into Cynthia's room. He wasn't in uniform. "Hi, Nico."

"Can I speak to you, please. It's important." He looked flustered.

"Sure." She moved toward the window, away from

people walking between the lobby and Poe wing. "Is something wrong?"

"The police talked to me about what happened last night. The detective asked me the same questions over and over. How near did I go to the dead lady? Was she wearing any jewelry? Did I take anything from the room? He asked about a fancy ring. He acted like he thought I stole it. You were there too. You saw me. I didn't take anything from the room." He chewed on his lower lip. "I could be fired if he tells my boss what he suspects. Can you help me?"

"I told him I didn't see you take anything from the room. I'll speak to him again." Though she hadn't convinced Roy the first time.

"Thank you."

Val thought of something else she could do for Nico, a long shot, but worth the try. "I'm going to say hello to a woman who's sitting in the lobby. I'd like you to wait half a minute, come up to me, and repeat what you just said. Pretend it's the first time you're telling me about the policeman's questions, but don't say that I was in the room with you. I'll act as if I'm hearing your story for the first time."

Nico frowned. "I don't understand."

"You know what *hearsay* is from your criminal justice classes?" When he nodded, Val continued. "If I tell the woman what you said, it's only hearsay, easy to reject as inaccurate. If you tell her, it will make more of an impression. Okay?"

He nodded.

As Val returned to the lobby, she thought about the righteous statement Willow had made to her and Granddad: "I wouldn't let an innocent person be punished." They'd been talking about murder, but the same rule should apply to theft. If Val's hunch about the ring was right, Willow would get a chance to prove how far she'd go to clear an innocent person.

# Chapter 11

Willow looked up from her phone as Val approached her. "I read over the contract from your grandfather. It's fine with me, especially since I don't have to pay him the bulk of it unless he succeeds."

Granddad was confident of his own abilities. "Send him a message agreeing to the terms, and he'll start working for you." Val pointed to Nico, who was walking toward them. "That's the security guard who was on duty last night and went into Cynthia's room."

Nico approached Val tentatively. "Can I please talk to you, miss?"

She nodded, and he once again described his experience with the police. She glanced at Willow and saw her sit up straighter when Nico mentioned a ring missing from Cynthia's room.

"The policeman thinks I stole a ring from the lady who died. I'll get fired if he tells my boss that."

Willow blanched.

Val said, "The police wouldn't tell your boss about their investigation until it's over."

Nico didn't look convinced. "I hope you're right. I'm on probation because I just started working here. I need this job." He started to leave and then turned back. "I'm sorry for interrupting you. Have a good evening."

Willow watched him leave, hugging herself. "He was talking about my mother's ring."

Val nodded. "You said Cynthia must have been wearing the ring when you and Trisha were in the room. Was she still wearing it when you brought back the key card?"

Willow hesitated. Because she'd had to consult her memory or because she was choosing her words carefully?

She licked her lips. "I didn't look at her hand. I freaked out when I saw she was dead."

Val had a spoon full of guilt ready for Willow. "I hope the detective figures out what happened to the ring for the sake of the poor security guard. New on the job, he's sent to check on a problem in Cynthia's room. I'll bet he'd never seen a dead body before. Must have spooked him. And now he's got a cop accusing him of theft. What a way to start a career."

Willow stuck her phone into the leg pocket of her cargo pants. "I have to leave." She rushed out of the hotel.

Her strong reaction gave Val hope that Willow's

conscience would plague her on her drive home, assuming she'd taken the ring. But if she hadn't, Val could come up with another more likely suspect than the guard. She wanted Roy to know all the alternatives.

She texted him. If he could spare a few minutes, she had information he might find helpful. His return text told her to meet him in fifteen minutes at the office where they'd talked earlier.

Val crossed the lobby and went into the Poe wing, hoping to find Birdie. With the afternoon's last panels ending, fest attendees milled around in the corridor. Val scanned the crowd without spotting Cynthia's nosy neighbor.

A cluster of people had gathered in front of the easel holding the fest's message board. One person pointed to it. What was attracting all the interest? Trisha stood at the edge of the group, craning her neck to read the board.

As Val approached the group, she studied the lower half of Trisha's face, the part not obscured by glasses and her cap. The volunteer's plumped lips and squared jaw resembled Patty Cook's. That, plus the similarity of their voices, which Claire had noticed, confirmed Val's belief that the food vlogger and the volunteer were the same woman using different names.

Bethany came up next to Val, looking perturbed. She pointed to a handwritten sign tacked to the board. "Did you know your grandfather was going to post that?"

Val read the notice: SEEKING WITNESSES! REWARD FOR INFORMATION ON THE WHEREABOUTS OF THE NERO WOLFE RECIPE BOX. IF YOU SAW ANYONE WITH

THE BOX AFTER THE BAKE-OFF, PLEASE CONTACT DON
MYER, AKA, NERO WOLFE'S GOURMET COOK, FRITZ.

Granddad's phone number and e-mail address
followed. "He didn't tell me he was going to post a
notice, but I don't see a problem. The recipe box
is missing. He'd like to find it."

Val glanced at Trisha, who'd now inched close
enough to read the sign.

Bethany folded her arms. "He could have said
*lost*. Instead, he used words like *whereabouts* and *witnesses*, as if a crime was committed. The sign im-
plies someone here is a thief."

Even worse, someone here might be a murderer—not what Bethany wanted to hear. "Granddad was trying to engage people who love mysteries.
I don't think the attendees will interpret his notice as
an affront to their honesty. They might even take it as
a mystery game."

Trisha sidled up next to Val and said quietly,
"Shouldn't I get the reward? I told you and your
grandfather where the recipe box was."

"But where is it *now*? My grandfather asked the
police if they'd found it. It wasn't in Cynthia's
bag."

"It must be somewhere in her room." Trisha
stomped away.

Val would bet Trisha had lied about the recipe
box to smear Cynthia. But once Cynthia was dead,
why double down on a lie? Maybe Bethany could
shed some light on Trisha's character.

Val turned to her friend, whose lips were puck-
ered as if she had a lemon slice in her mouth. "Do
you think Trisha is trustworthy?"

Bethany shrugged. "I'm just glad she's here. Most

of the volunteers have been at the fest previously. This is her first time, and she's been a trouper. If she hadn't signed up to be a volunteer, I'd have had to call on you to do more."

"When did she sign up?"

"A week or two ago. She was easy to slot in wherever I needed someone. The other volunteers wanted to attend the big sessions and the popular panels. Trisha was willing to skip them."

Because she had no interest in mysteries. She'd come to the fest to get back at the bake-off cheater, one way or another. But how had Trisha known Cynthia would be at the fest? When Bethany stepped away to respond to a text, Val pulled out her phone and brought up Cynthia's website. The date and location of the fest appeared prominently on the page where she listed her speaking engagements and cook-offs. She couldn't have made it easier for someone to track her.

Val's next stop was the office Detective Roy was occupying. When she was seated across the desk from him, she told him everything she'd discovered about Trisha. He jotted in a notebook as she talked.

When she finished, he put down his pen. "Trisha did nothing criminal. She promotes herself online with a different name and tries to look her best on video. Even if you could prove she wrote the anonymous notes, she'd have an innocent explanation. She left the note to your grandfather to keep Cynthia from cheating again. The note to Cynthia was spiteful, but even she didn't take it as a threat. Unless you have evidence that Trisha stole your grandfather's recipe box—"

"I don't. And I wasn't asking you to charge her with a crime. I'm just giving you background to help you when you question her. By the way, after you talked to Willow, she told Granddad and me she'd gone back to Cynthia's room."

"And found her dead."

"So she said. Trisha might have also gone back. When I saw Cynthia in the afternoon she had two key cards. Willow used the key from Cynthia's bag to open the door when she and Trisha took Cynthia to her room. Where was her second key card? Possibly on the desk or the floor. Trisha could have pocketed it when Willow's attention was elsewhere. When they left the room around 11:15, Trisha said she was going to drive home, but did she really do that?" After Roy didn't respond, Val continued. "The hotel must have surveillance cameras around the doors to the outside."

"Only at the main entrance, but not at the exit door in that wing." Roy dug a protein bar from his pocket. "If Trisha paid a return visit to Cynthia's room, was that before or after Willow did the same thing?"

Val paused to think. "Either way. If she went in after Willow left, Trisha could have been the person Birdie saw walking toward the end of the hall, where the stairwell is. Take those stairs two stories down and you're near the exit door closest to the parking lot."

"Without passing a surveillance camera on the way out. How do you explain the two key cards without prints?"

"Trisha dropped the key on the desk, stole the ring, and realized the key card had her prints on it. With two keys on the desk, she couldn't tell which card she used, so she cleaned them both and left."

"Who put the kettle on?"

Val shrugged. "The simple explanation is Cynthia woke up, felt woozy, and decided tea would help. She put the kettle on, crawled back into bed, and died. So nobody killed her."

"There's some evidence to the contrary, though it's not definitive. The doc ordering the autopsy called a friend at the state crime lab and got it on a fast track. Preliminary results suggest suffocation as a possible cause of death, and the alcohol and sedatives in her system would have facilitated that." Roy slowly unwrapped an energy bar. "You've made your point that the women who brought her to her room had the opportunity to take the ring."

Val sat back, relieved that he was considering alternatives to Nico as the ring thief. With her goal accomplished, she could focus on worming information from Roy. "Have you had any luck locating Loren Davis, the cousin who sent Cynthia a letter?"

"My people have searched Cynthia's place for that letter, her will, a family tree, or anything else we could use to trace her roots. So far, nothing's turned up." Roy stared at his snack bar as if trying to decide how to tackle it. "Davis is a common surname. We don't know where the cousin lives or even her age. She could be as old as eighty or as young as twenty, depending on how many times removed she is on the family tree. The fact that she sent a letter by mail makes me think she's on the older side."

"A young person might send an old-fashioned letter, not knowing how much technology a sixty-year-old woman uses." But the letter must have contained some form of contact information. "Perry Macon, the man whose business card I gave you, told me about the letter. Maybe he noticed a return address."

"I asked him. No return address, just a phone number in the letter. He didn't even remember the area code. Cynthia didn't pass the letter around. He was the only one who looked at it."

"Birdie Natter, Cynthia's nosy neighbor, is also in the book club. I wouldn't put it past her to have peeked at the letter while he read it. Have you talked to her yet?" Val suspected he hadn't.

"I'll speak to her before I leave today. She's on my schedule." Roy crunched down on a piece of his energy bar.

"Perry told me that Cynthia always put herself in the spotlight at book club meetings. She did that last night at the bar when she talked about the murder a year ago. She must have told the book club about it too. A staged murder during dinner, followed by a real murder later that night is quite a story. It's a mystery book club, so the members would have pressed her for details about what she saw and heard."

Roy laughed. "She wasn't at the hotel for the murder mystery dinner. Perry Macon and his wife were. They'd have seen Cynthia if she'd been there."

"So she lied last night." Val shouldn't have been surprised. "People who heard her didn't know it was a lie. She might have attracted the attention of someone who didn't want the truth about that old murder to come out."

"Obviously." Roy drummed his fingers on the desk. "I don't understand your interest in this case. We got to know each other when you were sleuthing because your grandfather was a suspect in a murder. The next time I ran into you, you were trying to solve a murder that took place in your backyard."

"When the victim was dressed just like me."

"So you had a personal reason. Why do you care about the death in a hotel of a woman you'd just met?"

A valid question. Val went for the easy answer. "I'd like to help my grandfather locate his keepsake recipe box, which Cynthia supposedly had."

"What if I told you we found the recipe box in her room after all? Would you forget Cynthia's death and enjoy the fest's made-up murders?"

"Definitely not." It took Val a moment to figure out why she was so invested in explaining Cynthia's death. "Because of the kettle. Without that kettle, I'd have slept well, learned of Cynthia's death in the morning, and given it little thought. But the whistle called me to the scene and made me part of it. Call me a ham, but I can't step out of the scene until the curtain comes down."

Roy smiled with his lips pressed together. "*I* will bring the curtain down. Don't ask me to reenact the crime, like you did once before. With an unsolved murder from a year ago and a suspicious death from yesterday, I'd like you to stay in the wings or, better yet, in the audience."

As an audience member, was Val allowed to hiss? She resisted asking that question. "I will remain offstage. Now it's time for me to exit left."

He applauded her exit.

He'd like nothing better than to close two murder cases at once. That left her and Granddad to solve the mystery of the ring and the recipe box. She went to the lobby to find Granddad and give him the news.

# Chapter 12

Granddad was on a sofa in the lobby, jotting in the small spiral notebook he always carried in his shirt pocket. He patted the cushion next to him. "Have a seat. Where have you been?"

"Talking to Roy." She plopped onto the sofa and told him what the detective had said.

When she finished, Granddad folded his arms. "He hasn't done squat about my recipe box."

"Your sign offering a reward for information might get some results. What's the reward?"

"A gift certificate to Dorothy's bookshop."

A win-win for him on two fronts. He wouldn't just get information but also curry favor with his lady friend. Val pointed to his spiral pad. "What have you been scribbling?"

"Notes on what Eric Reddish, the bartender, told me. He was helpful . . . until he got hostile."

Val turned to look at the thirty-something man behind the bar. With his brawny build, butch-cut hair, and impassive face, Eric could double as a bouncer. Easier to imagine him hostile than helpful. "Roy said Cynthia had alcohol and sedatives in her system. If her drink was spiked last night, the bartender was in the best position to do that. It's got to be harder for the person next to you at the bar to tamper with your drink without your noticing."

"It wouldn't have been hard last night. Eric said Cynthia swiveled her seat to talk to the people at the tables. She had her back to the bar a lot of the time. Unless she was cradling her drink, it was sitting there within reach of the people who sat beside her."

Val glanced at the U-shaped bar. With Cynthia's seat in the middle of it, someone spiking her drink risked being seen by the people along the sides. "Using her poison ring, Cynthia might have gotten away with nonchalantly spiking a drink. I'm not sure anyone else could have done it without attracting notice. But let's assume someone did. We know Dave saved a seat for her next to him, left for a while, and came back. So he had the opportunity to tamper with her drink. Did the bartender remember him?"

"Yup. He said Dave left the bar before ten, came back around eleven, and was still there when the bartender left for home at twenty minutes past midnight."

"Did Eric remember anyone else who sat near Cynthia?"

"Not by name, but he described people I recognized." Granddad glanced at his notes. "The journalist Greer stuck around awhile after Dave gave her his seat. And Willow moved over to the seat next to Cynthia's for a short time."

Val frowned. "Willow told us she didn't sit next to her stepmother." What else had she lied about?

"She didn't start out next to Cynthia." Granddad glanced at his notes. "At first there was a young guy between them. He didn't stay long."

"Guess he didn't like being sandwiched between a granny and a goth."

"Can't blame him. One of them never shut up, and the other never opened her mouth. Eric said Willow stared at her phone the whole time she was at the bar. A couple came in and asked her to slide over so they could sit together. That put her next to Cynthia, but when the couple left, Willow went back to the other seat."

"So Cynthia had an empty seat on one side. Was Greer still on Cynthia's other side?"

Granddad shrugged. "Eric didn't keep track of when she left. A lot of folks piled into the bar when the movie let out around ten thirty. One of them was Birdie, and she sat next to Cynthia."

Val was amazed. "Birdie told me all kinds of things about Cynthia this morning and never mentioned being in the bar with her."

"They probably didn't have a conversation. Cynthia was so out of it by then that she tried to pay her bar tab with her room key card. Then it took her a while to fish her credit card out of her bag."

Val straightened up. "Maybe she left that key

card on the bar." Who could have picked it up and used it later? "Did Eric say anything about Trisha moving near Cynthia?"

"Nope. And I won't get any more information from him 'cause I got on his bad side. Soon as I asked if he'd heard Cynthia talk about the murder a year ago, he clammed up and didn't come near me again. Too bad. I'd like to find out who was there to hear what she said."

"If there's any connection between Cynthia's death and the one a year ago, Roy will uncover it. He said Cynthia wasn't here when that murder happened." But the bartender wouldn't have known that. Val studied the man behind the bar. "I wonder why Eric reacted that way to your question about the old murder."

"He coulda been tending bar the night that murder happened. I ordered a beer when I first sat down. After he brought it, we were shootin' the breeze, and I asked how long he'd worked here. Year and a half." Granddad glanced sideways toward the bar. "Greer's still sitting at the bar. She came in just before I asked Eric about the old murder. She looked amused when he shut me down. I'll try to catch her at the reception and find out why."

Val glanced at her watch. "I want to change out of these clothes and freshen up before the reception."

As she stood up, a middle-aged woman tentatively approached Granddad. "I read the sign you posted about your recipe box. I saw something after the presentations at the bake-off last night that could help you locate it. Of course, I don't know if it will, but if you have some time now, I'll explain."

Val was sure Granddad would tell her whatever news the woman gave him. "See you at the reception, Granddad."

The reception was underway when Val arrived. A partition between two meeting rooms had been rolled back. Small standing-height tables had replaced the rows of chairs in the center, and the chairs now lined the back and one side wall. Along the opposite side wall was a buffet of cheese and fruits. Fest goers helped themselves to the food while servers poured wine at the front of the room.

Val scanned the attendees. Dozens of them wore "detective" hats, part of their costume for the Best Dressed Detective contest that would follow the reception. Aside from the Miss Marple hats and deerstalker caps, there were bowlers, cloches, fedoras, and even bonnets appropriate for a Jane Austen sleuth. Some wore costumes without hats. Harrison in a tuxedo held a wineglass in one hand and a monocle in the other, an aristocratic sleuth from head to toe.

Like Val, a third of the attendees wore casual clothes. She noticed Dave Proctor at a table with the two women who'd recognized him from a soap opera. She suspected he was scoping them out as possible restaurant investors, now that he'd lost Cynthia as a backer. Maybe he would succeed in turning lemons into lemonade this weekend.

Val finally spotted Birdie in the buffet line and darted across the room toward her. "Hi, Birdie. Have you enjoyed your day?"

The small woman nodded vigorously, making the feathers on her hat quiver. "Very much. And I went by the hospitality room twice to neaten up the display."

"Thank you. I forgot to do that." Val came up with a roundabout way to worm information from Birdie about the woman she'd seen last night. "I met Cynthia's stepdaughter, Willow, today and was struck by how tall she is. Was the woman you saw in the corridor last night also tall?"

"Everyone looks tall to me . . . even you." Birdie scanned the room. "The tables where we're supposed to stand and eat weren't made for petite women like us."

"I hate those tables too." Val refused to be side-tracked. "Do you remember if the woman in the corridor had short or long hair?"

"She had no hair." Birdie laughed. "I surprised you with that, didn't I? I mean that she had no hair showing. She had a black turban on her head, like you see on women getting facials in a spa."

"A turban. That's unusual in a hotel that doesn't have a spa." Trisha could have stuffed her ponytail under a turban, though it would have had a bump in the back. Val glanced at the front of the room and saw her queuing up for wine in her jeans, sweatshirt, and baseball cap. "Birdie, did you notice what kind of clothes the woman in the hall was wearing?"

The older woman acted as if she hadn't heard the question and turned her attention to the buffet table. "This is such a nice spread. All the different cheeses and fruits."

Val sighed. Birdie had all different ways of dodging questions. Maybe wine would loosen her tongue. "I'm going to get a glass of wine. Would you like a drink?"

"My wine's already at one of those tables." Birdie waved her hand in the direction of the tall tables.

Val wasn't sure which table she meant, but it shouldn't be hard to find her once she reclaimed it.

On the way for wine, Val stopped for a quick chat with Jordan. He confirmed Willow's story. He'd seen a woman with long dark hair and face piercings take the up elevator from the third floor around 11:45 last night.

As Val waited her turn for wine, Bethany came into the room, wearing a dress imprinted with bright green and blue peacock feathers. She'd dressed as Mrs. Peacock to promote the evening's events—mystery board games and the *Clue* movie.

Val motioned to her. "Do you want me to get you a glass of wine?"

"I'll grab one after I make the rounds of the tables. I'd like to get feedback about the fest and remind people about tonight's activities."

Val fully intended to forget them. She'd seen the movie, and playing murder mystery board games didn't appeal to her, especially when she had a real murder plot to ponder. "Granddad and I are going to eat dinner in the restaurant here. I'll text you when I know what time. Hope you can join us."

"Okey-doke." Bethany plunged into the crowd.

Val spotted Greer coming into the reception

with Granddad close behind. After he caught up
with her, they sat down in the chairs along the wall
and talked. With the line for drinks getting longer,
Val decided to save Granddad the trouble of queuing up. She'd get two glasses, one white and one
red, and drink whichever he didn't want.

By the time she had both glasses in hand, Greer
had left Granddad.

Val hurried over to him and held out the glasses.
"Red or white?" After he took the red, she sat down
in the chair the journalist had vacated. "What did
Greer have to say?"

"She explained why the bartender was peeved at
me. He was tending bar the night the murder happened a year ago. He didn't like being reminded
of it. She got a kick out of the way he shut me down.
He did the same thing to her last night when she
asked him about that murder, but she was more
persistent than I was."

"Pushiness goes with the territory when you're
a journalist. Did she say anything else about that
case?"

"There was a murder mystery dinner show and,
after it, some hotel guests went to the bar. One
couple got real loud. The husband had drunk a lot
and accused his wife of taking up with her former
boyfriend. She said he was insanely jealous. They
were still arguing when they went up to their room.
Later a fire was reported in their room. Husband
dead, wife fled." Granddad sipped his wine.

Though Val was used to his meandering before
he got to the point of his story, she hated being
kept in suspense. She nudged him along. "And the
wife was suspected, but there wasn't enough evi-

dence to try her. That doesn't explain Eric's negativity when you asked him about the murder."

"The police interviewed everybody the couple went near. Folks in the bar heard them arguing about the wife's ex-boyfriend. His name was Eric."

Val's jaw dropped. "The bartender was the boyfriend?"

"No, but he came in for some heavy questioning. The police never located Eric, the ex. The wife said he was a figment of her hubby's jealous imagination."

"Roy seems to think—or hope—there's a connection between that murder and Cynthia's death. I don't see it. The bartender couldn't have been involved in Cynthia's death. He was at the bar when she left at 11:15, and he was there an hour later, when I went down to the lobby to report the kettle whistling."

"Tending bar's a good alibi." Granddad pointed toward the door. "See the woman coming in now? She's the one who wanted a reward for telling me about the recipe box."

"What did she say?"

"After the bake-off presentations ended, when everyone was milling around the table at the front, she saw Trisha with the recipe box in her hand. That's all. The woman didn't see her pull it out from under the table or walk away with it."

"Not an eyewitness to the crime. Maybe someone else will come forward."

"I sure hope so." Granddad handed Val his half-empty wineglass. "I'll get us cheese and fruit. How about you find us a table so we don't have to balance the food on our laps?"

With a wineglass in each hand, Val searched the room for Birdie and spotted her at a table with Perry Macon. No point in trying to coax her for more details about the woman in the hall last night. Perry would probably scorn amateur sleuthing, as he had this morning, and make Birdie less likely to share what she knew. Besides, Val and Granddad would barely be able to squeeze in at the small table with two other people.

But they'd fit at the table next to Birdie's, where Claire stood alone. Val wended her way toward her former classmate and waved as she passed Birdie and Perry. Instead of waving back, Birdie clutched the edge of the table, grimaced, and dropped to the floor, taking her wineglass with her.

# Chapter 13

A lump formed in Val's throat as she stared at Birdie on the floor with her eyes closed and her hat askew. Leaving the two wineglasses on the table, Val knelt down next to the older woman.

"Birdie! Birdie!" No response. "Someone call 911," Val yelled over the din in the room.

"I'll call," Claire responded.

Perry crouched on the other side of Birdie and put his fingers on her wrist. "Her heart's beating. Slowly."

Birdie's eyes flickered open. She groaned and closed them.

Perry pointed under the table where there was a purse with a chain strap. "Look in there for her phone. Her son's number must be in it. His name's Jim."

Val picked up the purse. A foot away from it, Birdie's glass lay on its side, still in one piece after the carpet cushioned its impact. Red wine bled into the gray rug. Val unsnapped the bag's clasp, took out Birdie's iPhone, and said, "Hey, Siri. Call Jim."

When Siri responded, "Calling Jim," Val stood up and handed Perry the phone.

She fished her own phone from her shoulder bag and texted Roy, asking him to come to the room because of an emergency.

People from nearby tables clustered around Birdie. A hotel staffer excused his way through the group. He bent down to pick up the wineglass.

"*Don't touch the glass!*" Two women in the group around Birdie shouted in unison.

The staffer backed off, looking askance, apparently unaware that clue hunters surrounded him.

"It could be evidence," Jordan explained to him and dropped down by Birdie. "I can give CPR if she needs it."

Val looked around for Granddad. He was still going through the buffet, apparently unaware that someone had hit the floor.

Claire peered down at Birdie. "The 911 dispatcher said the first responders are coming. I hope she's okay. Is she a friend of yours?"

"No, we were thrown together as hospitality room volunteers. She and Cynthia knew each other well."

Claire's eyebrows rose. "Cynthia's the woman with the poison ring who died last night?"

"Yes." When Cynthia was showing off the ring at the bar, Claire had gone over to take a close look at it. Had she seen someone near Cynthia that the bartender hadn't mentioned? "Did you notice who was sitting next to her when you were looking at her ring?"

Claire shook her head. "I was laser-focused on that piece of jewelry." She tilted her head to the side and studied Val. "I can think of only one reason you'd ask that. Did someone steal that ring?"

That was the kind of conclusion Val would have jumped to. Mentally awarding her classmate amateur sleuth points, Val stuck with the facts. "I heard the ring was missing." She saw Roy at the entrance to the room. "Would you excuse me, Claire? See you later, I hope."

Val hurried to Roy. She explained what had happened and told him the first responders were on the way.

After checking Birdie, he took Val aside. "Don't make too much of this. She's an elderly woman."

"An elderly woman who witnessed someone in the vicinity of a suspicious death." Val held back from saying what she was thinking: *You said you would interview that woman today, but you didn't, and now it may be too late.*

Roy called the room to attention, announced that there was a medical emergency, and asked them to clear a path for the first responders. Anyone in the front half of the room should step to the back.

Most attendees complied quickly, though a few lingered to rubberneck, trying to catch a glimpse of Birdie. Claire was in the middle of the crowd at the back. Val went to the corner where Granddad stood with two plates of cheese and fruit. Bethany was with him. Val filled them in on what she'd witnessed.

Bethany nervously twirled the strands of her ginger hair. "This fest is cursed."

"*Cursed* is the word of the day," Granddad said.

Bethany sighed. "I'm going to have to back out of dinner with you two. The steering committee has to meet. Does the show go on as if we didn't have a death and a medical emergency and who knows what else tomorrow? This weekend was supposed to be fun."

Granddad patted her arm. "If you can break away, we'll be in the restaurant here. I reserved the same table we had for breakfast, the one in the corner where it's quiet. The reservation's for six thirty."

Greer elbowed her way through the group toward them. She sidled up to Granddad. "What do you know about the woman who collapsed?" The journalist held her phone ready to record his response.

Granddad shrugged. "Not much. She's a fest volunteer. I met her yesterday."

Bethany edged away from them, probably expecting the journalist to interview her next.

Greer waggled her finger at Granddad. "You're holding out on me. I told you about the murder last year."

Val doubted Greer had said more than what was in newspaper accounts anyone could read online.

Granddad held up his hands like a magician showing he wasn't hiding anything. "I can't tell you what I don't know."

"I saw that older woman sitting next to Cynthia Sweet at the bar after last night's movie ended. What do you make of that?"

Granddad scratched his head. "She must have eaten popcorn and gotten thirsty."

The journalist pursed her lips and walked off. Granddad winked at Val.

She glanced at the emergency team working on Birdie. A middle-aged man with round glasses that gave him an owlish look was coming into the room, probably her son. He followed the EMTs as they wheeled her out of the room.

Roy approached the fest goers, asked for attention, and held up his identification card. "I'm Detective Roy Chesterfeld. With your interest in murder mysteries, some of you might be dreaming up scenarios to explain what happened here tonight. They belong in books. In reality, it's not unusual for an elderly woman to fall down after a busy day and a drink or two. However, if you've seen or heard anything that would suggest otherwise, please report it. I'll be around for another few hours. The front desk knows how to reach me, or if you think of anything later, call the police. Just to be clear, we're interested in facts, not theories. Thank you for your attention and your cooperation. Enjoy the rest of your evening."

As soon as he left the room, the buzz began.

Harrison raised his voice and his monocle. "I must say, that was rather realistically staged, complete with a cop straight out of central casting. At last, we have a clue to this weekend's murder mystery. The first victim's name starts with a *C*. The second victim has a name starting with *B*. The solution to the weekend's mystery is the ABC murders, but with a twist. The killer is going backward in the alphabet, and the next victim's name will start with

*A.* Do we have any *Agatha*s or *Arthur*s here? Or other names starting with *A?*"

Perry's jaw clenched. "This wasn't staged."

A Poirot lookalike approached him. "You are a friend of the unfortunate woman?"

"We're in the same book club," Perry said curtly.

Trisha stepped forward. "I heard Birdie say she was in a book club with Cynthia. The same book club you're in?"

Perry nodded.

Harrison raised his index finger. "Aha! It's not the ABC murders. It's the book club murders." He pointed at Perry. "*You* might be the next victim."

Perry glared at him. "Pompous idiot! Have some respect for the dead and for—Never mind, you're incapable of it."

Harrison looked unruffled. Raising his voice, he said, "If anyone's interested in book club mysteries, stop by my shop and I'll point them out to you. I also have copies of Christie's *ABC Murders.*"

Perry turned on his heel and walked out of the room.

Val caught up with him in the corridor. She'd had enough of Harrison too. "I'm sorry, Perry. Birdie's in good hands now."

Perry sighed. "I was going to have dinner with her."

"If you'd like, please have dinner with my grandfather and me. We have a six-thirty reservation at the hotel's restaurant."

"Thank you. I'll do that. Maybe by then I'll hear from Birdie's son and find out how she is."

Val went back to the reception and ran into Granddad near the door.

"Where did you put our wineglasses?" he said.

"I left them on Birdie's table." Val could see that Birdie's table was empty. The hotel staff must have cleared it. She glanced at the next table, where Claire had previously been alone. Now Harrison was with her, probably regaling her with far-fetched mystery plots. "I'll get us some more wine, Granddad. Do you want to look for a table where we can squeeze in?"

"Nope. I wouldn't mind taking a rest before dinner."

"I'll skip the wine and do the same." They walked to the elevator. "By the way, I asked Perry to eat with us. He's feeling low about what happened to Birdie and waiting to hear from her son about how she's doing."

"I sure hope it's good news."

After joining Val and Granddad in the restaurant, Perry reported that he still hadn't heard from Birdie's son. "I had breakfast with her, and she was full of energy then. She might have had a delayed reaction to Cynthia's death."

Val wondered if Birdie had confided in him about what she'd seen last night. "She was very talkative when we were setting up the hospitality room. She told me she saw a woman in the hall just before midnight, around the time Cynthia died. Birdie wouldn't describe the woman, except to say she was wearing a turban."

Perry chuckled. "She told me more than that. I can add a detail to help you identify the woman. She was wearing a loose scarlet kimono."

Val frowned. A kimono didn't help her identify the woman at all. Maybe the point of the long, flowing dress was to conceal the size and shape of the wearer. Combined with a turban that hid the color and length of her hair, the disguise was complete.

Perry glanced from Val to Granddad. "I can tell from your blank looks that neither of you went to the movie after the bake-off Friday night."

"Nope. Val and I went to the bar."

"Birdie and I watched *Murder on the Orient Express*. Have you seen it or read the book?"

Granddad snapped his fingers. "Poirot hears a thud on his compartment door and peeks out. A woman wrapped in a kimono is fleeing down the corridor."

With that reminder, the scene flashed into Val's mind. "Like Poirot, Birdie only got a quick look at the woman whose back was turned."

Perry rocked his head from side to side. "But was that woman really there or only in Birdie's mind? She had trouble sleeping Friday night. She got out of bed, opened her door, and caught sight of someone in a kimono. I reminded her the same thing happened in the movie and suggested she was dreaming about the Orient Express."

Val nodded. "She told me she dreamed of being on a train and hearing it whistle." But then she'd woken up to a real whistle coming from Cynthia's kettle. That was well after midnight, and Birdie had seen the kimono woman before midnight. *Dreams can mess with your sense of time*, Val reminded herself. "How did Birdie react to the idea that the woman was a flashback to the movie?"

"Defiantly." Perry smiled. "She said she was as old as Miss Marple, and they both had all their marbles. She decided that if I didn't believe her, nobody would. They'd think she was batty and unable to distinguish between reality and a movie. So she made up her mind not to tell anyone else about the kimono."

Granddad said, "You seem to know her pretty well. Does she sometimes mix up what's real and what isn't?"

"She's never done it before, but it happens as people age, and she's past eighty."

*Never done it before* was enough reason for Val to accept Birdie's story. "Without mentioning the kimono, Birdie told me about the woman she saw in the corridor. I couldn't have been the only person she told. Maybe she was trying to find others who saw the kimono woman to prove you were wrong, Perry. Then she passed out after drinking some wine."

Perry folded his arms. "She always drank wine at our book club meetings without passing out. I believe the shock of Cynthia's death and a long, busy day were too much for her system."

He didn't know the role that an alcohol-and-drug cocktail might have played in Cynthia's death. Val didn't feel free to say what Roy had told her in confidence, but she could try nudging the lawyer to draw his own conclusion. "I realize you have a low opinion of amateur sleuthing, but the police are still here, looking into Cynthia's death. Someone might have been tempted to silence Birdie because she was watching what was going on near Cynthia's room last night."

Perry groaned. "I should have urged her to tell the police."

The server arrived with their dinners, cutting off further talk about Birdie. Perry ate robotically with no sign of enjoying his food. He might as well have dined on one of Roy's protein bars. Even that would have tasted better than the large helping of remorse the lawyer was apparently consuming now.

To give him something else to think about, Val broached a different subject she hoped he could shed light on. "The detective on the case is a friend of ours. He mentioned that Cynthia's will hasn't turned up."

"He'd like to find out who inherits?" Perry didn't wait for confirmation of his guess. "As of three days ago, she didn't have a will. She wanted my advice—free advice, I might add. She was never my client, so I don't feel contractually bound to keep our conversation private. She asked if she should make a will immediately or wait until Austin's estate was settled, when she'd know how much she had to play with, as she put it. I advised her to write a will as soon as possible. She could always modify it, if needed, at a later date."

"Surely she had some idea how much she'd inherit," Val said.

Perry shook his head. "Not from what she told me. Aside from their condo and a joint account, Austin kept his assets under his own name. After they married, he told her he was changing his will to take care of her and to be fair to his children. She expected to be the one who settled his estate, but he'd designated his daughter to do that."

Val tried to make sense of Cynthia's marriage. Her husband had kept most of his money where his wife couldn't get it when he was alive and didn't trust her to handle it once he was dead. Had she been a spendthrift? Or had his children convinced him she was a gold digger? He'd married her anyway, but he'd buried the gold, or at least some of it. "Since Cynthia was a beneficiary, shouldn't she have received a copy of the will?"

"It wouldn't have told her what she wanted to know," Granddad said. "Wills usually specify what percent of the total each person inherits, not what the amount is. It can take a while to track down all the assets and calculate their value."

"Exactly." Perry sipped his water. "As I told Cynthia, she couldn't expect to receive her inheritance so soon after Austin passed. The delay irritated her. She wanted to invest in a business and have a hand in its success. But she couldn't make plans without an idea of the estate's value."

Granddad asked the question on the tip of Val's tongue. "Did Cynthia have a particular business in mind?"

"A restaurant, a shaky investment with a high failure rate, but she wasn't asking me for financial advice."

So Cynthia's offer to fund Dave's restaurant made sense now. It dovetailed with her plans for a windfall. Val couldn't help thinking that Dave was more blessed than cursed when Cynthia died. Besides her initial investment, she'd have thrown in her two cents at every turn. And, given her craving for attention, she might have even demanded he name his restaurant after her.

Val wondered where the windfall would go now. "If Cynthia died without making a will, who would get her share of her husband's estate? Her closest relative?" Maybe the distant cousin who'd recently contacted her.

"That issue might not arise. Let me check something." Perry took out his phone and tapped on it while talking. "Most wills have a survivorship clause. Do you know what that is?"

Granddad nodded. "It says that beneficiaries cannot inherit unless they survive the will-maker by a specific length of time. Isn't it usually thirty days?"

"It can be longer, but that's the typical minimum. I'll check exactly when Austin died." Perry tapped his phone. "I just pulled up his obit. Thirty days ago today."

Val realized the date's significance. "Assuming Austin's will contains that standard clause, Cynthia wouldn't inherit unless she was alive today. But if she died before midnight, who would get the money?"

"Depends on what the will says. Sometimes children of the beneficiary inherit. Cynthia didn't have children, so it's likely her portion would be split among the other beneficiaries."

Val exchanged a wide-eyed look with Granddad.

Willow's insistence that Cynthia was dead before midnight suddenly made a lot of sense.

# Chapter 14

Perry tucked his phone away and tackled the rest of his huge Cobb salad. Val took his focus on his food as a signal that he was finished speculating on wills and inheritances.

Granddad frowned in concentration as he ate the last of his crab sliders, but Val doubted his meal was giving him food for thought. Instead, he must be chewing over Willow's actions in light of the survivorship clause Perry had described.

Val was convinced Willow hadn't told the whole truth. She must have taken the ring she believed was rightly hers. If that was all she'd wanted, she had no reason to tell the police she'd gone back to her stepmother's room and found her dead. But the terms of her father's will could have given her an incentive. She'd have wanted it on record that her stepmother had died before midnight.

Perry's phone rang, and he hurried out of the

restaurant to take the call. With most of the tables filled, the background noise made conversation difficult.

Val moved to the empty seat next to Granddad so she wouldn't have to shout across the table. She leaned toward him. "Let's assume the survivorship clause Perry described is in Willow's father's will. It explains why she'd claim Cynthia died earlier than other evidence suggests. It also gives her a motive to kill Cynthia before midnight."

Granddad raised a skeptical eyebrow. "A reason to lie and a motive to kill don't prove she did it. How do you explain the loose ends—the kimono and the kettle?"

"If Birdie dreamed or imagined she saw the kimono woman, we can stop trying to connect the kimono to Cynthia's death."

"I disagree."

"So you think there really was a woman in a kimono?"

"I didn't say that."

She wished he'd just spit out his theory instead of making her guess. If Birdie didn't dream about the kimono woman and the woman wasn't real, only one other option existed. "You're saying Birdie was lying? It crossed my mind this morning she might have invented the woman to get attention."

"Birdie could have another reason to lie."

Before Granddad could explain, Perry returned.

The lawyer stood by the table instead of sitting down. "Birdie will spend the night at the hospital. Her son says she's alert and responding to treatment."

Val released the breath she'd been holding. "I'm so glad. I was worried."

Despite the good news, the lawyer didn't look happy. "I'm still worried. Her vital signs suggested she might have taken something to calm herself down. She says she didn't. She felt fine until she had some wine. Her son had no idea she took anything like that. He's concerned she'll harm herself."

Val had visions of Birdie's son pushing her into an assisted living where her meds would be monitored. "She left her wine sitting on the table unattended for quite a while. Someone else could have slipped a sedative into it."

"That occurred to me too. She told me her wine was too strong. Maybe that was her way of saying it had an unusual taste. She's lucky she didn't drink more." Perry took out his wallet and put some bills on the table. "This should take care of my meal. I'm going to call my wife with the news about Birdie. Thank you for your company, and have a good evening."

Val watched him cross the room. "So much for Roy's idea that Birdie fell over from fatigue alone. I wonder if the drug was the same as the one Cynthia had in her system. Someone at that reception could have tried to shut Birdie up." But not Willow. She hadn't been there, either as herself or in her goth persona. Val sipped her water. "Now that you know Birdie might have been drugged, do you still think she lied about seeing the kimono woman?"

"Yup. Like every gossip, she craves attention. So she comes up with a mysterious figure everyone at the fest will want to hear about. But that's the icing on the cake. The woman in the kimono could be like the one in *Orient Express*—a red herring that distracts attention from what really happened."

Val thought a moment and gave up on guessing what really happened according to Granddad. "Go on, please."

"Birdie created the kimono woman as a suspect, someone to pin the crime on. Who was in the best position to enter Cynthia's room without being seen? Birdie. She peeks out her door. If she sees anyone, she closes the door and tries later. If the coast is clear, she crosses to Cynthia's room in three strides."

Val laughed. "Birdie killed Cynthia? You must be kidding."

"Didn't Birdie tell you that Cynthia invited other neighbors to tea but not her? And if Birdie had a good story to share, Cynthia had a better one?"

"Perry said she did that in the book club." The newcomer Cynthia had disrupted the club's dynamic, sidelining its founder, Birdie, and bringing Perry's wife to the brink of quitting. Still . . . "It's a flimsy motive for murder."

Granddad dismissed that with a one-shoulder shrug. "Her resentment of Cynthia simmered a long time before it boiled over. She was at the bar last night and could have spiked Cynthia's drink."

"I suppose you're going to say Birdie took the key card at the bar after Cynthia tried to buy drinks with it." When he nodded, "And tonight, what? Birdie drugged herself?"

"Why not? That makes her look like a second victim or, what you assume she is, a witness who had to be silenced. Of course, Birdie didn't swallow enough of her drugged drink to do any harm to herself."

Maybe Granddad was fixated on Birdie because she met Willow's criteria for someone who could have killed Cynthia well before midnight. "You think Birdie went into Cynthia's room before Willow returned to it?"

"Before, after, or both times. She could have gone in earlier to kill Cynthia and returned later. For sure Birdie was in the room around midnight, whether that was the first or second time she crossed the hall to go in. She knew about Cynthia's tea obsession and the whistling kettle. She filled the kettle and turned it on to make sure Cynthia was found at night."

Val didn't understand his point. "Why would she care about that?"

"If Cynthia isn't found until morning, it's not clear when exactly she died, so Birdie can't use her made-up kimono woman as a suspect. Also, Birdie wanted to enjoy the excitement she caused. It gave her lots to tell folks the next morning as they waited in line for breakfast."

While a young man cleared their table, Val pondered how to discourage Granddad's line of thinking without insulting him. When the busboy left, she said, "You should write a mystery novel, Granddad. That's too good a plot to waste. But you know what Roy will say. It's all guesses and no facts."

He folded his arms. "My theory fits the facts. Birdie had a motive and the opportunity. I've explained the kimono and the kettle. It's up to the police now. They can search Birdie's room for a sedative and check for her fingerprints or even DNA in Cynthia's room. I can't."

"Before you approach Roy, we should consider whether another scenario would fit the facts. What if the kimono woman in the hotel was real and saw Birdie peering out at her? Does that explain what happened to Birdie tonight at the reception?"

Before he could answer, the server offered them dessert menus.

Granddad didn't even look at his. "If you have Key lime pie, I'll take that."

"Yes, sir, we do. Coffee or tea with that?"

After Granddad shook his head, Val said, "No coffee for me either. I'd like the tiramisu, please."

"My beeramisu whetted your appetite for that." Granddad looked toward the restaurant entrance and waved. "There's Claire."

Val's college classmate approached the table. Her usual smile was absent, replaced by tight-lipped tension. "I was looking for you two. Have you heard anything about Birdie?"

Val noted Claire's clenched fist. "She's responding to treatment."

"That's such good news. Any idea what her problem was?"

Val didn't feel free to talk about another person's health. "As far as we know, it wasn't a major issue like a heart attack or stroke."

Granddad nodded. "She said she felt okay until she drank her wine."

Val was startled to see the color drain from Claire's face. "What's wrong?"

Claire gulped. "Birdie took my wine by mistake."

# Chapter 15

Val stared up at her college classmate. How could Birdie have drunk Claire's wine?

Claire must have noticed Val's confused expression. "I know it sounds crazy. I'll tell you what happened, and you can make up your own mind."

"Have a seat," Granddad said.

Claire sat down across from Val. "When I first arrived at the reception, I got a glass of wine and left it on a table that no one had claimed yet. I didn't want to carry it while I went through the buffet. After I filled my plate, a woman who'd gone to my panel came up to me. By the time we finished talking, the room had filled up. My wine wasn't where I'd left it, but on the table next to it. Birdie was drinking red wine at the table where I'd left mine."

With the tables crowded together and arranged haphazardly, Val could see how someone might go to the wrong one. "What did you do?"

"Nothing. I didn't want to make a fuss about it. I had a glass of wine in front of me that hadn't been touched. I was sipping it when Birdie fell on the floor."

Granddad stroked his chin. "What makes you so sure that Birdie drank your wine?"

"Because I know I drank someone else's wine. I watched the server pour my drink from a bottle of cabernet sauvignon. It's full-bodied and dark, almost opaque. The wine at the table where I ended up was lighter in taste and color—a pinot noir."

Granddad shrugged. "Colors don't look the same under different lights. Where they poured the wine, it might have looked darker than it did on the table."

"Possibly, but I saw both wines side by side when Harrison joined me at the table. He was drinking the cabernet. His wine was darker than mine."

Val was now convinced that the wines had gotten mixed up. "Birdie told Perry that her wine tasted strong. She must have had your glass." Val lowered her voice. "Let's assume someone wanted to knock you out. Is there anyone at this fest you'd previously met?"

"Not to my knowledge. I've never been to anything like this before. My friend Yvonne talked me into coming here with her, a weekend away for both of us. She writes mysteries with a female P.I. and would be here if she hadn't come down with laryngitis."

The server brought the desserts to the table.

Val looked askance at the mound of coffee-soaked cake topped with mascarpone. "This tiramisu is huge. Would you like to split it with me, Claire?"

Before Claire could respond, the server turned to her, "I'll bring another plate and spoon. How about coffee to go with it?"

"No coffee, thank you." When the server left, Claire said, "I made the mistake of having Irish coffee last night at the bar. I thought the whiskey would subdue the effect of the caffeine. No such luck. I was too full of energy to even think about sleeping until nearly midnight."

Granddad filled his fork with a chunk of Key lime pie. "What floor is your room on?"

"The fourth."

Willow had a room on the fourth floor too, and she'd gone down to Cynthia's room on the third floor when it was nearly midnight. Val glanced at Granddad. He must be thinking the same thing.

He raised the fork halfway to his mouth. "Did you see or hear anyone in the corridor outside your room last night."

Claire shook her head. "I was grading papers. It was quiet. When I got ready for bed, I realized I'd forgotten to bring my toothbrush. I called the reception desk to see if they had any. They did, so I came down around a quarter to twelve."

About the time Willow was leaving Cynthia's room. Struggling to hide her excitement, Val divided her tiramisu in half. "Did you see anyone on the way down?"

"Not on the way *down*. When I got to the lobby, I saw Jordan, who sat with us last night. He was talking to the desk clerk."

Val had seen him with Dave after midnight when she came down to report the whistling coming from Cynthia's room. "Did you happen to notice who was at the bar last night as you got out of the elevator?"

"I didn't take the elevator. I took the stairs in the wing. I never looked toward the bar."

Val gaped at her former classmate. "You avoided the elevator even though you were four flights up? You must be more claustrophobic than I am." And less safety-conscious.

The server brought the extra plate and spoon. Val put half her tiramisu on the extra plate and passed it to Claire.

Granddad balanced another bite of pie on his fork. "It's risky to go into a hotel stairwell alone at night."

"Tell me about it. I wish now that I hadn't, Mr. Myer. Someone was in the stairwell when I was going back up last night." Claire hugged herself as if she'd felt a chill. "It's a switchback staircase, a half flight with a landing platform where you turn to go up the other half flight. I'd gotten as far as the second floor when I saw a shadow on the wall at the half landing above. There was someone there."

Granddad frowned. "Was the person just standing still, lurking there?"

"The shadow showed arm movements. I reasoned that people doing things in empty stairwells might not want to be seen, and I didn't want to be seen watching them. I opened the door to exit the stairwell on the second floor. Before I got out, I checked to see if I was being followed. That was a mistake."

Val tensed up. "Why?"

"Because the light fixture by the door made my face clearly visible. The individual on the landing had leaned over to watch me and then ducked back when I looked up. That scared me. Later I felt silly about it, but I ran through the second-floor corridor toward the elevators. No more stairwells for me."

Val noted Claire's use of *individual* instead of *he* or *she*. She must not have been able to tell if it was a man or woman. "Did you notice anything about the person's size or clothing?"

Claire gazed past her, as if trying to bring an object in the distance into focus. "Medium-sized, not unusually tall or short. I got a glimpse of dark clothes. Hair is what I usually notice first, but a black hat completely covered the person's head, a little like a ski cap."

"Or a turban?" Granddad prompted.

Claire spooned up a bite of tiramisu. "Possibly, but not one that was wound into a peak like the turbans South Asians wear."

Granddad pressed his lips together as if holding back, but only for a moment. "Was the person wearing a dress, a robe, or"—he broke off as Val frowned and shook her head—"or something similar?"

"No. Anything like that would have made the shadow on the wall look different. The person wore pants."

As did nearly everyone at the fest. "Was that stairwell incident the only odd thing that happened to you at the hotel?"

Claire stared down at her dessert. "No, but the other one wasn't scary, just weird. When I went upstairs after the panel, the message light was blinking on my room phone. The front desk had received a call from someone who claimed that my house had been broken into and the door was open. I called my next-door neighbor, who's also the landlord, to check on the place. The door was locked, and nothing inside the house suggested a break-in."

"You live alone in the house?" When Claire nodded, Granddad continued. "That message was supposed to make you leave the fest in a hurry."

And the wine was the second attempt to get rid of Claire. Val was convinced that Claire had saved herself by fleeing the stairwell last night and that the wineglass switch had saved her this evening. She might not be so lucky next time.

Val had to warn her of the danger. "Here's what was going on around the time you were in the stairwell. Someone whose hair was hidden under a hat was seen near Cynthia's third-floor room, walking toward the stairwell. That was shortly before midnight. Not long after, Cynthia was found dead. Her death is under investigation. You should tell the police about what happened in the stairwell—and that phone message."

Claire bit her lower lip. "Can I report it to someone other than the detective who spoke to us at the reception?"

Granddad's head jerked back. "He's in charge of the investigation. You have something against him?"

Claire sighed. "He might have something against me. We talked this morning. He wanted to hear about the ring Cynthia was showing off at the bar last night. This evening, before the reception, he came up to me in the lobby and said hi. I didn't remember him and assumed he was attending the fest, so I introduced myself."

Val coughed to cover her laugh. It must have shocked Roy to run into the only woman on earth who'd ever forgotten his handsome face. "How did he respond?"

"He said we'd already met, told me his name, then turned on his heel and walked away." Claire blushed and used her fork to push her dessert around on her plate. "I'm going to tell you something I don't usually share. You've heard people say they never forget a face. The opposite is true of me. I have facial amnesia. I don't remember faces except for family members or close friends. I can't recognize people I've recently met or haven't seen for a while. You knew who I was from college, Val, but I didn't know who you were."

Val imagined how uneasy she'd feel not knowing whether she'd met someone before. "I'm sorry. That must be difficult."

"Fortunately, I see faces clearly when they're in front of me. I just can't store them in my memory. My case is mild. Some people have total facial blankness. They can't even recognize themselves. I've developed coping mechanisms, like memorizing hair. I recognize you now because your hair is like mine, but a little lighter and curlier. I'd have trouble if you grew your hair out or changed its color." Claire turned to Granddad. "After meeting you this morning, I know who you are by the white curls over your ears. But the detective's hair isn't unusual."

Val remembered how easily Claire had identified Trisha as Patty Cook by listening to her on a video without seeing her on the screen. "You're also good at remembering voices. They don't change as much as hair."

"Yes, but the detective gave me only one sylla-ble, which wasn't any help. People expect to be recognized by their looks. So I avoid situations where I have to greet anyone before hearing them talk, like in elevators. That's why I take the stairs, and it's good exercise. I went into the stairwell last night out of habit, not claustrophobia."

Granddad finished his last piece of pie. "And you ran into somebody there who probably didn't want to be seen."

Claire nodded glumly. "We saw each other's faces, and only one of us can identify the other."

Val couldn't think of a reason for Claire to ex-pose herself any longer to a threat she couldn't recognize or defend against. "You're not safe here. You should go home tonight."

"I can't. I promised Yvonne I'd take her place on tomorrow's panel. I won't be able to answer questions as the author of her P.I. book, but I can describe the book."

Granddad leaned forward, going eye to eye with Clare. "Your friend wouldn't want you to take chances. Tell the detective what happened in the stairwell. If he suggests you leave the hotel, do it."

Claire took a spoonful of dessert before re-sponding. "Yvonne's counting on me. I'll stay alert. I won't eat or drink anything that's been out of my sight. And I'll keep away from stairwells and other deserted areas. If you don't mind, though, I'd ap-preciate an escort to my room tonight."

Val wasn't satisfied with Clare's answer but realized arguing wouldn't do any good. "Of course. But first talk to the police. I know Detective Roy. Start by telling him about your face recognition issue." That should soothe his wounded ego. "Once he's aware of that, you'll find him a sympathetic listener. What you tell him may help catch a killer."

Claire agreed and finished her dessert while Val exchanged texts with Roy. She told him she had new information about Birdie and Willow, but that he might want to listen first to what Claire knew about Birdie's wine. He texted her to bring Claire to the office right away, and he'd talk to Val after that.

As Val led her to the tiny office that had turned into police headquarters at the hotel, she said, "Can you dress tomorrow in something really different from what you wore last night and today? The person in the stairwell only caught a glimpse of you and might remember your clothes and hair better than your face."

"I'll wear jeans and a corduroy jacket. I also have a scarf I can make into a bandanna to cover my hair."

"Perfect."

When Val returned to the restaurant, Granddad was looking over the bill with his credit card in his hand.

She sat down. "I hope Roy takes what happened to Claire seriously and comes up with a way to protect her." She reached into her shoulder bag for her wallet. "What do I owe you for dinner?"

"You paid for the pizza and drinks last night, so we're even." He put his credit card on the little tray with the bill. "If Claire's going to stick around, she'd be better off spreading the word that she doesn't remember faces."

"It wouldn't do much good. The person in the stairwell can't take the chance that she's lying." The phone message Claire had received gnawed at Val. "Whoever left the message with the hotel desk said Claire's *house* was burgled. How would a stranger know she lived in a house, not an apartment?"

Granddad took off his glasses and rubbed his eyes. "Like other folks on panels, she's in the fest booklet with her photo, her bio, and her website. That's enough to start digging up information about her online. It isn't hard to get someone's address, plug it into a map program, and see a street view of her place."

Val shuddered. So a would-be assailant could view Claire's house online, see it from different angles, and know where the windows and doors were. "You and I have caught the mystery-fest bug, Granddad. We've been treating Cynthia's death as a puzzle it would be satisfying to solve. Now we have a more important reason. Not solving the puzzle could have fatal consequences. If Claire saw Cynthia's killer in the stairwell, she isn't safe at the hotel, at home, or at work. This case can't stay unresolved for a year, like the previous murder here."

Granddad put his glasses back on. "At least you convinced Claire to talk to Roy."

Val wouldn't rely on Roy to figure out who was after Claire when he was focusing on solving an old murder. While Granddad signed the credit slip and tucked his card away, Val pondered what they could do without waiting for Roy. "Let's assume Birdie is a dependable witness. She saw someone dressed in a kimono walking toward the ice machine and the stairwell beyond it around the time Claire was using the stairs. I think we should check out the stairwell."

Granddad looked skeptical. "You expect to find a clue, like a thread from a red kimono?"

"No, I'd just like a sense of how much Claire could see from the second-floor landing and, even more important, how well the person on the half landing could see her. So you're going to play Claire, and I'm going to be the mystery person on the half landing."

# *Chapter 16*

Val and Granddad went into the empty stairwell on the second floor. She positioned him where Claire would have been after climbing from the first floor and turning to go up to the third floor.

Then Val bounded up the stairs to the half landing and situated herself as if she'd just come down from the third floor. Her shadow fell on the back wall. "Can you see me, Granddad?"

"No. The other half of the stairs are in the way. If I moved to the outer edge of the staircase, I might see you. That's not what I'd do. I'd stay closer to the inside railing, where I am now. From here I can see a double shadow on the back wall. The light fixture near the door here makes one shadow and the fixture on the third-floor landing makes another one. You're taller in one shadow and shorter in the other."

Val studied the overlapping shadows. The taller

one elongated her legs. It was clear she was wearing pants, but not whether she was male or female. If the person in the stairwell had worn a kimono, the shadow would have looked different. But what if the person had just removed the kimono before Claire looked up? "Watch the shadows carefully, Granddad." Val mimicked folding up a large piece of cloth like a kimono and stuffing it into her shoulder bag. "What did I look like I was doing?"

"The Macarena?"

Val laughed. "You're saying I looked like my arms were moving. That's how Claire described what she saw. Now please turn toward the door leading to the corridor and do what she did. Open the door and then look back at the half landing, where I am."

As soon as Val heard the door lever click, she stuck her head around the turn in the stairs, and peered down. When Granddad looked up, she could see his face. She jerked her head back.

"I saw your face for a sec, but not the rest of you," he said.

Face but no torso, exactly what Claire had described. Val hurried down the steps to join Granddad on the landing. "If Bram were here, he'd remind me that Sherlock would go on his hands and knees, looking for a bit of ash from a cigarette. Not me. Let's get out of this creepy place."

Granddad opened the door to the second floor. "What did we learn from this?"

"That my hunch could be correct." They walked through the corridor toward the elevators. "Let's assume the kimono woman took the stairs down, stopped halfway to the second floor, where I was standing, and removed the kimono. Claire came up the stairs from the first floor and was on the second-floor landing when the person stuffed the kimono into a bag, maybe the fest tote. That's what I was mimicking."

"Why did the person wear a kimono and then take it off in the stairwell?"

"She didn't belong on the third floor. With the turban and the kimono, she covered herself from head to toe so she wouldn't be recognized when she was near Cynthia's room." As they approached the elevators, Val took a moment to think of an answer to the second part of Granddad's question. "She removed the kimono because she needed to hide her identity only on the third floor. She had no reason to conceal it on other floors and didn't want to attract attention in that outfit."

Granddad pressed the button for the down elevator. "Hard to believe she just happened to have a red kimono with her. She must have found out that *Murder on the Orient Express* was gonna be shown this weekend."

"Easy enough. It was on the fest website as a highlight. She brought the kimono and turban to sneak around the hotel and do something she didn't want people to know she was doing, maybe to kill Cynthia."

"That makes it a premeditated kimono. The person wearing it certainly planned to do something in secret," Granddad said grudgingly. "But not necessarily murder. Using the stairs doesn't mean you're a killer. And besides, Willow said Cynthia was dead fifteen minutes before that."

"She'd say that whether it was true or not. She

inherits more if it's true. But she had no need to—" Val broke off as an almost-full elevator arrived and they squeezed into it. Once they were seated on a sofa in the lobby, she finished what she'd planned to say. "Willow had no need to dress in a kimono and go down to the third floor around midnight."

Granddad nodded. "She was in Cynthia's room earlier and had the chance then to swipe the ring and kill Cynthia, if she wasn't already dead."

"Yes, and she was disguised as a goth when she returned to Cynthia's room. Jordan saw her dressed like that when she waited for the elevator after leaving the room. Assuming the person Claire saw in the stairwell was the one who tampered with the wine at the reception, we have to rule out Willow. She wasn't at the reception."

"But Trisha was." Granddad eyed two women who paused to talk near the sofa and waited until they moved out of earshot. "Trisha coulda been the kimono woman. She was at the reception, and she's been up to a lot of no-good this weekend. Probably took my recipe box and slipped those anonymous notes to me and Cynthia. I thought of a way to connect Trisha to the note I received."

"How?"

He took a paper from his shirt pocket, unfolded it, and showed it to Val. "I found the anonymous note I got. I'd thrown it in my suitcase. See how *sabotage* is spelled wrong, with an *A* instead of an *O* in the middle? If you can get her to play trivia tomorrow, I have a question you can ask that'll tell us if she wrote the note. You're going to have the audience write down the answers for trivia, aren't you?"

"Yes, and it's easy to get Trisha there. I'll ask Bethany to assign her as the room monitor. Whether we can coax Trisha into answering trivia questions is another matter. What's the question you want me to ask?"

"Alfred Hitchcock made two movies with similar titles. In which one does a boy carry a bomb aboard a London bus—*Sabotage* or *Saboteur*? You know the answer?"

"No, but I'll guess *Sabotage*." When he nodded, she continued. "I like the question. Whatever answer Trisha gives, we'll find out if she's consistent in her spelling errors. If she is, what do we do?"

"Confront her. Her bad spelling is evidence she wrote the notes, she had the opportunity to slip them in our envelopes, and a witness saw her with the recipe box."

"You can try getting her to admit writing the notes and swiping the box." Val doubted he'd succeed. "But nothing points to her as a murderer. She acted out of spite, planting the notes and hinting that Cynthia stole your recipe box. She wouldn't bother doing those things if she planned to kill the woman who ruined her cake." A weak motive if Val ever saw one.

"Maybe that's what Trisha wants us to think."

"You have a devious mind, Granddad." And a rolling roster of theoretical killers, from Harrison to Birdie to Trisha. "The first step in getting rid of Cynthia was to drug her at the bar last night so she wouldn't fight back. Was Trisha in a position to do that?"

"Not according to the bartender, but he mighta been too busy to notice everyone who went near her. So far I count five people we know who could have tampered with Cynthia's drink." Granddad ticked them off on his fingers. "Dave, Willow, Greer, Birdie, and the bartender. Dave was in the bar from the time Cynthia left to go upstairs until the bartender went home for the night."

Val nodded. "I saw them both there when I came down to the lobby at 12:15. They both have alibis. Greer doesn't have any connection to Cynthia, no motive to kill her that we've uncovered."

"That leaves Willow and Birdie." Granddad smiled in triumph. "Birdie's still the best bet. Everything's explained if she's the killer. She made up the kimono woman, she put on the kettle to enjoy the excitement of Cynthia being found, and she drugged her own wine at the reception."

"Who was in the stairwell if not the kimono woman?"

"Coulda been someone doing a drug deal. If the person in the stairwell was the kimono woman and she killed Cynthia, how do you explain the kettle not whistling until fifteen minutes later?" When Val shrugged, he continued. "Did Cynthia invite the kimono woman in for tea and turn the kettle on? Then the kimono woman killed her before the water boiled, forgot to turn off the kettle, and left?"

"Even with that far-fetched scenario, the kettle would have whistled earlier than I heard it." Maybe Granddad was right about Birdie making up or imagining someone in a kimono.

"I've been meaning to ask you what the kettle looked like."

An image of it flashed into Val's mind. "Remember the stovetop kettle Grandma used for years? It was stainless steel and had a curved black plastic handle with a button to flip open the spout cover. Cynthia's looked like that, but it was electric. Behind the handle was a receptor to plug in the cord."

His eyes lit up. "Dorothy has an electric kettle like that. It's big, makes enough water for at least six cups of tea. Cynthia must have had a smaller version to take on a trip."

"No, she had a big kettle. How long does it take for Dorothy's kettle to start whistling?"

"A few minutes. Did you notice how much water was in Cynthia's kettle when you turned it off?"

"I pulled out the plug and never looked at the kettle again." Val steered the conversation from the kettle detour back to the main road. "So far we've focused on people with grudges against Cynthia. Let's not forget who benefits. The cousin hoping to inherit from her might be here under a different name."

"What's the cousin's name again?"

"Loren Davis. Roy said she could be in her eighties or her twenties."

Granddad's eyebrows shot up. "Eighties. Could be Birdie. That's gotta be a nickname. And Natter might be her married name. I'll see if I can dig up her birth name online."

"As long as you're looking up names, don't limit yourself to Birdie. One person we haven't considered because she doesn't have an obvious motive is our journalist friend, Greer Gordon."

Granddad craned his neck to peer around the lobby, possibly to make sure Greer wasn't in the vicinity. She wasn't, but he still lowered his voice. "She coulda been born Loren Greer Davis, married Mr. Gordon, and picked Greer Gordon as her pen name. It has a nice ring to it. I'll look her up too."

Bethany bustled toward them. "You two are sitting here with your heads together. Are you cooking up a scheme?"

"We're just feeding each other's fantasies," Val said. "Perry talked to Birdie's son. She's in the hospital, recovering well."

Bethany's tensed shoulders relaxed. "That's the first good news I've heard today. The fest board decided to continue with the schedule as planned. Are you going to play a mystery board game tonight, Mr. Myer?"

"Nope. I'm heading upstairs soon. Been a long day." He mimicked a yawn.

Val felt the same way, but she didn't want to let Bethany down. "I'll show up for the games, in case you need one extra person at a table. If you don't, I'd just as soon spend a little more time on my questions for the trivia session tomorrow. I'd also like to make up for the sleep I lost last night."

Bethany glanced at her watch. "We'll be starting in thirty minutes. Come by the game room then. I'll hold you prisoner only if absolutely necessary."

"Thanks. Can you do me a favor? Assign Trisha as the monitor for the trivia session tomorrow morning. I wouldn't want her to miss it."

"I didn't know she was a trivia fan. I'll take care of it."

"Great. See you in the game room."

As Bethany left, Val spotted Claire across the lobby, stood up, and waved to her. When she joined them, Val said, "How did everything go with Detective Roy?"

"Fine. He'd like to speak with you, Val. I think he wants you to vet me as sane." Claire smiled wryly. "Is it okay if I keep you company, Mr. Myer?"

"Sure. Have a seat."

Val could tell he wasn't happy about being left behind. He'd have liked to tag along and tell Roy his theory of Birdie as a cold-blooded killer. Val would have enjoyed watching the detective's reaction.

Claire had read Roy's purpose correctly. Val no sooner sat down across the desk from him than he asked her opinion of her former classmate.

"She strikes me as solid and trustworthy, not as a woman who'd try to make outlandish claims. But my opinion is based on limited contact with her. We took one class together in college. Though I haven't seen her since we graduated, I recognized her, but I'm better at faces than she is."

"That's a weird malady she has. It makes her vulnerable."

"I suggested she leave tonight and go home. She wants to stay over."

"Staying over is better than driving in the dark to where she lives alone. She won't be alone here. I've assigned an officer to take her to her room and patrol the floor she's on. Claire has a number to call when she's ready to go upstairs."

Val was satisfied that Claire would be safe tonight, but what about after that? "Will an officer be with her tomorrow?"

"I can justify an officer in the hotel tonight, but not during the day. I advised Claire to stay with other people and not go off on her own tomorrow. Too bad we have no description of the person in the stairwell."

"It could be the same person Birdie saw in the third-floor corridor. That was around the time Claire was in the stairwell. Birdie wouldn't describe the woman to me, but she did to Perry Macon." Val repeated what Perry had said about the woman in the kimono.

Roy jotted notes and looked up when she stopped talking. "Let me get this straight. You believe this woman in a kimono was in Cynthia's room and then entered the stairwell, where she was seen. The next day she tampered with Claire's wine because she feared Claire could identify her as being near the scene of the crime." When Val nodded, he continued. "You're assuming the person in the stairwell came down from the third floor, but Claire had no idea if the person was going up or down. She didn't see a kimono or a bag to stuff it in. She couldn't even tell if she'd seen a man or a woman."

"Nothing Claire said contradicts my theory." But the idea that Birdie might have seen a man in a kimono intrigued Val. "A kimono makes a good disguise for a man as long as no one sees his face close up."

"With a fresh shave, a lot of men would get away with it, even at close range. People focus on the shiny object—the costume—not who's wearing it." Roy leaned back in the desk chair and laced his hands behind his head. "Let me give you an example. A witness at the wine reception reported seeing someone stop briefly at a table that had nothing on it except a glass of red wine. The visitor put a plate of food and a second wineglass down on the table, stayed for ten seconds, and then took the plate and a glass away. The witness didn't notice if the wineglasses had been switched, but it happened at the table where Birdie ended up."

"And where Claire said she'd left her own wine. Did the witness describe the person who visited the table?"

Roy's expression turned solemn. "It was Sherlock Holmes. He'd stopped to take a pipe out of his mouth and put it in his pocket."

Val couldn't help laughing. "At least a dozen Sherlocks were at the reception."

"The witness noticed nothing except the costume. We checked out the Sherlocks who were hanging around after the costume contest. The witness ruled out only one of them—the female one."

"Even in a deerstalker hat and a Sherlock suit, a woman doesn't cut the same figure as a man." *Unless she's tall and solid like Cynthia's stepdaughter.* Val had scanned the people at the wine reception without seeing a woman as tall as Willow, but she'd skipped over the Sherlocks. Maybe Willow had been there after all and somehow slipped past the ticket taker at the door.

"Anything else you want to report, Val?" Roy picked up his pen as if he could tell she had more to say.

"Yes. The exact time when Cynthia died may be crucial to someone's prospects for an inheritance." Val related what Perry had said about the standard survivorship clause, the date when Willow's father died, and what that might mean for Cynthia's heir's inheritance. She ended with a question. "Do you know for sure when Cynthia died?"

"Not to the minute. The medical examiner wasn't called in until this morning. Based on the tests he did at seven thirty, he estimated her time of death at seven to eight hours earlier. Usually that's a distinction that wouldn't make a difference."

Val calculated that midnight was at the midpoint of that range. "In this case, it makes a big difference, assuming what Perry said about the will is true. Willow gets more of her father's estate if Cynthia died on the earlier side. What happens with the estate if you can't prove on which side of midnight she died?"

Roy scratched his head. "A court would have to decide that. Anyone convicted of killing Cynthia won't inherit no matter when she died because you can't profit from your crime. The remaining heirs wouldn't inherit by default. For them it still matters when she died."

Val glanced at her watch. "Time for me to solve another murder. I've been roped into playing Clue."

Roy cupped his hand over his mouth and whispered, "Colonel Mustard in the library with a wrench. Sorry for the spoiler." No longer whispering, he added, "I wish real cases were that easy to close."

# Chapter 17

After Val left Roy's office, she found Granddad still on the sofa in the lobby, but he was alone. "Where's Claire?"

"She called the number Roy gave her for the officer on patrol. The officer was an African American woman in plainclothes, six feet tall and broad-shouldered. Long as she's around, no one's gonna mess with Claire."

"I hope you're right." Val plopped down next to Granddad. "Roy told me the officer's only going to be here tonight. Tomorrow Claire has to rely on safety in numbers and not go anywhere alone."

"What else did Roy have to say?"

Val gave him a brief summary and added, "It's time for me to show up at the mystery game room. What are you going to do?"

"Hang out here to catch Dave. Willow hired me to find out who could have killed Cynthia in the half hour after she left the bar. Dave might be able to tell me who was at the bar just before and after she went upstairs, where they were sitting, and maybe even what time they left. The bartender would know that too, but I didn't get a chance to ask him before he stopped talking to me." Grand-dad eased himself off the sofa. "Gotta walk around before I get too stiff."

"If I get roped into a board game, I might not see you before you go upstairs. Let's meet for breakfast, same time as this morning."

Bethany greeted Val when she arrived at the game room. "I've already filled tables for a Sherlock Holmes game, a CSI game, and one Clue game." She pointed to a couple sitting at a table. "They're waiting for more people to play Clue with them. The game will work with three people. Do you want to join them?"

*Not really.* "Okay."

Val had enjoyed Clue when she was young. She liked the process of elimination to figure out who did it, with what weapon, and where. But after reading a couple of Nancy Drew books, Val had re-alized that the board game didn't ask the primary question in any mystery—why? Motive had no role in the game, and neither did the other *why* ques-tions that lead to solving a real murder: why that weapon in that place at that moment. The time was the sticking point in Cynthia's death.

Val exchanged introductions with the couple at the table and started dealing the cards. Before she finished, Bethany brought two late arrivals to the table. Val happily gave up her seat and left.

She got to her room just as Bram texted her—

*Call me when you can. I want to run an idea by you for our dinner tomorrow.* She flopped on the bed and speed-dialed him.

"How did the bake-off go?" he asked.

"So much has happened since then, it feels like a week rather than a day ago." She gave him an abbreviated version of the bake-off, the bar scene after it, and the whistling kettle that led to finding Cynthia dead. "Murder is suspected, but not definite. An antique diamond ring Cynthia wore last night has disappeared, and so has the recipe box you unearthed for Granddad in the attic."

"I thought the point of the fest was to talk about crimes in books, not commit them. Since you were the one who found Cynthia, murder is likely." His tone was teasing. "For a while I thought Bayport attracted dead bodies. Now I'm sure you're the murder magnet."

"Don't pick on me. Granddad might be the lure, or even Bethany. On the plus side, I reconnected with a woman I knew in college, Claire. She had a scary experience last night and might be in danger." Val told him about Birdie and the kimono woman, Claire's encounter in the stairwell, and the possible wineglass switch at the reception. "Claire didn't get a clear view of who was in the stairwell. She may be in danger even after she leaves the fest."

"Could the kimono wearer have been a man?"

"You have your Sherlock hat on, Bram. The detective assigned to the case suggested the same thing. Only the kimono wearer knows for sure." Val realized she'd been doing most of the talking. "On another note, how are things in Bayport?"

"Great. The assistant Mom hired for the shop is a fast learner and really good with the customers. Mom says she won't need me tomorrow. I thought I might drive to the hotel and pick you up. We'll take a detour on the way home and have dinner at a French country restaurant I heard about. It's not Paris, but it's the best we can do in this area."

The prospect of leaving the hotel for a French dinner lifted Val's spirits. "It sounds wonderful. I don't think Granddad will mind driving back alone. If he doesn't want to, he can hitch a ride with Bethany, and you and I will drive separately to the French country restaurant."

"I'd rather we drive together, but whatever works. What time should I come?"

Val would worry less about Claire if Bram, with his observation skills and quick reflexes, kept an eye on her. He agreed to be at the hotel before nine when Val explained why. She had another request for him. "Granddad told me your mother has an electric teakettle like the one Cynthia used. If you can bring it with you, we can run an experiment to determine when her kettle could have been turned on."

"By figuring out how long it takes the water to boil and the kettle to whistle?"

"Yes, with different amounts of water in it. Then we'll work backward from the time the whistling woke me to when Cynthia, or someone else, might have plugged in the kettle. We'll get a range of times, depending on the water level." Though the experiment wouldn't establish when Cynthia had died, it should show if the person in the kimono could possibly have turned on the kettle just before going into the stairwell.

"I'll run over to Mom's tonight and pick up the kettle. Do you want to hear about the French restaurant's specialties?"

"Definitely. Then maybe I'll dream about them."

They talked over the menu options for a few minutes before hanging up. Val finalized the script for the trivia session on her laptop. She added questions that anyone who'd attended the bake-off and the movies would be able to answer. She also incorporated the questions Harrison had given her and Granddad's suggestion for testing Trisha's spelling of the word *sabotage.*

Val had trouble keeping her eyes open any longer and went to bed, but dreams interrupted her sleep, and they weren't about French food. In one of them she was following a figure in a kimono who turned around to look at her, but had no face. Terrified, Val tried to run, but her legs wouldn't move. She woke up in a sweat with her heart pounding. In another dream she was trapped in a stairwell, endlessly climbing steps in a vain search for an exit door. It was dawn when she awoke from that dream.

Her subconscious had spent the night reminding her of the peril Claire was in. Unable to go back to sleep, Val dressed and went down for a pre-breakfast cup of coffee.

The restaurant wasn't busy. She asked for the table in the corner and sat facing the entrance so she could watch for Granddad, Bethany, and Claire.

Granddad showed up first. They both ordered coffee.

When the server left, Val said, "Did you learn anything new hanging around the lobby last night?"

"Yup. I asked Dave what he noticed Friday night at the bar. He sat down next to Cynthia just before eleven. Harrison came in at eleven, about ten minutes before Cynthia went out. He sat on her other side."

Val hadn't expected to hear that the bookseller had returned to the bar. "We saw him there earlier in the evening. He must have left and popped back in again for a nightcap. Did Dave overhear him say anything to Cynthia?"

"Nope. Harrison kept quizzing the bartender about the single malt whiskeys he had and the differences between them. Then he moved on to the brandy. Meantime, Cynthia nearly fell when she got off the bar stool and needed help getting to her room. Harrison paid right away when his drink came and took it with him."

"I'll stop by the book room before trivia and pump him for details about last night. I might have to buy something to prime the pump."

"Don't waste your money. Words gush from him constantly, but they're mostly a bunch of hooey. You'll probably hear another of his crazy theories about Cynthia's death."

The server came over to the table, poured coffee, and left menus.

Granddad studied the menu. "I'm ordering the big farmhouse breakfast. I may not have time to eat much at the luncheon before I have to go the podium and run the auction."

"The Swedish crêpes sound good to me." Val closed the menu and told him that Bram would be coming this morning and bringing Dorothy's kettle. "Did you find anything useful online about Birdie or Greer?"

"Birdie has nothing but a Facebook page with photos of her and her grandkids. Greer's on all sorts of social media, promoting her book. I couldn't find any other names either of them used or any secret ties to Cynthia."

Bethany came to the table, clutching her phone and looking flustered. "Someone sent me a link to a story in the Baltimore paper about Cynthia's death. Just from skimming it, I think we may get more media attention than we'd like."

Granddad sipped his coffee. "They say there's no such thing as bad publicity. Did Greer Gordon write the story?"

Bethany nodded. "She said the death this weekend echoed an earlier one at the hotel, after a murder mystery dinner. The only connection I could see is that both deaths occurred while a group of mystery fans were staying here. Total coincidence."

The server poured coffee for Bethany and asked if they were ready to order. Val and Granddad gave him their choices.

Bethany glanced at her menu. "I'd like the breakfast burrito and a fruit cup, please." Once the server left, she held up her phone. "Do you want to hear more about Greer's article, or should I just send you the link to it?"

Granddad shook his head. "The only kind of links I like at breakfast are made of sausage. What else is in her piece?"

Bethany swiped the phone. "Greer describes the

fest this weekend and says, 'At the hotel bar on Friday night, recipe columnist Cynthia Sweet hinted she knew who'd committed the murder a year ago. Before the night was over, Ms. Sweet was found dead. The police have not ruled out foul play. Some fest participants are assuming she was murdered and coming up with theories.' Greer mentions everything from the culprit in last year's murder wanting to silence Cynthia to the idea that she's the victim of a serial killer."

Roy's theory and Harrison's flight of fancy. Val said, "What else did Greer write?"

Bethany scrolled further. "Mostly gossip and innuendo. Cynthia's two husbands dying suddenly. Rumors of her cheating at a cooking competition. Uh-oh." Bethany glanced at Granddad.

His eyes widened. "What?"

Bethany squirmed. "Um. I'll read it. 'Among the fest attendees is a food writer whose ideas Ms. Sweet plagiarized to boost her column and secure a cookbook contract.' "

Granddad squawked. "Is that supposed to be *my* motive for murder?"

Bethany sighed. "I overheard some attendees talk about the rivalry between you and Cynthia, but I didn't expect a journalist to go there."

Val was tempted to tease Granddad by repeating his own maxim that there's no such thing as bad publicity, but his scowl stopped her. "What else is in the article?"

Bethany scrolled again. "Greer goes on about fictional murders inspiring real ones. She says the police are awaiting an autopsy report and haven't yet made a statement on the case."

No mention of Birdie, probably because Greer had to turn in her column before the reception last night.

Val glanced at the restaurant entrance as she'd done regularly since sitting down. She almost missed Claire with her blue-and-white bandanna covering her hair. The woman with her matched Granddad's description of the plainclothes officer assigned to Claire. "Excuse me. I'm going to talk to Claire. Maybe she'll join us."

Val skirted around the tables toward the restaurant entrance. The Black woman with Claire was in her thirties and made a commanding presence. She scanned the room the way a secret service agent guarding a VIP watched a crowd. Though she'd probably been up all night, she looked alert and ready to spring.

Claire greeted Val and introduced her and Officer Adams to each other.

A middle-aged woman approached the officer. "Excuse me, but are you Jordan Young?"

"No, ma'am."

"Sorry. The woman on the cover of Jordan Young's hairdresser mysteries looks a lot like you." She turned to Val, pointing at her name tag. "Your badge says you're a volunteer. Do you happen to know Jordan Young? I bought her book yesterday. I wanted to tell her how much I'm enjoying it, but I'm not sure what she looks like. There's no photo on her website."

"Yes, I know Jordan." Val surveyed the room and pointed to where the war veteran was sitting. "He's at the table by the window, talking to an older couple."

The woman's jaw dropped. "*He?* A woman salon owner is the sleuth in the book, so I assumed a woman wrote it. But with a name like Jordan, someone could be either male or female."

Val smiled. The same was true of her full name, Valentine, more popular for boys than girls. "Jordan will appreciate hearing that you like his book."

"I'll go right over and tell him. Thanks for your help." She crossed the room toward Jordan's table.

Officer Adams turned to Claire. "I'm going to take off now. Be sure to call the number I gave you when you're ready to drive home and stick with other people until then."

As she left, Val said to Claire, "Granddad and I have an extra chair at our table. Would you like to have breakfast with us?"

Claire looked apologetic. "I wish I could, but a woman interested in historical mysteries asked me to join her and her friend for breakfast. I won't be able to find her in a restaurant this full. I'll have to stand here, make myself conspicuous, and hope she recognizes me in my new duds."

It occurred to Val that Claire was also making herself conspicuous to whoever saw her in the stairwell. "My boyfriend, Bram, is going to be here today. If it's okay with you, he could shadow you this morning and fend off any trouble. He's not the pro that Officer Adams is, but he's really fit. He has good reflexes and a good heart."

Val expected and got pushback, but she persisted until Claire agreed. Noticing a woman standing and waving in their direction, Val said, "There's a young woman with long dark hair who looks like she might be waving to you. She's coming this way."

"That must be her. Yes, I see her now."

"I'll bring Bram over to your table when he comes."

The server was delivering breakfast when Val returned to the table. Her Swedish crêpes were topped with lingonberry compote, a feast for the eyes and the taste buds.

As she ate, her mind wandered. Had she made the same mistake as the mystery fan who'd assumed Jordan was a woman? "Cynthia told her book club about a distant cousin named Loren who'd contacted her recently. It's a family name going way back. I think of Loren as a woman's name, and Cynthia might have assumed that, but couldn't that be a man's name too?"

Granddad looked up from his plate. "There's an actor and a pro golfer with the first name of Loren, spelled with an *O*, like Sophia Loren's last name. But the other way of spelling it, like Lauren Bacall did, was more common for men than women when I was younger." He snapped his fingers. "I can check a geneology website for Cynthia's family. The site has family information from public records."

Bethany forked a melon ball. "How does it work, Mr. Myer?"

"You enter the name of someone's ancestor and any other details you know, like year of birth or death, a spouse, an occupation. Cynthia put her parents' names in the bio on her website. Her father was a writer, and her mother opened a bakery. If they're listed on the geneology site, I can get the names of their ancestors and keep going up the family tree to earlier generations. Parents, siblings, and children are all listed. If there's a *Loren* in the tree, it will say whether that name belongs to a son or a daughter."

Val nodded her approval. It made more sense to research Cynthia's family going back generations than to search for a link between her and the people who'd sat next to her at the bar. He'd already tried that without success.

Bethany finished the last of her burrito. "The hotel offered late checkout for one of the rooms the fest paid for. We need to be out of our room by noon, Val, but your room, Mr. Myer, is available until after the luncheon. Is it okay if we drop off our luggage there?"

"Of course. I really appreciate the free room this weekend. Breakfast is on me today."

"Thank you. Now I've got to run and make sure everything's ready for the morning panels." She stood up.

"Wait," Val said. "I have a favor to ask. Bram is coming this morning. Could you get him a badge? I've asked him to keep tabs on someone here, to make sure nothing else bad happens."

Bethany gaped at her. "A murder suspect?"

"No. It's a long story."

"I don't have time for a long story. I'll make him a volunteer badge."

Ten minutes later, as Val and Granddad finished their breakfasts, Bram came into the restaurant. He'd run into Bethany in the lobby. She'd given him a badge and told him where to find Val.

He hugged her and held up the shopping bag he'd brought. "Who wants the kettle?"

"I'll take it to my room," Granddad said. "We'll conduct our experiments there after Val's mystery trivia session."

Val drank the last of her coffee. "I have just enough time to go to the bookshop before the session starts. I want to buy a gift certificate for the trivia winner." And talk to Harrison. "Granddad, would you introduce Bram to Claire?"

"Yup. And I'll see you at trivia."

# Chapter 18

Val peered into the fest bookshop. Harrison, in the same three-piece suit he'd worn for the bake-off, was straightening stacks of books on a table.

He looked up as Val came in. "Good morning. I saw the notice of a reward for the Nero Wolfe recipe box. Did your grandfather get it back?"

"Not yet."

Harrison *tsk-tsk*ed. "A death, a theft, and then, last night, a woman keels over. This fest is jinxed. I usually sell a lot on the last day, customers buying books to take home. Sales may not be good this morning. I'm afraid people are leaving early for fear of what's next. And they might not come back for next year's fest."

"Really?" Val suspected he was overdramatizing. "Could the murder plots you were pushing have spooked them?"

"I was being facetious to lighten the mood."

If his theories about serial killers were meant to lighten the mood, Val shuddered to think what he'd say to dampen it. "If it's any consolation, your business is about to pick up. I'd like to buy a gift certificate to use as a prize for the trivia contest winner."

That was enough to put a smile on the book-seller's face. He rummaged in a leather briefcase, pulled out a postcard-sized certificate, and gave it to her, along with a pen. "You fill in your name and the amount. Then I'll ring up the sale and sign the certificate."

Val took her time filling in the blanks on the certificate. "I understand you were at the bar last night while Cynthia was still there. Did you have chance to talk to her?"

"No. She was too inebriated to carry on a con-versation. When she got up to leave, she had trou-ble staying on her feet. I was engaging with the bartender about his top-shelf whiskey. He wasn't particularly helpful. To be fair, he was distracted by customers clamoring to pay up. I must have waited fifteen minutes for my drink."

"Did the bar empty out, so you could savor your nightcap in peace?" Val hoped he'd tell her who else remained at the bar after Cynthia left.

"I didn't stay. I went out on the back patio to enjoy a pipe with my single malt. I sat upwind from where the cigarette smokers usually congregate. The bartender came out for a smoke, and so did the journalist, Greer. They had quite the heated conversation about the murder at this hotel last year. I caught only bits and pieces."

Greer's interest in that murder didn't surprise Val, but Eric's outdoor cigarette break did. She'd taken it for granted that he'd stayed in the bar until after midnight, when she saw him there with Jordan and Dave. Had he left the bar unattended, and if so, for how long? Val gave Harrison the certificate and her credit card. "Did you notice the time when the bartender took that cigarette break?"

"I went out around 11:30. The bartender showed up a few minutes later. Greer was hot on his heels. He smoked two cigarettes. That means he was there at least ten minutes." Harrison scanned her credit card. "You seem to have more than a passing interest in what was happening as midnight approached. Is that when Cynthia passed away?"

"I don't know when she died, but a lot of people were out and about at that time, in the elevator and the stairwell. Did you happen to see anyone when you came back inside?"

"I'd never climb stairs with an elevator available." Harrison gave her the credit card and the certificate he'd initialed. "I went inside a few minutes after the bartender did. It must have been ten minutes to eleven. The elevator I took was empty."

"Was anyone sitting at the bar when you came in?"

Harrison eyed a trio of women who'd come in and were browsing for books. "I didn't notice. Excuse me, I really must assist these customers." He hustled toward the women.

Did he really not notice who was at the bar? It wasn't worth pressing Harrison on that. Jordan could answer the same question. He'd gone down to the lobby at a quarter to twelve, so he'd know who was at the bar after that. And he could confirm whether he'd seen Harrison come in from the patio.

Val would look for Jordan later. She hurried toward the room where the trivia session would be held.

Granddad was standing across the corridor from the room. "Trisha's just inside the door, checking the badges of everyone going in."

"We have a few minutes until the session starts. I'll tell you what I learned from Harrison."

When she finished, Granddad said, "So the bartender left his post for a while. Working at the bar was his alibi for last year's murder. He mighta taken a break then too."

"That's something for Roy to pursue." Val noticed Dave coming down the hallway with the two women who'd recognized him from an old soap opera. The three of them went into the room for the trivia session. "Didn't Dave and the bartender alibi each other? I wonder if anyone can confirm that Dave stayed at the bar while the bartender was outside."

"We can check on that later, but now let's make sure Trisha plays trivia."

Once in the room, Granddad went around and gave each person an answer sheet. "One per customer. No teams allowed."

When Trisha, sitting in the back of the room, took an answer sheet without any coaxing, he beamed at Val. He returned to the front of the room and stood by the door to give answer sheets to any latecomers.

Val welcomed the thirty or so people in the room and asked them to mute their phones. She also warned them that using any electronic device—laptop, tablet, or cell phone—would disqualify them from the competition. Granddad drew his finger across his neck in a throat-slitting mime, and the audience laughed.

Always good to start with humor. "Would you please write your name at the top of your answer sheet, and we'll get started." Val waited for ten seconds. "Question 1. Arthur Conan Doyle, Alfred Hitchcock, and Stephen King all named the same author as their inspiration. Who was the writer?" Not a hard question for most mystery fans, especially those from Baltimore, where the football team was named for a poem by that author.

Next, Val asked Granddad's question about the Hitchcock movies and was glad to see Trisha writing a response. After another question about Hitchcock, Val switched to questions about Agatha Christie.

She read one that Harrison had contributed. "True or False: For the first stage adaptation of an Agatha Christie novel, the director wanted to shave decades off her detective and rename him Beau Poirot." Judging by the laughter in the room, Val expected most people to say the statement was false. Harrison had labeled it true.

He'd given her two questions about *Murder on the Orient Express,* and Val added one of her own. After those, she asked questions on food and mysteries. Anyone who'd gone to the bake-off would have an advantage answering those.

Then Val came to the last question, which favored those who'd attended last night's events. "So far, the answers have been worth one point each.

You can earn six points on this final question. What are the six weapons used in the original Clue game and in the movie based on the game?"

She gave the participants a minute to come up with the weapons, then asked them to exchange answer sheets for scoring and went over the questions again, taking oral responses from the audience.

When they'd gone through all the answers, she said, "Please put the score at the top of the sheet and return it to the owner."

Val collected the sheets and leafed through them to find the highest score.

Meanwhile, Granddad made an announcement. "If you went to Friday night's bake-off, you know that I write a recipe column focused on five-ingredient dishes. I've come up with a Murder Mystery Menu, from pre-dinner drinks to dessert. Each menu item has no more than five ingredients. You can invite your friends to a mystery dinner party or have a potluck and assign them each a dish." He waved a set of postcard-size menus. "I'll give a menu to anyone who's interested. You can find the recipes on my Web site, which is listed on the card."

This was the first Val had heard of his menu. As people read the menus he handed out, many of them laughed.

One woman said, "Will you come to my house and make the mystery meal?"

Granddad pointed to Val. "Speak to my granddaughter. She caters dinner parties." He showed her a card and waited for her reaction. She scanned the menu and smiled.

MRS. PEACOCKTAIL
HOT MISS SCARLET PUNCH
MR. GREEN SALAD WITH
COLONEL MUSTARD VINAIGRETTE
MRS. WHITE BEAN CHILI
PROFESSOR PLUM CAKE

She gave him back the menu. "You've given mystery fans something to remember you by."

"I thought it would make a nice souvenir of the fest. I have more menus to give out at the gala lunch."

He was no slouch at self-promotion. Val finished sorting through the answer sheets and found a winner without having to use her tie-breaking question. She announced the high scorer's name. One of the Miss Marples came up to receive the gift certificate. The audience applauded, and on their way out, some asked for extra copies of the Murder Mystery Menu for friends.

When the room emptied out, Granddad combed through the answer sheets and held one up. "Aha! Trisha spelled *sabotage* wrong, same as in the anonymous note. We're not just guessing she wrote the notes—we have proof." He pulled the anonymous note from his shirt pocket and unfolded it. He resembled a warrior, brandishing a paper weapon in each hand. "Let's see what she has to say for herself."

Val had a vision of him thrusting the answer sheet and the anonymous note under Trisha's nose and calling out her bad spelling in both. "Granddad, if you confront her with her spelling mistake, she'll think we set a trap for her. Which we did. She might not stick around long enough for you to ask about the recipe box. You'll have a better chance of getting it back if you don't antagonize her first."

His furry eyebrows rose. "So we're going to ignore the notes she sent?"

"No." Val took the answer sheets from him, put them in her fest tote, and headed toward the door. "We're going to have a friendly chat with Trisha. I'll mention the anonymous notes in a nonjudgmental way. You follow up by thanking her for saving you from Cynthia's evil scheme."

"You can make *my* note sound harmless, but not the one Cynthia got. That was a threat."

Val lowered her voice and kept walking. "Trisha doesn't know we saw it. I'll only bring up the note that you received."

Out in the corridor, Granddad glanced toward the fest table. "She's over there."

"Try to look nonchalant, not laser-focused on pinning her down." Val sauntered to the table. "Hi, Trisha. How did you like the trivia contest?"

"I was surprised at how much fun it was. I didn't expect to know so many answers, but you asked as many questions about movies as books, and I'm a big movie fan."

"My grandfather's a movie buff too."

He sat down in the chair next to Trisha's. "Yup. I used to own a video store and ended up with a big collection of classic films."

"I stream movies," Trisha said. "They don't take up any room that way."

A woman came to the table. "I'm not going to be able to stay for the luncheon. I'll leave my ticket in case someone else can use it." She handed it to Trisha.

"My boyfriend's meeting me here," Val said. "I could use that ticket for him."

Trisha passed her the ticket. "Here you go."

Val tucked the ticket into her pants pocket, put both hands on the table, and leaned toward Trisha. "We've been trying to figure out an odd thing that happened on Friday. My grandfather received an anonymous note in the fest envelope you gave him. We talked to the volunteers who assembled those envelopes. It looks like you were the only one who was alone with them and could have slipped the note into his envelope."

Trisha's shoulders tensed. "You have no idea how many volunteers—"

Granddad interrupted her. "I'd like to thank you for telling me Cynthia might mess with my dessert. I made sure she didn't get anywhere near it. From what I heard, you weren't so lucky. No one warned *you* about her before she tampered with your dish, Patty Cook."

The volunteer's brows rose in surprise, but she said nothing.

Val imagined the options running through Trisha's mind. Deny everything, including her alias and her history with Cynthia? Or cop to sending the anonymous note and accept praise for it?

"My Trisha hat failed. It didn't make me invisible," the volunteer said wryly. "Dave Proctor didn't let on he recognized me from the bake-off we were in with Cynthia. He must have told you I was Patty Cook."

"It wasn't Dave," Granddad said. "Your cap, glasses, and ponytail were enough to fool him."

"He's easily fooled. He believed Cynthia when she claimed she didn't ruin my cake." Trisha shook her head at his stupidity. "I left you a note so she wouldn't get away with cheating again. I didn't bother warning Dave. But I left her a note, thinking it might make her pull out of the contest. Didn't work. She could never come out on top except by cheating. Her recipes were nothing special."

Val wondered if Trisha would admit so readily to the other offense Granddad held against her. "Cynthia's recipes might not be special, but the box of Nero Wolfe recipes *is* special to my grandfather. It's been in our family for a couple of generations. It has sentimental value."

"And enough money value to make it felony theft in this state." Granddad paused. When Trisha didn't respond, he continued. "The box is still missing, but my reward notice led to information about it. Some folks told me they saw you with it after the bake-off."

Behind her glasses, Trisha blinked rapidly as if to get rid of an irritant in her eye. "When I was collecting the name tents after the bake-off, I noticed the box under the table. I wanted to check what kind of recipes they used way back then. I flipped through them and then put the box down."

Where had she put it down? Val made eye contact with Trisha. "You told us yesterday that the box was in Cynthia's tote bag. When did you first notice it there?"

"After I helped her up to her room. Her bag was gaping open on the floor."

Granddad frowned. "That's funny. The box wasn't there when her things were collected after she died."

"Then someone took it after I saw it there." Trisha met his steady gaze. "You look like you don't believe me. You think I have the box. Well, I don't."

Granddad sighed loudly. "That's too bad. If I don't get it back today, I'll have to make a theft report to the police and my insurance company."

Trisha's eyes behind her large glasses flashed at his veiled threat. "The police are welcome to search my car and my house. They won't find the box. I told you where I last saw it, and I'd appreciate it if you'd stop hounding me."

Granddad's shoulders drooped. He'd given up on getting the recipe box from her.

Val thought of a way to nudge the volunteer closer to the truth. Though willing to insinuate that Cynthia was a thief, would Trisha let someone other than Cynthia take the rap? "There's only one explanation, Granddad. The other woman who helped Cynthia upstairs must have taken the box. She told us she didn't see it when she was looking for the room key in Cynthia's bag. Of course, that's what she'd say if she'd grabbed the recipe box. Trisha, did you see her near Cynthia's bag when you were in the room?"

Trisha hung her head and rubbed the nape of her neck. After ten seconds, she looked up. "I took the recipe box from under the table Friday night so Cynthia would be blamed. It was payback for her cheating. At the bar I couldn't get close enough to slip it into her bag. I did it in her room when the other woman wasn't looking." She turned to Granddad. "I'm sorry I took your box."

"How did you plan to get it back to me?" His tone suggested she'd made no such plans.

"I was going to tell you it was in her bag, which I did Saturday morning. Then you'd ask her for it, and she'd have to return it."

"And she'd look like a thief caught with stolen property." Granddad crossed his arms. "Your plan didn't work out, so what are you going to do now to get my recipe box back?"

Trisha shrugged. "I can't do anything. Whoever went into Cynthia's room after I left must have taken the recipe box. The police ought to be able to find out who was there." She turned to a woman approaching the table. "Can I help you?"

Granddad stood up and walked toward the lobby with Val. "An apology is all well and good, but it doesn't bring my box back. Maybe she kept it for herself and stashed it where no one else would find it."

"Then you'd better hope her conscience starts bothering her more than it does now." As they reached the lobby, Val noticed someone else who might have a guilty conscience. Cynthia's step-daughter, Willow, sat in a chair with a cell phone to her ear. Val pointed her out to Granddad. "There's your client."

Granddad's cell phone chirped, and he answered

it. "Good morning . . . Sure. We're right here in the lobby by the reception desk."

Willow looked around and motioned them to join her.

Granddad clicked off his phone. "She wants to talk to us. She can't expect a full report from me after less than a day."

Val said, "Fingers crossed that she's here to give you information, not get it."

# Chapter 19

As Val and Granddad approached Willow, she tucked her phone away. She was wearing black slacks and loafers instead of the cargo pants and clunky lace-up shoes she'd worn the day before. Granddad sat down on a chair near hers, and Val stood between them.

She smiled. "I'm glad you aren't tied up this morning. I've been trying to reach the detective who interviewed me yesterday, but he isn't in the office where we met."

"I can text him," Val said, "if you have to reach him quickly."

"The business card he gave me had the police department's number. I left a message for him. He'll probably get back to me before long." She looked around the busy lobby. "Do you two have a few minutes to talk . . . in private?"

They adjourned to Granddad's room, sitting

where they had the day before, Willow in the cushioned armchair near the window, Granddad at the desk, and Val on the edge of the bed.

Willow fingered a gold band on her right hand. "I don't want an innocent person held responsible for what I did." She twisted the ring around and showed them the side that would normally be on top. Sparkling gems—square, triangular, and pearshaped—adorned the shell of a gold turtle. Its tiny head peeked out from under the shell. "This is my mother's ring, now rightfully mine. I took it from the nightstand in Cynthia's room. She was dead, and I was afraid her heirs wouldn't return it to me. I came here to tell the detective so he doesn't accuse anyone of stealing it."

By confessing, she might also keep the police from charging her with theft. Willow must have known yesterday that Val suspected her and would talk to the detective.

Mesmerized by the charming piece of jewelry, Val understood its attraction for Willow and Cynthia. "You may have to turn in the ring to escape prosecution for theft."

"I'm prepared to do that. I'll plead my case to Cynthia's heirs and, if necessary, buy the ring from them." Willow turned to Granddad. "Please don't hold it against me that I didn't tell you this yesterday."

Granddad tugged his ear. "It's not the only thing you kept to yourself. We found out that your father died less than thirty days before Cynthia did. That might mean her portion of his estate goes to you and your brother. Is that true?"

"Yes, but it's not like I was counting the days. I

expected Cynthia to live a lot longer. When I told my brother she was dead, he reminded me that she had to be alive yesterday to inherit anything from Dad."

If Val were on a jury in Willow's trial for murder, she'd find it hard to believe that the will's executor and beneficiary could be ignorant of such a crucial date. "That clause in the will gave you a motive to kill Cynthia before midnight on Friday."

Granddad nodded. "You might want to look around for a criminal defense lawyer."

Willow's foot tapped a silent rhythm on the rug, the only sign of nervousness she showed. "I was hoping you'd find someone who could have killed her in the half hour before I found her dead."

He sat back and crossed his arms. "Here's what I learned. An unidentified person was spotted near Cynthia's room close to midnight, but no one reported seeing anyone there earlier, before you went back to the room. Thing is, we haven't come across anyone with as strong a motive as you."

Willow's foot jiggled faster. "I guess I'd better look for that defense lawyer. What do I owe you?"

Granddad waved off the question. "If I dig up the information you're hoping for, I'll pass it on to you. Then you can pay me."

She stood up. "I'm going to wait in the lobby until I hear from the detective. It doesn't make sense for me to spend an hour driving home and then have to come back, like I did yesterday."

Val pulled out her phone. "I'll text him to ask when he'll arrive here and let you know what he says." After Willow left, Val looked up from her phone. "You fired your client so nicely that she didn't even realize you were doing it. Do you think she killed Cynthia?"

Granddad raised one shoulder in a half-shrug. "Can't rule it out. She mighta confessed to a lesser crime so she looks innocent of a worse one."

True, but there were still loose ends Val couldn't tie up. "If Willow took the ring, killed Cynthia, and left the room at 11:45, when Jordan saw her at the elevator, what explains the kimono person, the stairwell incident, and the spiked wine? Those things might have nothing to do with Cynthia's death, but her kettle whistling after midnight is something we have to explain."

Granddad snapped his fingers. "Here's what mighta happened. Willow takes the ring while Cynthia's sleeping, rushes out, and forgets to leave the key card. Back in her room, she realizes how easy it would be to kill Cynthia. Willow goes back and does the job."

"But first she puts on a red kimono, which she just happens to have?"

"It's not a kimono. It's a silky bathrobe or one of those long, loose things women wear who sell incense and crystals."

"A caftan." Though Willow didn't strike Val as the incense-and-crystal type, caftans were sold as loungewear. "Okay, I accept that Birdie could have mistaken a caftan for a kimono, especially when she saw only the back of it. What do you think Willow does after putting on a caftan?"

"She takes a plastic bag to Cynthia's room, smothers her with it, and puts on the kettle. Why the kettle?" He stared at the ceiling. "Willow hopes the whistle brings someone to the room by midnight to verify the time of death. She leaves and Birdie sees her in the hall going toward the stairwell."

Granddad's explanation for the whistling kettle wasn't bad, but it didn't explain why it took fifteen minutes for the kettle to whistle or who was in the stairwell. "To get back to her room, Willow would climb up the stairs, not go down them. She wouldn't have been the person Claire saw from the second-floor landing."

"Like I told you before, the kimono wearer and the stairwell lurker could be different people."

"The kimono wearer *might* be an outlier, but the murderer, the stairwell lurker, and the wine spiker are probably the same. That person feared Claire could identify him or her as being nearby when a murder occurred." Val stood up and paced the room. "If Willow feared being identified, she'd have left the hotel early yesterday and never come back. Instead, she returned and sat in the lobby, visible to everyone passing by yesterday afternoon and this morning."

For a change, Granddad couldn't poke holes in Val's argument. "I'll buy that a person afraid of being recognized would want to leave early. Doing that might look suspicious if it's a change of plans. And some folks can't leave because they're working—Eric tending bar, Harrison selling books, Greer interviewing folks for her newspaper column." Granddad ticked them off on his fingers.

"And panelists wouldn't want to miss a chance to promote their books." Val reached into her tote for the fest schedule and checked it. "Of the people we've met, the ones on panels today are Jordan,

Greer, and Claire, who's filling in for her mystery-writer friend. Dave isn't on a panel. Hmm. Once he played his part as Bunter, he had no reason to stay at the fest."

"Except pitching to possible backers for his restaurant."

"He came to the trivia session with two of his prospects. I wonder what questions he got right." Val pulled the answer sheets from her fest tote and leafed through them until she found the one with Dave's name on it. She focused on his answers to three questions. Then she checked how others had answered the same questions.

Granddad craned his neck to see what she was doing. "What are you looking at?"

"Dave correctly answered two hard questions about *Murder on the Orient Express* that a lot of people missed—the objects in the victim's compartment and the clue that could have implicated any of four passengers. But he gave the wrong answer to this question: What unlikely clue or red herring did Poirot find in his own suitcase? Nearly everyone else got it right."

"The red kimono. Hard to miss because Poirot makes a big deal of it. Could be a touchy subject for Dave."

"Yes, but it's not proof." Val's phone dinged. Roy had texted her back. She scanned his reply. "Roy's got a lead on last year's murder. He won't be here until this afternoon at the earliest."

Granddad tapped his fingers on the desk. "We can't wait around for him. I'm going to look up Cynthia's family tree to find a Loren Davis. What are you going to work on?"

"Alibis. I'll try to verify what Harrison said about the bartender going out for a smoke. If the bartender was outside long enough to smoke two cigarettes, he can't confirm that Dave was at the bar then." Val stood up. "When is an alibi not an alibi? When two people alibi each other and we learn one of them wasn't there the whole time. That means the other one doesn't have an alibi."

"The bartender mighta asked Dave to cover for him and tell customers he'd just stepped out. How do we find out whether Dave stayed at the bar the whole time?"

"Jordan Young would know whether Dave was in the bar for some of that time. Jordan's panel is going on now, and he'll be signing books afterward. I'll talk to him and to Greer. She'll be signing books too. She can confirm what Harrison said about her and the bartender smoking and talking outside."

"We're moving full steam ahead this morning. Anonymous notes traced to their source. Missing ring located." Granddad reached into the shopping bag Bram had given him and pulled out the electric teakettle. "If we can figure out this kettle thing, we might have the whole shebang solved before Roy shows up."

And Claire could go home without worrying that someone from the fest would come after her.

# Chapter 20

Val took the elevator down to the first floor and hurried toward the Poe wing. If she'd known a murder was going to occur this weekend, she'd have packed homemade cookies, and not only as comfort food. Cookies loosened tongues and usually blunted any resistance to answering questions.

She couldn't bake a batch of them here in the hotel, but buying books might have the same positive effect on their authors as cookies would.

Like the other writers sitting at tables in the corridor, Jordan and Greer eagerly chatted with readers while autographing books for them. Val zipped into the bookshop, bought Greer's *Mysterious Murders of the 1920s* and Jordan's *Hairsay Evidence,* and went back out to the corridor. Five readers were waiting in the line at Greer's table. Val went first to Jordan's table and stood behind the two people in line for his signature.

She advanced quickly to the front. "Hey, Jordan. I hope your panel went well."

"Got some new fans, so the fest was worth it." He opened the book she'd handed him, signed it on the title page, and put one of his promotional bookmarks in it. "How's the fest goin' for you, Val?"

"Not as well as I expected. Cynthia's death wasn't the only bad thing that happened. Someone in the stairwell frightened Claire just before midnight when she was walking upstairs. I've been asking people who were up at that time whether they noticed anyone hanging around looking or behaving strangely."

"Is Claire okay?" When Val nodded, he continued. "Aside from her and the night clerk, I didn't see another soul in the lobby when I took the elevator down to the bar."

"At a quarter to twelve?"

He nodded. "The only sign of life was a half-finished highball left on the bar. No bartender."

And no Dave, who'd claimed to be there then. Had he or someone else left that unfinished drink? "It's odd that the bar was empty."

"Right. It was supposed to stay open 'til midnight. I checked with the front desk to see if the bar had shut down early. The clerk said it was open and the bartender must have slipped out briefly. I waited at the bar, and he showed up before long."

"What time was that?"

"Midnight minus ten. He told me the bar was closing in ten minutes, but he'd be happy to serve me two drinks for the price of one since I'd had to wait." Jordan gathered the bookmarks strewn on the table into a neat stack. "Can't blame the guy for shutting down the taps promptly. Even after midnight, he was busy getting the bar set up for the next day."

"That's why he was there when I came down at a quarter after twelve. You were there with Dave. When did he join you?"

Jordan shrugged. "A couple of minutes after the bartender returned. Dave had time to finish the drink he'd left on the bar and order another one. He'd gone out to his car to pick up a bag he'd forgotten to bring in."

How long could it have taken Dave to fetch something from his car? No more than a few minutes. Unless he could name someone who'd seen him after the bartender and Greer went outside around 11:35, Dave had no alibi for almost twenty minutes. That shot him up to number one on Val's suspect list. And he could have been the person Claire had seen in the stairwell.

Val tamped down her excitement. So far she hadn't discovered a motive for Dave to kill Cynthia. The alibi the bartender had given him had kept her from digging for one, but now that had changed. And even if Dave wasn't the killer, he might be a witness. "Maybe Dave went up to his room to stow the bag and saw someone in the stairwell. I'll have to ask him."

Jordan shook his head. "Don't bother. He brought his bag to the bar and put it on the floor between the bar stools."

Val conjured an image of the bar after midnight, Jordan and Dave sitting there and, yes, a small bag on the floor, an expandable duffel like the ones athletic club members carried into her café after they'd exercised. It could be folded into a small pouch and, when expanded, it had just enough room for a change of clothes, or maybe a kimono and turban. "Thanks, you've been a great help, Jordan."

"No problem. If you have any other questions, you can catch me at the gala lunch. I'm sponsoring a table there and was thinking about gathering the same group as we had at the table Friday night. We can compare notes about the fest."

And about the crimes that took place at it. "Count me in. See you there."

Val glanced at Greer's table. The line of readers wanting her autograph had dwindled.

When the last of them left, Val approached her. She congratulated Greer on her newspaper column that morning and asked her to sign a book.

With little prodding, Greer filled in the blanks in the mental timetable Val was creating for Friday night. When the people who'd seen the movie thronged into the bar, Greer left and sat in the lobby, waiting to catch the bartender when he was free. Becoming impatient after half an hour, she checked her watch frequently and knew within a minute or two when the last few bar customers left. She confirmed what Harrison had said about his visit to the patio and hers. She also pinpointed when Dave had been at the bar and when he hadn't.

By the time Val stepped away from the table to make room for an autograph hunter, she could fill in a schedule of what had happened in the bar and lobby Friday night around the time Cynthia was killed.

The corridor had emptied out. Probably most

fest goers were either attending the final panels or checking out of their rooms. Val sat at the table where Jordan had been signing books, opened the notes app on her phone, and recorded the timing details before she forgot them. She started with eleven o'clock, when Cynthia, Trisha, Willow, Dave, and Harrison were all at the bar. When she finished the timetable, she inserted what had been happening near Cynthia's room during the same period and some unresolved questions.

11:10 Cynthia, Trisha, and Willow leave bar. Dave and Harrison at bar, Greer in lobby.

11:15 Willow and Trisha drop off Cynthia in her room.

11:30 Harrison goes out to the patio with drink and pipe.

11:35 The bartender and Greer are outside. Dave still at the bar.

11:40 Greer goes to her room. No one at the bar.

11:44 Willow goes into Cynthia's room and leaves a minute later. *Was Cynthia dead by then?*

11:45 Willow and Jordan wait for third-floor elevator. Willow takes the up elevator to her room. Jordan goes down to the bar. Claire is at the front desk to pick up a toothbrush.

11:50 Claire starts back to her room. Harrison leaves the patio for his room.

11:50–11:55 Claire sees someone on the stairs. Dave returns to the bar.

12:05 Whistling kettle wakes Val. Cynthia likely dead or would have woken up. *Who turned on the kettle and when?*

12:10–12:15 Val goes to lobby, sees bartender, Jordan, and Dave, and talks to night clerk.

Val studied the schedule. If Cynthia was dead before 11:44 as Willow claimed, the people who were in the bar or out on the patio couldn't have killed her. Harrison, Greer, and the bartender had solid alibis. Dave would have been pressed to get from the bar to Cynthia's room two stories up, spend the five minutes Roy said it would take to smother her, and leave the room before Meredith got there. On the other hand, if Cynthia had been alive around midnight, Harrison or Greer could have killed her, though Dave couldn't have because he was back at the bar. But, unlike Willow, none of those three had an apparent motive. Willow had the opportunity to kill Cynthia at any point from 11:15 on, but she couldn't have tampered with Claire's drink the next night. Dave had the opportunity to kill Cynthia roughly between 11:35 and 11:55, and he was at the reception where Claire's wine was spiked.

Val's phone dinged with a text from Granddad, telling her he was in the lobby. She tucked her phone away and went to meet him. With checkout time over and most fest attendees at panels, the lobby was less busy than usual. She spotted Willow at a table near the bar, sipping from a cup. A huge half-eaten croissant was on the table.

Granddad was in an armchair across the lobby from the her. From there he'd have a clear view of the bar and the door to the patio. Greer might have sat in that same place Friday night, tracking the movements of everyone going in and out. But Granddad was poring over his laptop.

He looked up from the keys as Val approached. "Bethany's finishing her packing in my room. We had to move her stuff and yours there at checkout time. At least you'd put your stuff in a suitcase. Her clothes were still on hangers when we moved them."

"She hasn't had much free time this weekend."

"She had time after we moved her clothes over. But instead of packing, she made a video call to her dog. She wanted me onscreen with her, so the dog could see me when I said hello. I told her I had something else to do."

Val laughed. "What? You skipped a face-to-face with Muffin?"

"Yes, to explore Cynthia's family tree. Bethany will text me when she leaves the room. Then you and I can go up there and experiment with the kettle. Did you make any progress?"

Val nodded. "Jordan and Greer filled in some details about Friday night." Val perched on a small but sturdy metal side table next to his chair and showed him the timetable.

He scrolled through it for a minute and then returned her phone. "The bartender is the only one with a solid alibi from the time when Cynthia left the bar until you went down to report the whistling. Any of the others could have killed her before you heard the kettle whistle."

Val glanced at the two suspects that were in the lobby now, Willow sitting at a table and Dave standing near the hotel's main entrance. He checked his watch, looked around, and broke into a smile when the woman who'd recognized him as a soap opera actor came up to him. They'd apparently planned to meet each other. He pointed to an unoccupied love seat. Two side chairs were at right angles to it. She chose a chair with wood arms, and Dave sat at the end of the love seat near her chair.

Val pointed toward him with her thumb. "Dave's sitting over there. I want to drill down into his background to look for a motive. He acted in a soap opera, but I can't remember the name of it. He also had a part in *Law & Order*. Is there a site with a searchable list of TV actors' names?"

"Yup. IMDB, the Internet Movie Database. It tracks the casts of movies and TV shows."

Val searched the database for Dave Proctor and, finding no match, looked for David Proctor. One actor had that name, but he'd been in a movie a hundred years ago. Maybe the database didn't include all cast members of all soap operas or the dead bodies from *Law & Order*. "I can't find him in the database."

"Maybe he used a different name for acting and then went back to his real name." Granddad rubbed his forehead as if he had a headache. "It's mighty hard to solve a crime in a hotel with suspects who are all strangers. If they came from Bayport, I could get the skinny on them from the old-timers."

"And I'd have baked treats for the suspects and be invited in. Then I'd get to know them by their books, the photos or doodads they display, and, if I'm lucky, what's in their kitchens." She glanced at

Granddad's screen. It had been idle long enough to go blank. "Did you discover anything about Cynthia's ancestors?"

"Yup. I had to trace her family back three generations before I found a Loren, and it's spelled like Sophia Loren. It was the maiden name of Cynthia's father's grandmother. She had a son and a daughter around the turn of the twentieth century. Cynthia is descended from the son. The daughter's first name was Loren, spelled the same as the mother's maiden name."

"Cynthia told her book club she had a great-aunt Loren who married a man named Davis. That's the person you found."

"Right. She married John Davis. I went up the tree two generations from Cynthia's parents. To see if the name Loren Davis shows up in later generations, I have to hop over to the other side of the family and trace the descendents there." Granddad peered at his screen for less than a minute. "Not a lot of side branches in that family. Cynthia's great-aunt Loren had one child, a son named Loren Davis."

"So within three generations, the name started as a surname, turned into a girl's first name, and then a boy's first name."

"The name shows up in the next generation too. The male Loren Davis had a son with the same name, born in 1948. Junior died quite young, in the early 1970s. He was childless. His father outlived him, but he's dead now too."

Val's elation drained away. "Huh. Did the name disappear too?"

"It's not in the tree. Only dead people are listed.

But there's something interesting here. The Loren Davis who died young had a sister." Granddad's eyes lit up. "Wanna guess the name of the man she married?"

Val glanced across the lobby at Dave. "Give me a moment." She went back to the movie database and tried a new variation on Dave's name—Davis Proctor. She found a match. "Her husband's surname must have been Proctor. Davis Proctor was in the cast of a soap opera. He had a few other TV credits. In his publicity photo he looks like a younger version of our Dave. Can we find out for sure that Dave the actor belongs in Cynthia's family tree?"

"The names on the site are linked to obituaries. I'll check the Proctors' obits for the names of surviving family members." It didn't take long. "Sure enough. The last paragraph in both obituaries lists Loren Davis Proctor as the only surviving child. The sister of the Loren Davis who died young named her son after him."

"So Dave dropped the first name for his acting career. And he dropped the last name when he contacted his cousin Cynthia." Val put the brakes on her speculations. "It's tempting to assume he killed her. He had a motive as the blood relative who'd inherit from her if she didn't have a will naming another heir. But how would Dave know whether she had a will? Even if he did, he was back at the bar before midnight, when we think Cynthia must have been alive to turn on the kettle." Val brought the timetable up on her phone and showed it to Granddad again.

He didn't bother looking at it. "Sometimes having an alibi is more suspicious than not having one. Dave coulda had an accomplice." He closed his laptop and scooted forward in his chair.

Val was surprised by his sudden move. "Are we leaving? I was going to text Roy that we've identified Cynthia's cousin."

Granddad stood up. "Hold off on that. Let's see what Dave has to say for himself."

"Roy isn't going to like that. He should be the one to confront Dave."

Granddad looked down at her. "When's Roy gonna be here? Might not happen before everyone leaves the hotel. You're the one who said Claire's not safe even at home unless the killer is caught before the fest ends."

"Why don't we try the kettle experiment before we—" She broke off. Granddad was already on his way across the lobby. She hurried after him.

# Chapter 21

Val caught Granddad's sleeve, slowing his march toward Dave. "You want to probe Dave's family connection to Cynthia? Fine. But don't ask him what he was doing when he left the bar Friday night. Leave that to the police. We don't want him to know we suspect him of killing her."

Granddad waved away her concern. "Don't worry. I'll stay in my own lane."

As they approached Dave, Val read the name tag of the woman sitting in the armchair near him. Her unpronounceable consonant-heavy surname was paired with a first name that suited her perfectly—Angela. Her hair, white waves sweeping back from her face toward golden tresses, looked like a halo.

She smiled. "You're Dave's friends from lunch yesterday. Nice to see you again. Won't you join us?"

"Thank you. We'd like that." Granddad claimed the other armchair in the grouping.

Dave made room for Val next to him on the love seat.

Angela turned away from him toward Granddad. "The trivia contest you two ran was such fun. Did you attend any interesting panels this morning?"

"No, I've been practicing my detective skills." Granddad beamed. "I've taken private investigator courses and have a sideline in that."

He'd taken a single course online, but Val didn't correct him. She put on her best blank face.

Angela's eyes lit up. "You're really a detective? That's fascinating. I'd love to hear about some of your cases. I guess you can't talk about them for privacy reasons."

"I can't say anything about my clients, but I can tell you about something surprising I just came across. Dave here is related to Cynthia Sweet, the woman who died suddenly Friday night. In fact, he's her only living relative."

Angela peered at Dave. "You didn't mention she was related to you. I had no idea you were grieving. I'm so sorry."

Val glanced sideways at Dave. His face was turning radish red. Even actors couldn't control blushing. Or maybe anger at being confronted with the truth had suffused his pale skin with color.

With him at a loss for words, Granddad piped up. "Don't feel bad that you didn't know. Dave kept it to himself. He didn't even tell the police detective investigating her death."

Val glared at him for mentioning the police.

Angela sat up straighter. "Investigating her death? So it's true she didn't die of natural causes. I overheard that, but I assumed these mystery fans were letting their imaginations run wild. Have the police announced the cause of death yet?"

"No." Val said curtly. Time to steer the conversation back to family matters. She turned to Dave. "Cynthia wasn't aware of any living blood relatives, or so she recently told a friend. Did you set her straight, Dave?"

Her yes-or-no question made him hesitate for five seconds. "I had a good reason not to. A rift in the family a century ago never healed." He leaned toward Angela. "I hate to bore you with family history."

"It won't bore me." Angela looked as if she'd relish the story.

Val was sure he wouldn't be telling the story if his prospective backer hadn't been there.

Dave made eye contact with all-ears Angela. "In the late 1920s, my great-grandmother married a man named John Davis. Her parents were leery of him. Her father went bankrupt in the Great Depression. Davis offered to take over the mortgage on the family home and let his in-laws live there at no cost."

Val tried to keep his family straight. Dave was a generation down from Cynthia. His great-grandmother was the Loren Davis whom Cynthia had mentioned and Granddad had found in the family tree.

Angela leaned forward. "It's heartwarming that the man disliked by his in-laws ended up saving the family."

Dave grimaced. "Not for long. As the Depression wore on, he reneged on his promise, evicted his in-laws, and sold the house." Dave shook his head in disapproval of his forebear's behavior.

"What a terrible thing to do," Angela said. "But not unforgivable if he needed the money to take care of his own."

"The other side of my family considered it unforgivable ever after." Dave's tone had changed, his resentment bleeding through. "History is written by survivors. And John Davis wasn't one of them. He disappeared, leaving a wife and son to fend for themselves. Her parents recovered financially, but refused to see their daughter. Her brother scorned her too. She and her child, my grandfather, had to stand in breadlines. From then on, both sides of the family were cursed."

Curses again? Yesterday over lunch Val had heard Dave chalk up his professional setbacks to a curse. Maybe that word had been part of the family lore. "What makes you say they were cursed?"

"Only one person from each generation made it past middle age. My grandfather had two children, a son who was killed in Vietnam and my mother. Before I was born, she had a stillborn son, and she died when I was barely twenty. On the other side of the family, in that same generation, Cynthia's brother committed suicide."

And, as Val and Granddad had learned yesterday, Cynthia's husbands had died too, but at least they'd made it to retirement age.

Angela *tsk-tsk*ed. "Those tragedies should have brought the family together."

"Absolutely," Dave said. "My branch of the family reached out a couple of times. Nothing came of it. My mother used to say that hate was an inherited trait in the other branch."

Granddad shook his head. "Hate is learned, not inherited. It can be unlearned."

Dave raised an eyebrow. "I hoped that was true. After my California job went up in smoke, I moved to this area, where the other branch of the family still lived. With premature deaths on both sides, Cynthia and I were the only two left. I tested the waters by writing her a letter, suggesting we get together. I thought a letter would give her more time to think about her response than if I showed up on her doorstep or called her."

"But you didn't sign the letter with your full name," Granddad said.

Dave's jaw dropped. "You have good sources. I used only my first and middle name, Loren Davis, because Cynthia might recognize them as family names."

*Lame excuse.* Val didn't say what she was thinking: Adding *Proctor* to the name wouldn't have interfered with Cynthia's recognition.

"Did you get a response from her?" Angela asked.

"No."

Another *tsk-tsk* from Angela. "She owed you the courtesy of a reply."

Val was weary of Dave's pity-me routine. "Cynthia was dealing with the death of her husband when she got your letter. Maybe she'd have answered it, given more time." But her time had been cut short, possibly by Dave himself.

He looked at Angela while responding to Val's

question. "I could have waited longer, but I had a backup plan. Cynthia's website convinced me we shared a love of food and cooking. If we met as strangers and bonded, I would break the news about our family connection and reconcile with her. But the curse struck again."

His outreach to Cynthia had started earlier than he was letting on. Val doubted he'd competed in the same bake-off with her six weeks ago by coincidence. He'd begun to butter her up then, defending her against Trisha's accusation of sabotage. How long had Dave been staking out Cynthia as a potential source of funds? Long enough to know when her husband had died.

"You poor boy." Angela patted his hand resting on the sofa arm. "Now you're the only one left."

Perry Macon came up to Val and Granddad. "Sorry to interrupt. I wanted to let you know Birdie's being released from the hospital right now, and she insists on going to the luncheon." He glanced at Dave and Angela. "She's the woman who needed emergency help last night at the reception."

Angela put her hands together as if praying. "I'm so happy to hear she's recovered, but it would be better for her if she didn't rush back here."

Val agreed. With her tendency to second-guess her assumptions, she couldn't rule out that Birdie had been the target of the drugged wine, slim though that chance was. Birdie would be safer staying away from the fest. "Can't her son talk her into going home?"

Perry shook his head. "He tried. He couldn't convince her. At least he'll be here with her and take her back to the hospital if she has any problems. I'll see if I can scare up a lunch ticket for him."

When Perry left, Granddad's phone dinged. He glanced at it. "Bethany's left the room," he mumbled.

Val saw a chance to cut short his interrogation of Dave before it strayed into police matters. She stood up. "Granddad and I have an appointment." With a teakettle.

Granddad took his time getting up. "Nice meeting you, Angela. Maybe we'll see you at the gala lunch. Are you staying for it?"

"I'll definitely be there. How about you, Dave?" When he nodded, Angela picked up the fest tote on the floor next to her chair. "But first, I have to go meet a friend. See you all later."

While waiting with Granddad for the elevator, Val glanced back at Dave and caught him watching them. He looked away quickly. "Dave's trying to figure out what we're up to, Granddad."

"I have to hand it to him. He made himself sympathetic when he explained why he didn't tell Cynthia they were related. I wonder how he'll explain his alibi falling apart."

"Not having an alibi for the time when she might have been killed doesn't wrap up the case against him. Being related to her isn't a motive to kill her. Why would he think he'd inherit her money? She confided in a lawyer, Perry, and told him she hadn't made a will yet. Can you see her telling Dave that she had yet to make a will?"

"No, but don't forget the grudge built up over the generations. We only have his word that she was going to invest in his business. She mighta checked up on him, found out who he really was, and told him she wouldn't give him a dime."

The elevator arrived, and two people joined them inside it. They stopped speculating about Dave. The kettle experiments should tell them whether Dave could have killed Cynthia and started the kettle before he returned to the bar.

Fifteen minutes later, Val answered a knock on Granddad's door and opened the door to Bram.

She felt a pang of fear. "Where's Claire?"

Bram strolled in. "I was replaced as her bodyguard. Two ex-policemen are with her now. They're writing a novel about law enforcement in Washington, D.C., during the Civil War. They may hire her to edit their book for historical accuracy. She's talking to them now and is going to sit with them at lunch."

Granddad must have noticed Val's anxiety. "They'll do a better job watching over her than Bram can do alone."

But they didn't know she might be in danger, and Claire probably wouldn't tell them that.

Bram pointed to the desk, where the kettle was burbling but not yet whistling. "How's the experiment going?"

Granddad swiveled around in the desk chair. "We finished one test with half a kettle, and now we're timing how long it takes to whistle with twice as much water. And we cooled off the kettle before starting the second test." He pointed to a large glass on the desk. "We used that to measure how much water we put in each time. In our first test we boiled about two cups of water. Val said that was about right for the little teapot she saw in Cynthia's room."

She nodded. "The kettle took four minutes to whistle. So the latest time a half-full kettle could have been plugged in was one minute after midnight. With less water, it could have been plugged in two or three minutes after midnight. That means either Cynthia was alive after midnight to start the kettle or someone else plugged it in after she was dead." But that person couldn't have been Dave, who was at the bar then.

The kettle gave a full-throated whistle. Val checked the stopwatch on her phone, noted the time on the hotel pad, and pulled out the plug.

Bram picked up the kettle. "My mother always boils more than half a kettle even when she's making only a cup or two of tea. It's pretty full now. How long did this much water take to boil, Val?"

"Eight minutes. Makes sense. Twice as long for twice as much water. So the kettle would have needed to be turned on three minutes to midnight for me to hear it at five after." But Dave couldn't have done that either. He had been back at the bar for several minutes by then. He'd have needed to put even more water into the kettle to delay when it whistled. Val pointed at the kettle. "For our next experiment, we'll fill the kettle to the brim. When we see how long it takes to start whistling with the maximum water, we'll know the earliest possible time someone could have turned on the kettle."

Bram shook his head. "The kettle is as full as it

should be. There's a little more room in it, but if you fill it to the top, the water will spill out once it starts boiling. The desk would have been wet by the time the security guard let you in. Did you notice any water on it?"

"No, and the water wasn't boiling over when I got to the kettle." She exchanged a disappointed look with Granddad. "Dave is the only suspect we've found with a reason to make it look as if Cynthia had lived past midnight. But he couldn't have killed her, set up the kettle to whistle five minutes after midnight, and returned to the bar when he did. Darn."

Granddad sat bolt upright in the desk chair. "Ice! If you start with ice in the kettle, it'll take longer to come to a boil. I woke up Friday night when someone used the ice machine across from my room. I looked at the clock. It was just past 11:35 when I heard the racket from the machine."

"Let's see how long it takes for the water to boil starting from ice." Bram grabbed the ice bucket. "I'll get the ice. We'll stuff as much into the kettle as we can." He left the room.

Granddad tapped his head with his forefinger. "It's funny how that noisy ice machine popped into my mind. I didn't even think about it yesterday."

"I have a niggling feeling I forgot a detail I heard early yesterday, when I was focused on getting other information. Maybe it will come to me while I get the kettle ready for the next experiment." Val took the kettle to the bathroom, poured out the hot water, and ran cold water into it.

As she reviewed what she'd heard on Saturday morning, she realized what she'd missed. Birdie had been chattering about so many different subjects that Val hadn't followed up on one of them— a man Birdie had seen visiting Cynthia at her condo.

Val dried the kettle and put it back on the desk. "I'm going downstairs to see if Birdie's here yet. I have to talk to her."

"Can't you wait until our ice experiment is over?"

"No. I planned to talk to her last night. She ended up being carted to the hospital. Once she gets here today, she might decide not to stay for the lunch after all, and I'll miss her again."

# Chapter 22

Val found Birdie easily, but getting near her was difficult. She was at the fest table with a covey around her. Perry sat next to her, doing a crossword puzzle, and her worried son hovered nearby. A number of people stopped to greet her and wish her well. Though pale, she seemed to enjoy the attention.

As Val waited to get closer to the fest table, Jordan came up to her. "I'm filling up my table at the luncheon. Same group as we had for the bake-off plus a few. Harrison and Trisha will be there. I'll ask Claire too, when I see her. I hope you and your grandfather will sit with us."

"We will, but Claire made plans to sit at another table. My friend Bram came this morning. He can take her place."

"Okay. I just found out the tables seat eight. Feel

free to ask two more people. I want to go finish a chapter before lunch."

"I'll take care of filling up the table." She'd check if Bethany and another volunteer could join them, possibly Perry, unless he wanted to sit with Birdie and her son.

"Thanks. It's table ten. Talk to you later."

Val was finally close enough to Birdie to claim her attention. "I'm really happy to see you back here. Everyone was worried about you."

"The hospital took good care of me, but it was hectic. Hard to get any rest there." Birdie finger-combed her wispy white hair. "I'm anxious to go home and sleep the rest of the day, but I didn't want to miss the luncheon or the auction. I'm going to bid on something I really want."

"My grandfather's going to be the auctioneer. It should be fun." Val noticed Dave walking by. She bent closer to Birdie and lowered her voice. "I need your help, but it's confidential. I'd rather other people not hear us talking."

Birdie whispered. "My son won't let me out of his sight. The only place I can get away from him and Perry, my two guards, is in the ladies' room. How about you and I go there and we can talk in the hall outside it?"

"Perfect." The corridor near the restrooms had less traffic than the area around the fest table. Birdie's son accepted Val as his mother's escort.

After visiting the restroom, Val and Birdie huddled near the exit to the parking lot.

"What can I help you with?" The older woman looked delighted to be needed.

"You told me yesterday that a young man visited Cynthia not long after her husband died. I was wondering if you've seen him since then." Maybe in the last two days?

"I wouldn't recognize him. I didn't see him up close. I was inside when they walked by my door on the way to her condo. It's next to mine."

Val tried to hide her disappointment. "But you knew he was a young man."

"I saw him when he was leaving. I have a view of the building entrance from my window. He went out of the building and crossed the parking lot. It was the day we had that late-season snow. From four stories up, I couldn't tell much about him, but he didn't walk slow and careful like an older man would when it's slippery. That's how I know he was young."

Val visualized looking down at a man four stories below. Not much to see except the top of his head. "What color was his hair?"

Birdie sighed. "I can't help you with that. The hood on his parka covered his head."

"Could he have been a repairman fixing something in her condo?"

"No. She'd gone out for two hours and came back with him. They must have met somewhere. I heard them talking when they were going from the elevator to her place. I didn't want to look nosy and peek out, so I just cracked my door open. After she unlocked her door, she said, 'Welcome to my humble abode.' I grabbed my donation envelopes and rushed over there before they got, um, involved in anything, if you know what I mean."

Val resisted a mischievous urge to ask Birdie what she meant. "Were you collecting for a charity?"

"Yes, the Maryland Food Bank. Cynthia's husband, Austin, always wrote a fat check for it. I was hoping for a donation from Cynthia and the man she was with."

And also hoping to satisfy her curiosity about that man. Val shared that curiosity. "It's a wonderful charity. Were you successful?"

Birdie shook her head. "I got only as far as the hall in Cynthia's place. She told me she'd contribute, but not yet. She said that a silly clause in Austin's will kept her from inheriting any money until he'd been dead thirty days. But once the estate was settled, she would donate so much that the media would cover it. The food bank would get lots of publicity."

And so would Cynthia. "She died before she could make the donation?"

"That donation and more. She told me that when Austin's estate was settled, she would draw up a will and name the food bank as one of the beneficiaries. All her money would go toward fighting hunger in the world."

And nothing would go to family. Val could hardly contain her excitement as she framed her next question. Birdie's answer could be critical to the case against a member of that family. "Do you think Cynthia's visitor could hear her when she was talking to you?"

"Certainly. It's not a big place, and she wasn't speaking quietly." Birdie cupped one hand around her mouth like someone revealing a secret. "I believe she said those things so he'd think she was kind and generous."

If that man had been Dave, he'd have realized the narrow window of opportunity he had for getting rid of Cynthia. By looking up her husband's obit, he could pin down the day she'd qualify for her inheritance. He knew she intended to will her money to charity after inheriting. Even the small risk that she'd write a will the next day was enough to make Dave act.

But Val had no proof that Dave had been Cynthia's visitor. Even if Birdie couldn't describe the man, maybe she could recall a detail that would eliminate Dave. "Was the man you saw leaving the building a big guy?" If yes, it wasn't Dave, who was slimmer and shorter than average.

"His puffy parka made it hard to tell how heavy he was, but he definitely wasn't tall. A tall man would have longer legs and would tower over the cars."

*All I saw was his leg a second before the door closed.* Birdie had said that yesterday about the man who'd visited Cynthia's hotel room before the bake-off. "Could the man in the parka have been the same one you saw going into Cynthia's room on Friday afternoon?"

Birdie frowned. "He wasn't tall either. He could have been the same man."

Val was convinced Dave had been Cynthia's guest for tea that afternoon and he'd swiped a key to her room then. He'd gone to her room shortly after she'd gotten back the key card she'd mistakenly given Val. Cynthia probably left that key card lying around. Easy for Dave to pocket it, and she wouldn't miss it. She never seemed to remember where she put her key.

Val noticed Birdie looking down the corridor with glazed eyes and realized she'd kept the older woman standing too long. "You've had a hard weekend. I can't thank you enough for taking the time to answer my questions. Let's go back to the fest table. Hang on to me if you'd like."

Birdie clasped Val's arm as they walked. "You're a good listener. Will anything I said help identify Cynthia's killer?"

"It might. I'll pass it on to the detective in charge of the case." Val crossed her fingers that Roy would show up soon.

"Here comes my son. If he asks what we've been talking about, don't say it had anything to do with a murder."

"I won't. You've been a huge help."

After turning Birdie over to her son, Val went through the lobby toward the elevators. The table where Willow had sat was empty. Maybe she'd given up on talking to Roy and gone home. As Val waited for an elevator, she looked out the window and glass door to the hotel's patio. Willow was out there doing laps, not in the pool, but around it, walking briskly.

Cynthia's stepdaughter might not need a criminal lawyer after all, if the case against Dave continued to strengthen. Birdie had bolstered that case, though she hadn't clinched it. Granddad's experiment with ice in the kettle might take it a step further.

Two minutes later, Val was back in Granddad's room with him. "How did the experiment go?"

Granddad smiled like the cat that got the cream. "Filled with ice, the kettle took sixteen minutes to whistle."

Val high-fived him. The timing fit with her hearing the kettle whistle at five after twelve. "At eleven minutes to midnight, Dave could have plugged in the kettle, after killing Cynthia, and walked down the corridor in a kimono toward the stairwell. He started down the stairs, where Claire saw him before she ducked into the second-floor hall. He then hurried to the first floor and reached the bar seven or eight minutes before midnight, while the ice in the kettle was still melting."

Sitting on the edge of the bed, Bram grinned. "A watertight alibi if I ever heard one."

Val groaned at his pun. "The scheme was worth more than an alibi to him. If Cynthia lived until after midnight, she would have died a much richer woman, with her husband's money added to her own. As her only relative, Dave would inherit from her in the absence of a will. And Cynthia's neighbor just explained how Dave might have known those things." Val related what Birdie had told her.

Granddad said, "Unless Birdie can swear Dave was the man who visited Cynthia, we can't prove he knew about Cynthia's inheritance or her not having a will."

Bram shrugged. "The only thing that matters is what he did Friday night. Take us through that step by step, Val."

She perched beside him on the bed. "After the bake-off, Dave saved Cynthia a seat at the bar and ordered a drink for her. He sat next to her for the first half hour and had a chance to add a sedative to her cocktail either then or later. We saw him leave a little before ten. He went back to the bar an hour later."

Granddad piped up, "Val made a schedule of what happened based on what witnesses told her. Cynthia left the bar at ten after eleven. Dave stayed there until the bartender went out on the patio around eleven thirty. No one saw Dave at the bar for about twenty minutes after that. If he was going to kill Cynthia during those twenty or so minutes, what's his first move when he leaves the bar?"

The answer was obvious to Val. "He'd go to his room, where he'd already set out what he needed to get away with murder. He put a kimono over his clothes and a turban on his head. I think he also picked up an expandable duffel bag in his room, folded it small, and tucked it in his pants pocket or waistband. When I saw him in the bar after midnight, he had a bag like that next to him, expanded enough to hold the kimono and turban. He wouldn't have had the time to drop off his costume in his room before going back to the bar to establish his alibi. Do you know where his room was, Granddad?"

"Yup. When we were making our desserts Friday night, I complained about my room being near the third-floor vending room. Dave said his was right below it. He was on the second floor near the stairwell. I figure he could be up there in a minute from the bar, and it wouldn't take more than thirty seconds to put on a kimono. Then he went up to the third floor and stopped at the ice machine."

Bram held up his hand as if stopping traffic. "Why didn't he get ice on the second floor?"

The answer occurred to Val. "When I went to get drinks for us at the bar on Friday night, a woman asked the bartender for ice. She told him the ice machine on the second floor wasn't working."

Granddad said, "Dave didn't need to go out of his way to stop for ice on this floor. Based on when I heard the ice machine, he could have gotten into Cynthia's room a few minutes before 11:40."

Val continued the story. "He let himself into the room with the key card he'd snatched when he was in Cynthia's room for tea in the afternoon. On Friday night he barely managed to suffocate Cynthia when Willow knocked on the door and then opened it with a key card she'd taken. Now what does he do?"

Granddad stood up. "We gotta act this out. Bram, you stand at the head of the bed as if you'd just killed Cynthia. I'll go out to the hall, knock on the door, and use the key card to get in. When you hear the lock click open, try to hide without me seeing you."

"Wait a minute, Granddad. The room was probably darker Friday night. Willow said the hall light was on when she went into the room." Val turned on the hall light, walked over to the window, and pulled the blackout drapes across it. She sat in the armchair near the window. From there, she could see both Bram and the door. "Cynthia was lying on the side of the bed near the window."

Granddad went out of the room and closed the door behind him.

Bram leaned down near the bed. At the sound of a soft knock on the door, he straightened. When the lock clicked, Bram zipped behind the drapes. He was hidden before the door had fully opened.

Granddad closed the door softly and crept toward the head of the bed. There he turned on his cell phone's flashlight and mimicked picking up the poison ring from the bedside table. He shone the light onto the pillow. "Willow claimed she saw Cynthia was dead and hotfooted it out of there." He dropped his key card on the desk and hustled toward the door. He opened it wide and then closed it, but didn't go out to the corridor.

Val said, "That took about a minute. That's how long Willow said she was in the room."

"I didn't see Bram or hear him moving." Granddad switched on the light in the room and looked around. "Now I can see a bulge in the drapes, only because I know he's hiding somewhere. Willow could have come in and gone out without ever knowing Dave was in the room."

Bram pushed the drapes aside. "Dave wouldn't have been able to see her behind the drapes, but he would have heard the door close and known when she left the room."

"She told Granddad and me that she left at 11:45. Once she was gone, Dave filled the kettle with ice and plugged it in. He went back along the corridor the way he'd come. That's when Birdie, in the room across from Cynthia's, noticed someone in a kimono heading toward the stairwell. He was hurrying down to the bar to set up his alibi."

"So he's the person Claire saw in the stairwell?" When Val nodded, Bram continued, "He must have planned everything before he came to the fest. He packed a kimono to conceal his identity from other people or surveillance cameras in the corridor. For the plan to work, though, he needed Cynthia's key. He couldn't depend on getting hold of it."

"True, but he's a creative guy," Val said. "He probably intended to wangle an invitation to late tea or to help her to her room after drugging her cocktail. But once he picked up the key when he was in her room for afternoon tea, he didn't need to risk being seen with her later. No matter which scenario played out, he'd make sure he was with people somewhere else when the kettle whistled."

Bram sat on the bed. "Why didn't he wait until after midnight to kill Cynthia?"

"Because the bar closed at midnight," Granddad said. "From then on, Dave couldn't count on anyone being in the lobby to give him an alibi, except the desk clerk, who wasn't going to watch him every minute. And Dave banked on everyone assuming Cynthia died of natural causes. The police probably would have put the case on the back burner if Val hadn't alerted them that Cynthia's ring was missing."

Val couldn't take full credit. "Two key cards without fingerprints made Roy suspicious. Willow must have wiped off the key card she used, and Dave the one he used."

Granddad held out both hands, his palms up. "Ta-da! The keys, the kimono, and the kettle, all explained."

Bram folded his arms. "Now that you two have figured it out, how will you prove it?"

# Chapter 23

Val reached into her shoulder bag for her cell phone. "We came up with the solution. The police can track down the evidence, but some of it might disappear after Cynthia's killer leaves the hotel. Roy had better get here before then. I'm texting him."

Granddad rested his chin on the back of his hand like *The Thinker* sculpture. When Val put away her phone, he said, "If Roy doesn't show up real quick, how do we keep Dave away from Claire during lunch?"

Bram said, "I'll watch him. You'll need to point him out to me." He turned to Val. "Can you make sure he doesn't sit at the same table with Claire?"

"Jordan invited us to share his table and asked me to invite two more people. See if you can get Dave to join us. He hangs around people he hopes will put up money for his restaurant." As an in-

vestor in tech start-ups and his mother's book-
store, Bram fit the profile. "Introduce yourself to
him as a backer of small businesses and convince
him to sit with you at lunch. By the way, I have a
ticket for you."

Bram pulled a ticket out of his shirt pocket.
"Bethany already gave me one."

Granddad straightened up in the desk chair.
"Why don't you give Willow the extra ticket, Val?
She can confirm some of what we're going to tell
Roy."

"Okay. If I see her in the lobby, I'll ask her to
join us." Hardly anyone turned down a free lunch.
"Bram, you and I should go down now, but separately. It's better if Dave doesn't see us together.
When I see him, I'll text you where he is and what
he's wearing so you'll recognize him." Val's phone
dinged with a message from Roy. She scanned it.
"Roy will be here in an hour. The luncheon will
still be going on."

Val walked Bram to the door, gave him a quick
kiss, and returned to the desk where Granddad
sat. "What are you going to do until lunch?"

"I have a plan. You go on ahead. I'll see you
downstairs."

Uh-oh. Nothing made Val more uneasy than
Granddad with a plan. No use asking him to tell
her about it. He either hadn't worked out the details yet or didn't want her to know them because
she might object. She sighed and left the room.


Val glimpsed Dave talking on his phone in the
lobby and texted his location to Bram. She then

ran into Nico and assured him that the police were likely to hear from the person who stole the ring. He thanked her profusely.

She felt uneasy when she didn't see Willow in the lobby. Had she changed her mind about confessing to the ring theft and gone home? Val went out to the patio, noticed Willow coming up the path from the pond, and coaxed her into going to the luncheon, saying Detective Roy would be there later.

When they went into the ballroom, Val was relieved to see Claire at a table far from Jordan's. Willow and Val were the last to arrive at Jordan's table. The chairs on either side of Granddad were empty. Val claimed the one that gave her a view of Dave across the table. He looked small sandwiched between the brawny Jordan and the broad-shouldered Bram. Willow took the seat between Jordan and Granddad. Harrison sat to Val's right with Trisha on his other side, next to Bram.

Jordan had left party favors at each place—bookmarks and a pocket comb with his name and *The Hair Salon Mysteries* printed on it. He'd provided a bottle of champagne and a pitcher of orange juice for mimosa lovers. Val filled her champagne flute with straight OJ. The glasses in front of Granddad, Bram, and Jordan were bright yellow like hers, while the others had paler drinks from the champagne they'd mixed with the juice.

Servers brought plates with quiche and salad during welcoming remarks by the fest committee chair.

Once she'd finished talking, Harrison treated the table to a monologue about trends in mystery fiction based on his sales over the weekend. "Today's readers want to know, not just whodunit, but what to cook for dinner, so we have a veritable feast of culinary mysteries. And books featuring women as Victorian PIs and World War II spies are coming on strong."

As he droned on, Val tuned him out.

Halfway through lunch, Jordan asked what everyone's favorite part of the fest was. When no one responded, he persisted. "What did you like best, Willow?"

Not an easy question for a woman who hadn't registered for the fest, but only hung around its fringes.

She paused before answering. "I found the whole weekend . . . stimulating."

"Me too," Granddad piped up, probably to forestall any request for Willow to be more specific. "The best was the Friday night bake-off. What about you, Val?"

"My favorite part was meeting someone from my college years and discovering we had a lot in common." And learning that Claire was in danger had made the weekend that began with a death even worse.

Harrison raised his glass. "Besides champagne, my favorite part of the fest was totaling up the book sales I made." As everyone laughed, he guzzled from a glass that had no hint of orange juice in it.

Then it was Trisha's turn. "I enjoyed last night's reception. You can't go wrong with wine and cheese and people wearing funny clothes." She adjusted her big glasses and peered at Dave. "Why did you show up as Sherlock Holmes and then change out of your costume?"

Granddad's foot nudged Val's under the table. They'd seen Dave at the reception, but not in a costume.

He downed his pale drink before responding. "You've confused me with someone else."

Trisha shook her head. "I was standing by the door. You came in as Sherlock Holmes. Fifteen minutes later, you were there without your costume. What happened?"

Dave reached for the champagne bottle and refilled his glass. "It's a case of mistaken identity."

No, it wasn't. Trisha had just provided the missing piece in the case against Dave. He was the Sherlock seen at the table where Claire had put her wine. After leaving a glass of drugged wine there, Dave had ditched the costume he no longer needed.

Val's phone dinged with a message from Roy. He was waiting outside the ballroom to talk to her.

She excused herself from the table and met him in the corridor. She briefed him on Dave's family connection to Cynthia, his motive for killing her, and the timetable that showed how he could have committed the murder and contrived an alibi.

After listening attentively, Roy said, "I'd rather not make a public move yet. I'll keep an eye on Dave and speak to him when lunch is over. Where is he sitting, and where is Claire?"

"Dave is the small man across from me at table ten. Claire is sitting on the other side of the room. Willow is also at my table, and she's been waiting since early this morning to talk to you."

"I wish I could have been here earlier. A man's who's just back from a year abroad contacted us. He didn't know about the murder here last year until he read the newspaper article this morning. Turns out he'd overheard the victim's wife describe how to get away with murder. He thought it was a theoretical discussion, but it was the plan she executed. His evidence should get us a conviction."

Wrapping up the year-old murder this morning and this weekend's murder this afternoon would do wonders for Roy's career. Val was sure he'd give it his all.

When she returned to her seat, dessert was being served, and Granddad was going to the podium to conduct the auction. She'd missed the announcement of the bake-off winner. Harrison filled her in. Granddad's dessert had been the official judges' choice, and Dave won the people's choice award. He showed her his plaque, looking the happiest Val had seen him all weekend. That wouldn't last long. Roy had slipped in and now leaned casually against the wall near the door.

Harrison excused himself, saying he had to leave early for another engagement.

A program at each place included the list of auction items, and Granddad moved briskly through them. Experience as his church's auctioneer served him well. He smoothly coaxed higher bids by reminding bidders of the literacy charities that would benefit. Dinners with authors, baskets of books, and naming rights to characters in the next books by various writers went for top prices. Birdie won the right to have a character named after her.

After auctioning off everything on the list, Grand-dad held up a bulging fest tote. "Now we come to a final item that's not on the auction list. You might think it's just another swag bag, but what's in it makes it unique. What we have here is a *murder kit.*" He drew out the last three syllables.

The hum of conversation in the room quieted. Val had no inkling what he was going to do, but she assumed her role was to watch Dave's reactions. She read polite interest in his expression.

Granddad made a show of opening the fest tote and peering into it. "Aha! This is a collection of things that can disguise a killer's identity and the time of the murder. Let's take a look at them."

Val cringed inwardly. He was doing a show-and-tell of what they'd explained to Bram. Would Granddad name the culprit or only tip him off that he needed a lawyer? Either way, Roy wouldn't like it. Though Val didn't have a good view of the detective's face across the room, she noticed he'd stopped leaning against the wall. He stood ready for action.

Dave remained expressionless, but he gulped down champagne with a water chaser as if his mouth had turned dry.

Bethany crept over from the next table, sat down where Harrison had been, and hissed, "What's your grandfather doing? It's not on the program."

"I'm as surprised as you are," Val whispered.

Granddad reached into the bag. "What have we here?" He held up a folded piece of red cloth about two foot square. "Looks like a red kimono."

Gasps and laughs came from the audience. Val recognized the material, though no one else would.

He was displaying the top of his burgundy-colored pajamas, making sure the sleeves and buttons didn't show. Across the table from her, Dave clutched his glass so tightly that his knuckles were white.

Granddad stuffed the pajama top back in the bag. "On the Orient Express, Hercule Poirot glimpses a woman in a kimono. That kept him from recognizing her. A kimono could also disguise a man, especially if his head was completely covered by a hat, like this one in the kit." Granddad briefly held up his black knit cap, not a turban, but it sufficed to make his point.

Dave put down the glass he'd drained, his body rigid.

"Let's see how the killer in the kimono planned to get away with murder." Granddad pulled out a raffle ticket. "This is a coupon for a free drink at the hotel bar, useful when the culprit needs an alibi for the time the murder took place . . . supposedly."

Bethany looked askance at him, and Dave fidgeted in his chair. Val saw Roy moving along the room's side wall. He stopped where he had a good view of Dave. Willow stared at the podium with a puzzled frown.

Granddad reached into his bag again and held up a bulging plastic bag. "In case you can't tell, this bag is filled with ice. What's a bag of ice doing in a murder kit? Combined with the next thing in the bag, it can fudge the time of death."

With everyone focused on him, Val might have been the only person to notice Dave's eyes darting left and right. He glanced behind him, possibly to find the quickest way to the exit.

Granddad pulled the electric kettle from the bag. "Starting with ice instead of water delays when the water will boil and the kettle will whistle. It can make it look like the victim put water on for tea a few minutes before it boiled, though she'd been dead already for fifteen minutes."

Dave stood up. Bram jumped to his feet, blocking Dave on one side.

Jordan rose and put his hand on Dave's shoulder, towering over him on the other side. "You okay, buddy?"

Dave looked like a panicky caged animal. When Roy came toward him, Dave's shoulders slumped.

He hugged himself. "It's true!" His agonized cry drew everyone's attention. A hush came over the room. "I set up an alibi to get away with murder. But I couldn't kill her. *She was already dead.* Someone else did it, but I still needed the alibi."

Val's surprise was mirrored in the faces of the others at the table. She took Dave's outburst as putting his own spin on Cynthia's death, denying his guilt as most murderers would.

Roy spoke so quietly that only those at the table with Val could hear what he said to Dave. "Please come with me, sir. And don't do anything foolish. Police officers are on the premises."

"I'm innocent," Dave howled, as Roy hustled him out.

Willow watched them leave, round-eyed with shock, her hand covering her mouth. Bethany sat speechless and immobile.

Trisha frowned. "Was that a put-on or was he telling the truth?"

Good question. Was it possible Dave *didn't* kill

Cynthia? The timetable Val had created flashed through her mind. Change one detail in it and, yes, it was possible.

If Willow had gone to Cynthia's room five minutes earlier than she'd claimed and stayed longer than she'd admitted, Dave might be innocent of murder. Based on when he was last seen at the bar, he could have entered the room before Willow, but he wouldn't have had enough time to smother Cynthia. He might have been standing over her, ready to kill her, when Willow came to the door.

Granddad tapped the microphone. He'd been silent long enough to make Val wonder if his thoughts mirrored hers.

"In case you haven't figured it out, the murder kit I showed you relates to the death here Friday night." His words electrified the room. "Now I gotta ask for some help from you, just a show of hands. Did anybody see a person in a kimono in the hotel between 11:30 and midnight on Friday?"

Only Birdie raised her hand.

"Thank you." Granddad continued. "What about a woman with long dark hair, dressed in black, with rings and sparkly things around her nose and mouth? Did anyone notice her around that time?"

Val now understood why Granddad had presented their murder theory in public. This was his last chance to find witnesses.

Willow's eyes were downcast, while everyone else at Val's table was scanning the room for upraised hands.

Greer popped out of her seat. "I saw her. When I took the elevator from the lobby to the fourth floor and got out, she was disappearing into the other elevator going down. I went to my room and checked my e-mail. That was at 11:40."

So Willow *had* lied about when she'd left her room, lied to the tune of the five minutes it would take to smother Cynthia. Dave didn't know it yet, but Greer had just lifted the curse on him. Thanks to a woman who time-stamped her every memory, he might not spend the rest of his life in prison.

A man in a Stetson raised his hand, one of the anti-Christies Harrison had pointed out Friday night. "I saw that woman in black right around that time. She was going into a room on the third floor."

That must have been Cynthia's room. The evidence against Willow was mounting. The Stetson guy would need to be more specific about the time, but Val had enough information to act. She stood up. She'd made a strong case to Roy for Dave's guilt, but now she had to find the detective and convince him that Dave might be telling the truth.

She rushed out of the room and sped down the deserted corridor. She sensed a person behind her. Before she could turn, strong hands gripped her by the shoulders and shoved her into an empty meeting room.

# Chapter 24

Willow shut the heavy door to the corridor and blocked it with her body. "Don't scream. I don't intend to hurt you."

Val would be crazy to believe that. She'd scream if she thought anyone would hear her. She sized up her chances against her opponent. Cynthia's stepdaughter had size and weight in her favor, but Val was younger and fit. Even so, she'd rather talk than fight. "I've already told the police what you did. You can't—"

"You're lying. You just figured it out. And I don't want you telling the police." Willow leaned against the door she was blocking. "I didn't come here to kill Cynthia. Dave wore a disguise to get away with murder. I wore one to keep her from recognizing me. Yes, I trailed her to get my ring if she left it lying around, but I never planned to kill her."

Val inched away from the woman. Her plans had changed on Friday night, and they might change now too . . . and not for the better.

Willow gazed across the room at the windows. "Grief is supposed to lessen over time, but it comes in waves. It overwhelmed me when I saw her drunk in bed. She kept my father from his family at the end of his life. She fed him foods no diabetic should eat. With him dead, she would live like a queen off his money. I couldn't bear it." She took a deep breath. "The hotel laundry bag should have been in the closet, but it was on the bed, tempting me." She buried her face in her hands, sobbing.

But she still blocked the only exit from the room. "Any jury would sympathize with you, Willow, as long as you admit what you did." And don't commit another crime. "You're not ruthless like Cynthia. And you won't let an innocent person be punished for her death." Though calling Dave innocent was a stretch.

The door Willow leaned against rattled and burst open. Pushed forward, she lost her balance and fell as Bram and Jordan charged in.

Bram hugged Val. "Thank God you're okay! I didn't notice Willow leave. When Jordan told me she followed you, I rushed out, but we couldn't find you."

Jordan was bending over Willow. "She's all right. I don't think anything's broken."

Her bones weren't broken, but she was. Val hoped the mental stress of Willow's grief would argue for a lenient sentence. Some grieving people never got past despair and killed themselves.

Willow was stuck at the anger stage and had killed the person she blamed for her grief.

With Jordan's help, she stood up and looked at Val. "I didn't mean to scare you. I wanted to turn myself in and tell my own story. And I wanted you and your grandfather to understand how it happened."

As Val took out her phone, she glanced at the poison ring on Willow's finger. It had proved poisonous to her. Val texted Roy that Dave hadn't killed Cynthia, Willow was ready to confess, and the police had better come quickly before she changed her mind.

He was there in a minute and hustled Willow away.

Jordan returned to the ballroom, where people were straggling out. Val held Bram back to tell him what Willow had said while they waited for Granddad.

Claire joined them outside the ballroom. "I'm not sure I understand what happened in there. Is the man who jumped up and confessed the person who saw me in the stairwell?"

Val nodded. "He was there on his route from Cynthia's room to the bar. If you could identify him, you'd destroy his alibi. It's toast now, so you're safe from him. And he's in police custody." She brought Claire up to date on his and Willow's roles in Cynthia's death.

"Cynthia, Dave, Willow. Their lives intertwined and fell apart in the space of two days. Somehow I got in the middle of it." Claire pulled off her bandanna. "Thank you for helping me out of it. I wanted to thank your grandfather too. People are lined up to talk to him, and I couldn't even get close. Please say goodbye to him for me."

"I will." Val took out her phone. "Let's exchange numbers. We should try to get together again soon. You're welcome to visit us in Bayport. We have a big house with three guest rooms. It's beautiful along the Chesapeake, and it's an easy drive from Washington."

"Thank you. And you let me know if you're coming to the Washington area."

After they texted contact information to each other, they hugged and Claire left.

Birdie came over to say goodbye. Val assured her, and her skeptical son, that her observations had been crucial in solving the mystery of Cynthia's death.

Val saw Trisha heading for the door to the parking lot and said, "I'll be right back, Bram. Keep an eye out for Granddad."

She caught up with Trisha. "Before you go, I have a question. It's about Dave. Did you notice what he was doing when he was dressed as Sherlock Holmes?"

"I saw him do one odd thing. He was carrying a glass of wine, took out a swizzle stick, and stirred the wine. Then he put the swizzle stick back in his pocket. It was red wine so it probably stained his clothes."

Val could think of no reason to stir that wine unless he'd added something to it. "Did you see Dave drink that wine?"

"No, I went to get some cheese. The next time I

saw him, he'd changed clothes. More questions? Ask me anything except where the recipe box is. I can't help you with that."

"I know. You don't have it anymore."

"I'm glad you believe me. I don't think your grandfather does." Trisha turned on her heel and left.

By a quarter to three, the Bayport contingent had gathered in Granddad's room. He sat in the armchair, Bram lounged against the wall, and Bethany, uncharacteristically quiet, was shifting items around the suitcase she'd already packed.

Val sat on the bed. After getting off the phone with Roy, she updated the others on what he'd said. "Dave and Willow are at police headquarters. We were right that Dave went into Cynthia's room a minute before Willow did. He hid behind the drapes while she was there, came out when he heard the door close, and found Cynthia dead. Bottom line, Dave's in the clear, and Willow is on the hook for Cynthia's death."

Granddad folded his arms. "He should be charged with other crimes even if he didn't commit murder. He stole Cynthia's key card, spiked her drinks at the bar, and tried to drug Claire's wine, with Birdie ending up in the hospital because of it."

"Roy will try to charge him, but Dave's acting experience makes him a convincing liar. He claims Cynthia gave him a key card and invited him to her room for a nightcap. So far, no one has come forward who *saw* him slip anything into Cynthia's cocktails or into the wine at the reception, but Roy will keep looking for a witness. A search of Dave's belongings might turn up evidence." Like a tell-tale swizzle stick with residue of the drugged wine Birdie drank.

"He darned near pulled off the perfect murder," Granddad said. "He told us his mother fed him mystery books when he was growing up. I guess that explains his elaborate plan. He sure had me fooled with his *I'm-cursed* scene when we told him Cynthia was definitely dead. He'd known that for twelve hours."

Bram said, "If Dave's such a good actor, he should have projected calm about the so-called murder kit. Why did he blurt out a confession in front of everyone?"

Granddad hit the chair arm with his fist as if it were a gavel. "He knew we had the goods on him."

Val thought of another reason for Dave's outburst. "He wanted to make the point that someone else had been in that room. And he had an audience for his big scene. He and Cynthia were cut from the same cloth. Ambitious, eager to be the focus of attention, and willing to do anything to come out on top."

Granddad grunted. "Doesn't seem right for him to inherit money from the woman he planned to kill. At least he won't get any of her ex-husband's money. She didn't live long enough for it to pass to her. I suppose that means Willow inherits twice as much from her father, but where she's going, she won't get a chance to spend it."

Bethany zipped up her suitcase. "So she killed Cynthia for the inheritance?"

Val tilted her head from side to side, weighing how greed and grudge, combined with grief, led to the murder. "Willow blamed her father's death on Cynthia, but she killed on impulse. Once Cynthia was dead, though, money motivated Willow. She insisted Cynthia died earlier than the police thought and hired Granddad to find people who could have killed her."

"Yup, but she didn't want me to pin the murder on a particular person, just muddy the waters about the timing of it." Granddad checked his watch. "How soon are we supposed to be out of this room?"

"Six minutes," Bethany said. "I still need to arrange things in my backpack."

"I'll take the large bags down." Bram picked up Val's overnight bag and Bethany's suitcase. "I'm going to call my mother from the lobby. She'll enjoy hearing about the starring role her kettle played. Meet you downstairs."

When Bram left, Granddad turned to Bethany. "I'm sorry I had to go off script at the end of the auction, but it was the only way to wrap this up before folks scattered. Val and I couldn't talk to everyone at the fest individually. The microphone gave me a chance to ask a hundred people questions in one fell swoop."

And he loved being the showman, but Val kept that thought to herself. He'd justified his stunt.

"I accept your apology," Bethany said, "and I owe you one in return." She reached into her backpack and pulled out the Nero Wolfe recipe box.

Granddad looked thunderstruck. Val was less surprised. Two images sprang into her mind— Bethany standing near Cynthia's tote bag while the guard checked Cynthia for signs of life and Bethany clutching her stomach a minute later. She'd hidden the recipe box under her bulky sweater and feigned sickness to hurry out of the room.

Granddad frowned. "Where did you get the box?"

"I took it from Cynthia's tote bag when Val and I found her dead. You wouldn't have gotten it back quickly from whoever took possession of her things. I saw no reason to make a fuss and brand a dead woman a thief when I could return it to you after the fest."

Granddad looked peeved. "You coulda saved me a lot of worry by giving me back the box."

"I was afraid someone saw Cynthia steal it, and if you had the box after she was murdered, you might be questioned about how you got it back. Then it would come out that I took it from the scene of a crime. I was going to mail it to you anonymously. I'm sorry." She handed him the box.

He clutched it. "It's okay. I'm awful glad to have it back."

She smiled with relief. "And I'm glad that you solved the murder and that an outsider did it, not one of the fest goers. Maybe they'll come again next year, even though the gala luncheon ended with a man dragged off protesting his innocence."

Granddad tucked the box into his suitcase.

"Half of them thought it was part of the entertainment. They'll come back *because* of it."

Val nodded. "And they'll never attend another mystery weekend quite like this." Though it wasn't the murder-for-pleasure weekend Val had expected, she would come back next year. She patted Bethany's back. "You put on a great fest, my friend."

# Acknowledgments

Over the last fifteen years I've attended dozens of mystery fan gatherings, but none in the last fifteen months because they were all cancelled. Missing them, I created a fictional mystery festival. The characters in the book are not based on anyone I've ever encountered at such events. Some of my festival's happenings mirror those at real mystery fan weekends, but the bake-off and the murder are invented. The year-old crime is based on a 1990s murder at a hotel on Maryland's Eastern Shore. As in this book, the crime occurred shortly after the killer and victim had attended an interactive murder mystery show at the hotel.

The valuable artifacts that disappeared at the festival have real counterparts. Currently you can find book-shaped boxes with Nero Wolfe recipe cards for sale online. Also online is the *Antiques*

*Roadshow* episode with an appraisal of a Renaissance-revival poison ring similar to the one in this book.

I'm grateful to many people who contributed key ingredients to *Bake Offed*. Mark Bergin, crime writer and retired Alexandria, Virginia, police lieutenant, explained how the police would respond to and process the scene of an unattended death like the one in this book. Mystery writer and forensic consultant D.P. Lyle, MD, provided details about the medical aspects of the crime and its investigation. I appreciate your help. Any mistakes in the book on those subjects result from my misunderstanding.

My critique partners and fellow crime writers, Carolyn Mulford and Helen Schwartz, performed their magic on this book as they have on the seven previous ones in the series. They brainstormed with me, gave me chapter-by-chapter feedback, and edited the full manuscript. Thank you for your advice and your friendship, Carolyn and Helen.

My husband, Mike Corrigan, also read and commented on this and the other books in the series, as did Nora Corrigan, Cathy Ondis Solberg, and Elliot Wicks. Thank you all for giving me feedback that made the book better. I'm indebted to Carolyn Mulford for doing a final edit under a tight deadline. Special thanks to my nephew, Gregory Berman, for the blue cocktail he created as part of the Murder Mystery Menu.

I'm grateful to my agent, John Talbot, who brought the Five-Ingredient Mystery series to Kensington Books. I'd like to thank my editor, John Scognamiglio, and my publicist, Larissa Ackerman, as well as the production, marketing, and sales teams at Kensington Books for continuing to bring out books at a time when we needed them more than ever.

Special thanks to the organizers and volunteers of Malice Domestic, Bouchercon, Left Coast Crime, Sleuthfest, Killer Nashville, the Suffolk Mystery Authors Festival, and similar gatherings. You make it possible for mystery lovers to come together and celebrate the books we love.

Finally, I'm thankful for readers who enjoy mysteries and keep them alive. I've talked with many of you at mystery conventions and festivals. I hope to see you and other mystery fans at future book events. Until then, happy reading—and eating!

# The Codger
# Cook's Recipes

# Mrs. Peacocktail

*This drink is made with Hpnotiq, a blue liqueur made from vodka, cognac, and fruit juices. There are no substitutes for it.*

1 ounce Hpnotiq
2 ounces gin
1 ounce lime juice
Optional: dash of blue agave syrup
Blueberries

Combine the liquid ingredients in a cocktail shaker. Shake, pour into highball glass with ice, and top with seltzer if desired. Garnish with fresh blueberries, preferably small ones.

Serves 1.

Recipe created by Gregory Berman.

## Hot Miss Scarlet Punch

*The first recipe here makes a generous single serving. The second one makes enough for a crowd. For a tangy drink, use a dry white like sauvignon blanc or Italian pinot grigio. For a sweeter version, use a Riesling, a white zinfandel, or a dessert wine.*

3 ounces cranberry juice cocktail
1½ teaspoons brown sugar
scant ½ teaspoon ground cloves
scant ½ teaspoon ground cinnamon
2.5 ounces white wine

Heat the first four ingredients in a small saucepan. Bring the mix to a boil. Reduce the heat and simmer for five minutes uncovered. The ground spices remain in the punch. Add the wine and heat the mixture before serving in a glass or a large punch cup.

Serves 1.

4 cups cranberry juice cocktail
⅓ cup brown sugar
Cinnamon sticks, 1 for cooking and optionally
    more as swizzle sticks
3 teaspoons ground cloves or 4 whole cloves
1 750-milliliter bottle of white wine

Combine the cranberry juice, brown sugar, cinnamon stick, and cloves in a large saucepan, and bring them to a boil. Reduce the heat and simmer for five minutes uncovered. Remove the spices. Add the wine and heat the mixture before serving. Serve in glass or large punch cups.

Serves 12–14.

Adapted from a recipe for Hot Scarlet Wine Punch in *Better Homes and Gardens 500 Five-Ingredient Recipes*, 2002.

## Mr. Green Salad

5 ounces fresh baby spinach (or any leaf lettuce)
1 large Haas avocado
½ cup halved seedless green grapes
Your choice of ingredients for contrast color:
   grated carrots, radishes, orange sections
Optional: Feta cheese

   Wash and tear the spinach or lettuce into bite-sized pieces.
   Cut the avocado into chunks.
   Combine the ingredients in a large bowl.
   Toss with Colonel Mustard vinaigrette.

Serves 6.

## Colonel Mustard Vinaigrette

*This is a classic vinaigrette that can be used on any green salad.*

1 small garlic clove, grated or minced
¼ cup white balsamic, white wine, or rice wine
    vinegar
2 teaspoons Dijon mustard
¼ cup olive oil
Kosher salt and freshly ground black pepper to
    taste

Whisk together the grated garlic, vinegar, and mustard in a small bowl.

Gradually add and whisk oil until tiny drops of oil are dispersed in the vinegar mixture.

Season with salt and pepper.

Add the dressing to a bowl of green salad, toss to combine, and serve immediately.

Makes ½ cup.

## Mrs. White Bean Chili

The basic recipe makes a vegetarian chili. Add cooked chicken for a meat version.

4 cups vegetable or chicken broth
4 15-ounce cans of white beans (navy or Great
    Northern), drained and rinsed
2 cups salsa verde (mild, medium, or spicy,
    depending on your taste)
1 14.5-ounce can petite diced tomatoes
2 teaspoons adobo seasoning, or more to taste
Optional: 2 cups cooked chicken, cubed or
    shredded

Combine the broth, half of the beans, and the salsa in a soup pot. Cook on medium to high heat until the mix simmers. Add the adobo seasoning.

Using an immersion blender, whirl the mixture to make it thicker, but not quite smooth. You can also blend the soup by batches in a standard blender.

Stir in the remaining beans and the diced tomatoes. Add chicken if using. Bring the mix to a boil and turn down the heat to simmer it for 15 minutes.

Ladle the soup into bowls and garnish with your choice of toppings: shredded cheese, sour cream or yogurt, avocado chunks, tortilla chips.

Serves 6-8.

## Professor Plum Cake

½ cup unsalted butter, softened
¾ cup sugar
1 cup self-rising flour, sifted (or all-purpose flour plus 1 teaspoon baking powder and pinch of salt)
2 eggs
8–10 pitted and sliced red plums, enough to cover the top of the batter in a single layer
Optional: 1 teaspoon cinnamon

Preheat the oven to 350 degrees.

Cream together the sugar and butter in a large bowl.

Add the flour and eggs and beat the mixture.

Spoon the batter into a 9-inch spring form pan (or 8- or 10-inch cake pan).

Arrange the plum slices on top of the batter in a single layer. If desired, sprinkle with cinnamon.

Bake for 45 minutes. Let the cake cool. Remove the sides of the spring form pan before serving.

Serves 8.

Adapted from a recipe for Plum Tort by Marian Burros, via the *New York Times*.

# Nero Wolfe's Lemon Sponge Cake

*This recipe is essentially the same as the one Rex Stout included in* Too Many Cooks *and in the recipe box given out at the whistle-stop publicity tour for the book. It specifies using an* **ungreased tube pan**, *sometimes called an angel food pan. Angel food and sponge cakes don't contain any leavening. The air whipped into the egg whites makes them rise. The batter will cling to the sides of a straight-sided tube pan, causing the rest of the batter to rise. This will not occur in a Bundt pan with fluted sides.*

6 eggs separated, using 6 egg whites and 5 yolks
1 cup of sugar, sifted twice
½ lemon (1 tablespoon lemon juice plus the
    grated rind from half the lemon)
1 cup flour, sifted twice
¼ teaspoon salt

Preheat the oven to 325 degrees.

Beat 6 egg whites until stiff and beat in ½ cup sugar.

In a separate bowl, beat 5 egg yolks until thick. Mix in the lemon juice and rind. Beat in the remaining ½ cup sugar.

Combine the two egg mixtures. Sift the flour with the salt. Fold it into the batter.

Pour the batter into an ungreased tube pan. Cut through the batter with a knife a few times to break up any air bubbles.

Bake for 1 hour.

Turn the pan upside down on a rack and let it stand until cold.

Loosen the edges of the cake and let it drop out of the pan.

Adapted from a recipe in *The Nero Wolfe Cookbook* by Rex Stout.

## Beeramisu

*This dessert has alternating layers of cake and fla-vored cream. You can assemble the layers in a trifle dish, large bowl, or individual dessert cups, at least 2½ inches tall.*

¾ cup heavy cream
8 ounces mascarpone
¼ cup coffee liqueur like Kahlúa
1½ cups of Guinness stout
Slices of Nero Wolfe's sponge cake *or* crunchy
    Savoiardi ladyfingers
Optional: 1 tablespoon cocoa powder for
    sprinkling on top

Beat the cream, mascarpone, and coffee liqueur with an electric mixer on low speed until the ingredients are combined. Beat on medium speed until the mixture thickens enough to be spread, but before it turns to butter. Refrigerate the mixture until you're ready to assemble the cake.

Pour the stout into a wide bowl or pie plate. Dip a cake slice or ladyfinger into the stout, quickly remove it, and place it on the bottom of your dish or dessert cups, cutting if needed to fit the shape of the dish. Repeat until the bottom of your bowl or cup is covered with a single cake layer. Spoon the cream mixture over the bottom layer and smooth it out.

Repeat dipping and placing another cake layer on top of the cream. Spoon the cream mixture over the second layer and smooth it out. If you have a very deep bowl or dish, and enough cream mix left over, create a third layer in the same way. The top layer should always be cream.

Refrigerate small dessert cups for at least two hours before serving.

For beeramisu made in larger dishes or bowls, refrigerate at least six hours. Spoon the beeramisu onto plates or small bowls for serving.

If desired, sift or sprinkle cocoa powder over the top layer.

Store leftovers in an airtight container for up to 3 days.

Serves 6.

Adapted from a recipe by Pieter Vanden Hogen on sunset.com.